# Tidings *of* Comfort *and* Joy

## HOLIDAY LOVE SERIES

## Marie Savage

*Katie
Happy Reading!
Marie Savage.*

Tidings of Comfort and Joy
Copyright © 2017 Marie Savage

This is a work of fiction. Names, characters, places, organizations, and events portrayed in this book are either the product of the author's imagination or are used fictitiously. Any resemblance to actual persons, living or dead, events, business establishments, or locales is entirely coincidental. All rights reserved. In accordance with the U.S. Copyright Act of 1976

Second edition August 2017

Cover Design: pro_ebookcovers

Editing: Prima Editing and Proofreading Services

Interior Formatting: T.E. Black Designs
www.teblackdesigns.com

# dedication

This book is the beginning of a dream of mine. A dream I have shared with only a few special people in my life. Now with their encouragement and strength, I am ready to share with the world.

To my family, especially Keith, Jenna, Lauren, Mileena, and Madeline thank you for always being in my corner cheering me on and respecting my writing time.

To my day job cheerleaders Amber, Elizabeth, Heather and Lisa, thanks for listening to me rant about edits, deadlines and go on and on about books.

Finally, to my best friend, lover and dear husband Larry. Thank you for encouraging me to pursue my dream and for not thinking I am nuts. Your support means more to me than you will ever know.

# CHAPTER
## *one*

"COME ON, JULIE, YOU HAVEN'T been out with us in a long time. It will be fun. Mike's coworker Ryan is very cute." Holly nudges me with her shoulder as she hands me another ornament. Stretching, I reach up as high as my five-foot-four frame will allow, so I can get to that bare spot near the top of the tree. Ever since we arrived this morning at six o'clock, Holly has been trying to convince me to go out with them. Earlier, the morning rush made it easy to avoid her as we were both too busy for chitchat.

It has slowed down now, so we decided it is the perfect time to put up the diner Christmas tree. Well, that isn't exactly true. Carl, our boss, decided we should go ahead and put up the tree. As for myself, I couldn't care less about Christmas. Holly, on the other hand, is enjoying herself, singing along with Bing Crosby's "White Christmas." Her off-key vocals have me and a few nearby customers cringing, but that doesn't stop her. That's Holly though, she loves the holidays, and she isn't afraid to let everyone know it. Well, when your mother names you Holly, because you were born the day after Christmas, it kind of makes sense.

Holly isn't the only one with the Christmas spirit. As I look around, it seems everyone is in the holiday mood. This morning alone, I have had several orders for Carl's famous pumpkin spice pancakes with eggnog flavored whipped cream. He caught the pumpkin spice flavor fever back in September, when all around, all you saw was pumpkin spice this and pumpkin spice that. The cinnamon smell in the air has my stomach growling, reminding me that break time is soon.

I look over at Holly, who is now dancing in place to "Rocking Around the Christmas Tree." What a goofball. She couldn't wait to start playing Christmas music this morning. Carl and I are just glad she waited until the day after Thanksgiving. If it had been up to her, we would have been playing Christmas carols the day after Halloween. She is even dressed festively this morning with a bright green sweater, reindeer earrings, and a Santa pin on her red waitress apron. I guess it is safe to say I am dressed for the holiday as well, just not Christmas. I am wearing my black T-shirt and black jeans. After all, it is Black Friday.

She hands me another ornament, nudging me in the shoulder again, and causing me to almost drop it on the floor. Luckily, I had a good hold on it. She is not letting the subject of tonight go. She is right, it has been a while since I went out and socialized, but the truth of the matter is, I haven't missed it.

"Stop bumping me, Holly, you almost made me drop it." I smile as she does it again. "Stop! I told you I would think about it, but I have some things I need to do first." I giggle as she does it again. Who am I kidding? I know that answer will not be good enough for her. She is like a dog on a bone when it comes to my social life, or should I say lack thereof. She is not going to stop until I give in.

"Then hurry and do them and come out with us. You're twenty-three not eighty-three, and there will be plenty of time to be a crazy cat lady and knit all day when you are a gray haired old granny." She continues to hum along to the tune as she sets the empty box down on the table and opens the last box of ornaments. We saved the best for last. These are the special ones with all the branches of the military insignia on them.

"I have a dog, Holly, his name is Bo, and it's crocheting not knitting," I correct her as I walk around the tree, making sure every spot is decorated. I may not be enjoying this as much as I used to, but I still want it to look nice.

"Knitting, crocheting, needlepoint, whatever, it doesn't matter, you always hide away at home. You need to get out and mingle. It is not healthy to stay home alone all the time." She hands me another ornament as she turns and scans the diner, making sure everyone is good. It is ten o'clock and only a few patrons remain, but experience knows the second wave will be arriving soon.

Shaking my head to her statement, I continue decorating the tree. I don't feel the need to explain myself to her or anyone else, for that matter. My home is my sanctuary, the place I feel safe. I don't have to put on a brave face and pretend to be happy. I can let my emotions go and no one is there telling me not to cry, and it will be okay. I could be doing far worse than crocheting in the comfort of my home.

"I didn't see you complaining about the scarf you saw on Pinterest, and begged me to make you." I raise my brow at her as she gives me her famous Holly eye roll. We have had this discussion before, in fact, we argued about it yesterday.

Like many times before, I zone the conversation out, and think of other things. Like this Christmas tree, for example. I may not be in a festive mood, but I love this tree. It is a white artificial tree that Carl and I found on clearance three years ago. That was just after Jason had left for Afghanistan. I knew it would look perfect with the red and blue and other patriotic ornaments we found. I even found some red, white, and blue bows on the Fourth of July that make the tree just gorgeous.

We get many compliments from the customers on it. It stands as a tribute to our soldiers—the ones still fighting and those we have lost. It has been almost a year now since my brother's death, and I know I am avoiding the social scene. Maybe Holly is right, even if I don't appreciate being called out on it—I am too young to be hiding away at home.

Unlike Holly, I am not big on the whole going out and hanging with people scene. I am also not a huge fan of being set up on dates, but who really is? I guess I wouldn't mind finding a guy that I liked, but as Holly says, I am too picky. I really wouldn't go as far as calling me picky since I live in a small town and the options are few. Especially when most of the single male population that is your dating age, were also good friends with your brother. That alone leaves me at a disadvantage. No one would dare date Jason Walsh's little sister.

Don't get me wrong. I have had guys be brave enough to ask me out, but I usually end it after the first date. I just didn't feel the spark with any of them. That is Holly's and my term for the special connection you have with someone that triggers thoughts of a relationship, marriage, and growing old together. Well, that's how I explain it. Holly defines the spark as the moment where,

Hey, I want to get to know you, turns into BOOM, I really want to get to know you better. It's the spark before the fireworks, as she likes to refer to it.

Well, I really wouldn't know personally, because I have yet to find it with someone, but I have read about it many times. Since I am home a lot, I read a lot, with romances being my favorite, of course. In each one I read, the couple share a moment, a connection—a spark. One day, I want that with someone. I really do. Of course, if I continue to hide at home, as Holly says I do, I may never find it. Maybe I should go out with Holly and meet this Ryan guy. Who knows? Maybe he can ignite that spark.

It is easy for Holly to call me picky, because she found her spark with someone. Mike is perfect for her; they go together like peanut butter and chocolate, her phrase, not mine. Where Holly is loud, opinionated, and gets excited very easily, her boyfriend Mike is more laid back and quiet like me. He reminds me of Clark Kent, with his good looks and dark rimmed glasses. Of course, Holly lets me know about his Superman skills in the bedroom, which makes it very difficult to be around them at times.

Mike Tanner is also a good friend of mine. He joined our class at Clover High School, our sophomore year. He became best friends with my brother Jason and an immediate part of our group. Holly was in love with the new boy, almost instantly. She faked being lousy at trig and asked him to be her tutor. He gladly accepted, even though her GPA was much higher than his. They have been dating ever since. Opposites attract, so they say, and it stands to reason that Holly would be dating Mike and be best friends with me. I love her as the sister I never had, even if she gets on my nerves sometimes, like now.

Holly softly touches my shoulder, no longer bumping me. I am relieved, as I am sure she has bruised me good by now. I glance over only to turn my head quickly. Damn her. She is giving me those sad Holly eyes that she knows I can't stand. She is not playing fair now. She reminds me of those abandoned animal commercials that I have to quickly turn the channel from before I start crying. She must really want me to go out with her tonight if she is stooping to the sad eyes.

"Of course I love it when you make me things. I am just worried about you. You used to hang out and have fun, but ever since ..." She stops suddenly when I frown at her. The expression on her face tells me she knows she is pushing it. Placing my hand on top of hers and patting it gently, I know she means well and is not trying to hurt my feelings.

"Unlike you, I like hanging out at home." She starts to interrupt me, but I gently squeeze her hand. "And I get what you're saying." I sigh as I am about to give in. "You win. I will go out with you guys tonight." I feel a little defeated but maybe it will be okay. At least for now it will get her off my back.

"Really?" she says too loudly as she wraps her arms around me, giving me a big hug as she is jumping us up and down. We are causing quite the stir with the customers beginning to look at us like we are crazy. I struggle to get out of her embrace. I don't like being the center of attention like she does. She finally releases me, her sad eyes gone, and her face lit up brighter than the lights on the tree.

"Hey, slow down, before you get too excited. It is just a group friend thing, right? I am not ready to date anyone yet, even if he is cute."

Holly starts nodding in agreement; she probably still can't believe I said yes. That would make two of us. "Yes. Yes, it can be a total group thing." She reaches over and hands me the last ornament. "Julie, you gotta promise me you will give Ryan a chance. You haven't dated anyone in a long time and Ryan could be the one, you know?" She smiles as she starts putting the empty boxes back in the storage tub. She is pleased with herself, I am sure. She prides herself on her matchmaking skills.

"Fine." I turn to the tree again as I prepare to hang the Marine Corps Christmas ornament at eye level so it will be easily seen. I pause for a moment as I look at the ornament in my hand, while my finger traces around the glitter insignia. I miss you, Jason. I can't believe it has been almost a year now. My vision starts to blur with the unshed tears building up in my eyes.

"Looks really nice, girls." Carl comes out from the kitchen area and stands next to us, admiring his Christmas tree. I blink a few times and quickly place the ornament on the tree. I am able to keep the tears from falling this time as I take a step back to admire my work. When I look over at Carl, he is smiling as he continues to look at the tree. Luckily he didn't catch my solemn expression.

Carl is short, stocky, and bald but has one of those faces that you can't help but like. He swears he looks like Paul Newman, but I would say he looks more like Ernest Borgnine. He is a retired Air Force crew chief and the owner and manager of Hill Top Diner in our small town of Clover, Alabama. He insists the Christmas tree in his establishment be decorated to honor the military. It has been a tradition since he opened the place ten years ago. Anyone who knows Carl knows he is very patriotic and he will sit and talk your ear off with his Gulf war stories. He is my boss, my dear friend, and even though he wasn't married to my Aunt Gina, I still consider him family.

"Miss, can I get more coffee, please?" Holly and I glance over at the man sitting at the counter as he holds up his empty mug, before looking at each other.

"I'll get it; it is time for your lunch break, anyway,"

Holly says as she grabs the coffee pot and heads toward the front counter.

"Thanks, Holl. We will talk more later about tonight."

Carl follows me as I start walking to the back storeroom to grab my things. I take my sweater off the wall hook and slip it on; the weather is getting much cooler these days.

"So what's going on tonight?" Carl casually asks as he is pretending to straighten the items on the storage shelf. I am amused by his attempt to act like this is a casual conversation when I know he is fishing for some answers. He is constantly worried about me, and like Holly, he doesn't like to see me sitting home alone. I can't help but smile, knowing that he would be nosy.

"Holly asked me to join her and Mike tonight for dinner and some bowling." I pause, thinking I might leave it at that but decide to come clean and get it over with. "And Mike's friend will be joining us." I look over at Carl, waiting for his reaction.

"Oh, yeah? Well I think that is good." He stops messing with the items on the shelf and faces me. The huge grin on his face makes me wonder if he and Holly aren't in cahoots on this plan to get me out of the house. "Yes, that's good. You should get out and be around people your own age." He turns back to the shelf.

I decide to tease him a little for that jab. "Seriously? Are you tired of me helping out at the Legion Hall then?"

He turns back to face me, the smile gone now, and his worried look has me feeling a little guilty. "No, of course not. You know better than that." The frown remains and I can't take it. I feel like a jerk now, all because of that look he has. It is almost as bad as Holly's sad eyes.

Before I leave to step outside for a few minutes, I walk over to him, patting his shoulder and kissing his cheek. "Yes, I know. I am just giving you a hard time."

He smiles again, pulling me in for a fatherly bear hug, and I don't mind because he is the closest thing I have to a father now. He releases me but isn't done with the questions. "How are you really doing, sweetie? Are you and Bo getting along okay?"

Now this is a topic I enjoy talking about—my pal Bo. His formal name is Bocephus but I call him Bo for short. He is a yellow Labrador retriever and also a retired member of the Marine Corps. He was my brother's service dog when they both were stationed in Afghanistan two years ago. Back in May, I was awarded custody of Bo in a leashing ceremony at Lackland Air Force Base. Carl played a major role in making that happen for me. Having Bo home with me has helped me cope a little better over losing Jason. "We are doing just fine. He is a good dog and great company."

Carl nods and smiles. "That's good. I know Jason would be happy that Bo is home with you."

I nod back. I am tight-lipped, not wanting to discuss Jason right now. Carl must sense my sudden withdrawal and stays silent. He tiptoes around the subject of Jason, in fear that I will start crying. It is a valid concern, especially right now. After a few seconds, I decide to break the awkwardness. "I am going to take a break outside—back in ten." I walk back to the shelf to grab my can of half drank soda and the breakfast sandwich Carl made me earlier and head outside to the back of the diner. I am grateful that Carl remains silent. He knows not to push too much.

As soon as I open the door, the cold air hits me, that and

the sour smell of the dumpster. I forgot that today is trash pickup day, and boy does it need it. I start rethinking if I want to take my break outside after all. I could be sitting inside listening to Holly go on about tonight and Carl watching to see if I am going to have a meltdown. So, maybe outside isn't so bad. Pulling my sweater tighter around me, I decide to tough it out as I head for the blue milk crates we use as chairs. Moving the crates around, I position myself so the wind isn't hitting me as bad. The smell from the dumpster is not quite as strong now, but it is enough that the desire to eat my breakfast sandwich has gone away. Stuffing it into my sweater pocket, I pull my phone out.

It is a beautiful morning, even though winter is approaching fast. The gas station next to us is busy with holiday travelers filling up on gas and fast food. We were very busy this morning with travelers visiting family, and of course, shoppers. So far, I have made some great tips. Holly and I always volunteer to work the day after Thanksgiving because we know the tips will be good. Something about Christmas time makes people more generous. I used to be out just like these folks, a few years ago. I haven't been Black Friday shopping since Aunt Gina died, and I smile as I think of how we would push through the crowds and find bargains with the best of them. God I miss her so much.

Scrolling the Facebook news feed on my phone, I see many friends posting pictures. Everyone, it seems, is getting ready for Christmas. Decorating the diner tree will be as festive as I get this year. Of course, I will buy or make presents. I will also help Carl with the Legion Hall Christmas party for the low income families, like I've done every year for as far back as I can remember.

I keep scrolling on Facebook but never comment, only clicking a few likes if I see something good. I don't hang out with anyone on here. Most of them are classmates from high school who I haven't seen much of since we graduated in 2011. The only friends I see on a regular basis are Carl, Holly, and Mike. The truth is, the only reason I see them as much as I do, is that we work together.

Holly is right. I don't socialize enough but I find it so hard to connect with people. Even in school, I was known as Jason's sister and not as Julie. Jason was the popular one. He was always in sports and clubs and I was the quiet one who stayed in the library during breaks and lunch.

I get bored with Facebook and move on to my favorite app, Pinterest. I want to find something nice to make Holly for Christmas. Holly and I have been best friends since kindergarten. Both of our last names start with W, mine being Walsh and hers Winston. We were always next to each other in classes and we just clicked. We were together so often that we were sometimes mistaken as being sisters instead of friends. We always get a good laugh about that. She is taller than me at five foot nine compared to my five foot four. She has curly strawberry blonde hair and I am a straight-haired brunette. We both have blue eyes, though, but mine are a lighter shade. Even though she can be a pain in the butt sometimes, she is my best friend and I love her like a sister.

She comes from an unconventional large family, with eight brothers and eight sisters. I am not joking. Can you imagine, during the holidays? Seventeen kids, two parents, grandparents, sibling spouses, and grandkids all in one household. She is telling me all the time how she envies my privacy but she and I both know that having family is a blessing. Holly's family welcomed Carl and I over for Thanksgiving yesterday. Even though it was chaotic with so many people, I have to admit, it was nice not being alone for a change.

I continue to look down at my phone, admiring all the neat pins and finishing up my soda. As I am looking at all the crochet ideas, I absentmindedly crush the can in the middle. It is a habit I have when I am about to throw it away.

"If you are done with that, can I have it?" A man's voice startles me, causing me to drop the can and almost fall back on the unsteady milk crates. I am not used to anyone coming back here, but I still should pay more attention. My eyes are first drawn to the military boots and pants worn by the man.

"Jason?" I whisper as I continue looking at him. The boots and pants are where the military uniform ends. I see he is wearing an old and torn blue hooded sweat jacket with a flannel long sleeve shirt peeking out at the arm cuffs. Everything is baggy on him, like he is wearing a few sizes too big, and he stands quite a few inches taller than me. He has to be at least six feet tall. He is definitely no soldier with his long unkempt hair and scruffy beard.

As I continue to inspect him, my mind finally registers that no, this is not my brother. I mean it can't be, he is dead, but this guy looks so familiar. When my eyes make contact with his, a feeling comes over me, making it almost hard to breathe. I am shaking but I don't think it is from the cold, maybe it is because for a moment I thought I was seeing a ghost. I notice he is looking at me strangely.

"You, okay, ma'am?" he whispers back.

I continue to stare into his eyes, trying to figure out their color. They look blue, but not like any blue eyes I have ever seen. I have to stop myself from walking closer so I can get a better look at them. He continues to stare at me as well, but I bet it is only because I am acting weird.

After I come back to my senses, I am a little peeved by the sneakiness of his approach.

"You frightened me. You shouldn't sneak up on people like that," I scold him. I begin to realize that he is most likely a homeless person and I probably should be careful about what I say. The warning bells of stranger danger go off inside my head. They are also telling me I should get my butt back inside the diner. There is something about him, though, that makes me stay put. He seems younger than the homeless people I have seen before. He looks like if he had a nice haircut and a shave he could be handsome. I have seen homeless people before, but no one quite like him.

"You should be more careful and pay attention to your surroundings," he scolds back, and I pick up on his accent, which is little different than the southern drawl around here.

Who does this guy think he is, telling me what to do? His statement irks me with its familiarity. It sounds like something Jason would have said to me under the same circumstance. I am so tempted to stick my tongue out at him, as I would have at Jason if he had said that. Taking a moment to reflect, however, I realize he does have a point. "You're right. I guess I should be more careful."

Both of us are now standing in awkward silence as we continue to stare at one another. I try to look into his eyes again. I want to figure out their color, but he looks away, avoiding eye contact with me.

"Well, anyhow, sorry I frightened ya." He turns and begins walking away, but I don't want him to go just yet. There is something about him that makes me want to find out more.

"No, wait!" He pauses, turning to look at me again. I bend down and pick up the can I dropped and walk over to him. "You wanted this, right?" I hold the can out to him, and he stares at it for a few seconds before looking at me again. Now his beautiful eyes look sad, and a lump builds up in my throat as a pain hits my chest. I recognize that look because I see it every morning in my own mirror. The look I try to hide from the world as I try to put on a brave face.

Again he looks away, avoiding eye contact with me. Maybe I am embarrassing him. He pulls his hand out of his jacket pocket and holds it out to me, as I note his large and very masculine hands. A childhood memory comes to me, suddenly; Daddy reached his hand out to me just like that on my first day of kindergarten. I was so scared, but when my little hand was in Daddy's large one, I felt safe. I must be losing it, because I have an overwhelming desire for him to take my hand and hold it. When he takes the can from me, my mind comes back to the present.

"Thank ya, ma'am." He quickly puts his hand back in his jacket and looks at the ground again. It is hard to tell whether he is shy or ashamed.

The feeling of wanting to help him overwhelms me as I start feeling around in my pockets. I realize I don't have any of my tip money on me. I feel bad that all I have to offer him is an empty soda can. My hand reaches my jacket pocket, feeling the sandwich there. Pulling it out, I hold it out to him. "Here, would you like to have this?"

He looks at me and then at the sandwich and then back at me, before shaking his head. "No, thank ya, ma'am."

I am dumbfounded; why would he refuse it? He must be hungry if he is out looking for cans to turn in for money. Maybe he doesn't trust me. "No, please, it's good, I am just not hungry."

He looks at the sandwich but makes no attempt to take it. Why is he being so stubborn? After all it's just a sandwich.

"If you don't take it, I'll just end up throwing it away." I look back over at the milk crates. "You can sit over there out of the wind and eat it, it's okay, really."

It takes him a moment to decide as he looks around. It is as if he is expecting to get in trouble for being out here. He slowly makes his way to the crates and sits. I hand him the sandwich and step back, just in case he tries something. I don't think he would, but you never know nowadays.

"Thank ya, ma'am."

The fact he keeps calling me ma'am is bringing back Holly's statements of me acting like an old lady. I watch as he unfolds the wrapper and takes a bite, the biscuit crumbs falling into his beard as he tries to wipe them out. I continue to just stare at him. Watching him, I start wondering what he would look like if he had a nice haircut, shave, and better clothes. Something tells me he would be very good looking.

He is so young; I would guess maybe late twenties at most. I am not used to seeing a homeless person this young, not that I ride around checking them out, of course. A chill runs down my back as I wrap my arms around myself, not sure if it is the cold or this man that is getting to me. He continues to stare out at the parking lot. Occasionally, he will look my way, but he is still avoiding eye contact with me. He finishes chewing before he speaks.

"You should go back inside; it's cold out here," he says as he takes another bite. Here he is homeless, cold, and hungry and he's worried about me. Again, it reminds me of something Jason would have said to me. What is the story with this guy? I definitely want to find out, so I decide to introduce myself.

"I'm fine, thank you. My name is Julie, by the way. What's your name?" I start rocking back and forth on my heels, nervous energy making it impossible to stand still.

Again he waits until he has no food in his mouth before speaking. I am surprised by his manners. It may be judgmental, but I wouldn't expect someone who is homeless to be worried about proper eating manners.

"Ben." He takes a final bite, finishing the sandwich, and again wiping his beard to remove the crumbs. He ate that quickly; he must be starving. I could get him more to eat inside.

"It is nice to meet you, Ben. Would you like to come inside the diner? It's nice and warm in there and I could get you a cup of coffee and maybe something more to eat." I am hoping he will accept, so I can talk to him some more. For some odd reason, I want to know his story.

"No, thank ya, ma'am." He starts looking around again, like a stray cat getting ready to bolt at any second.

"Are you sure? I know my boss won't mind." At least I hope Carl would be cool with it. He usually likes to help people.

"No, ma'am, I am fine out here, but thanks."

Okay the ma'am thing has to stop. "It's Julie." I remind him again.

"Yes, I know," he responds, still avoiding eye contact with me.

Okay, wow, this guy seems as frigid as the weather today. I really shouldn't care, but for some crazy reason, I do. I am so bad at being the one to get a conversation going, but he definitely isn't jumping to do so. "So ..." I realize my next question of, Do you live around here? would seem pretty lame, since he is homeless. I stare down at his boots and the question pops out. "Are you in the military?"

He finally looks at me again in surprise and then he follows my eyes to his boots. "No, not anymore ..." he pauses, raising his eyebrows, "Julie." He finally says my name, but it came out sounding a bit sarcastic. This time he doesn't look away, so I continue to engage in this conversation.

"So you are a veteran?" It is the only conclusion I can come up with based on the fact he is wearing authentic military garb. I hear him sigh, before he answers. Why is he acting so irritated with me? Am I being paranoid?

"Yes. Marines." He looks away again, as if admitting that is something to be ashamed of. My brother was a Marine and would say it with pride.

"Well, thank you for your service." He doesn't look back at me. What the hell is going on? A veteran should not be walking around hungry and homeless. Carl would want to help him, I know it. I want to show my appreciation with more than a cold sandwich and empty soda can, so I try one more time. "Ben, are you sure you wouldn't like to come inside the diner, so I can buy you a proper breakfast and a hot cup of coffee?"

He looks at me and frowns. "I said no thank ya, you don't owe me." He stands up and I fear I may have insulted him in some way. His face is hard to read, especially with that horrible beard.

"On that I would disagree, but I won't push you, so please sit back down." I start rubbing my arms as the frigid wind keeps cutting through me. He continues watching me, not looking away as he was before.

"You should get back inside ... Julie. You're obviously very cold right now."

There he goes emphasizing my name again. He is teasing me just like Jason used to and it gets my stubborn side going again. "And as I told ya ... Ben, I'm fine." Which isn't exactly true, since I continue to rub my arms, getting colder by the second.

"Suit yourself, I reckon." He looks away, yet he doesn't walk away and I could have sworn I saw him smirk. Maybe I am not getting on his nerves as much as he lets on.

"So have you been hanging around here long?" As soon as the statement leaves my lips, I realize how silly it sounds. He must have thought it was amusing too, when he finally gives me a smile.

"No, I just arrived here last night. I hitched a ride with a truck driver." The smile on his face is inviting so I continue on.

"Where are you from?" His accent is a little different than mine, so I know he is not an Alabamian like me.

"Texas." He pauses, looking away again, his smile gone. "Town called Kerrville." He has that faraway look again. I recognize that look, when someone is remembering something they wish they could forget. I do it daily. Pausing, I wait for a moment, to let him chew on whatever bad memory our conversation is stirring up. I check my phone; my break is almost up.

"Are you thinking about staying here in Clover?" I blush as I realize how I just sounded like some giddy school girl. He looks at me and once again rewards me with a smile. Maybe he has a thing for giddy school girls. He may be a little messy with the hair falling in his face, his beard in desperate need of a trim or better yet a shave, but he has a beautiful smile. I could stare at that smile for hours, stringy hair, beard, and all.

"I don't know yet, but it doesn't seem like a bad place to be so far." That accent of his and the way he just said that, has me tingling inside. Is he flirting with me? I don't know why but I like this guy. Our eyes lock on to each other's, a bond forming in just the few moments that we have been talking. It's crazy but I feel like I know him, but that's not possible. He just seems so familiar. Well, one thing looks for certain as he continues to smile at me, I am pretty sure I have just made friends with a homeless person.

My phone alarm goes off, surprising me as I struggle trying to shut it off. Looking back up, the connection is now gone and I hate that I have to go back inside. I wonder if this is it or if I will see him again. I start walking to the door, but turn before going inside. "I have to go. It was nice meeting you, Ben. If you change your mind, feel free to come inside and warm up, coffee and donut on me."

His smile grows bigger this time as he starts laughing. Obviously, I said something he thought is funny, but what? I hesitate at the door as I laugh with him. For some odd reason, the sound of his laughter is contagious. Once again, I am reminded of Jason. Anytime I heard his laugh, I would laugh too, whether I found whatever he was laughing at funny or not.

"What? What's so funny?" He has a great laugh too, even if I don't get why we are laughing.

"It's nothin'." He stops laughing but continues to smile at me. "Thank ya, Julie. It was nice meetin' ya too." That smile and those eyes, so warm but yet so lonely.

Now I am the one embarrassed. "Okay, well take care. Maybe I will see you around?" I open the door, blushing as I pause yet again, because I don't want to say goodbye.

"Maybe, ya will." He gives me a wink and turns, walking away.

I step inside, immediately feeling the warmth of the diner. I hurry and put away my things before heading back into the dining room. At first I want to tell Carl about him, but the little voice inside my head says don't do it. I like the fact that Ben is a secret friend, and I think for now, I will keep it that way.

Later that afternoon, my shift is over and I sit in my car waiting for it to warm up before leaving. Throughout the day, I kept watching the dining area hoping he would come in, but he never did. I even checked out back, but he was gone. My thoughts, since I met him this morning, have been of nothing but him. Holly even tried to talk to me about tonight and I was only half paying attention. In my mind, I keep seeing those intense eyes staring at me, and I have so many questions. I am a woman on a mission now. I want to know why he is homeless. I want to know why a US veteran is not getting help. I want to know if he is going to be warm tonight. I want to help him. I want to get to know Ben.

# CHAPTER
*two*

TRAFFIC IS REALLY CRAZY THIS afternoon, but I finally make it home. I pull my car into the driveway and park in front of the garage. I would love to be able to park inside it but there is too much stuff in there. This is the house I grew up in, and now live alone in, except for Bo, of course.

It is a decent size, three bedroom, two bathroom, ranch-style home in the country, just outside of town. It sits on two acres of land with an assortment of fruit trees as well as pecan trees. During the harvesting times, it can be a chore to keep up with, but I make a little side cash with the fruits and nuts of my labor, so I can't complain. On the inside, I try keep it exactly the way my parents and Aunt Gina kept it, with only necessary improvements and small deviations from the original decor. Holly has been begging me to update it, but I just can't. It is important to me to keep it the way I remember it as a little girl.

I know it is crazy, but it makes me feel like I am not alone. I can still see Dad sitting in the same brown recliner, watching football, and my mom getting on him for not using a coaster when he sets his beer on the coffee table. Mom is still in the lemon yellow kitchen, wearing her blue apron, and making her famous banana bread. I can see Aunt Gina and me sitting at the kitchen table, preparing comfort packages for Jason and the troops overseas.

I did change a few things; my old bedroom is now my craft room and I sleep in the master bedroom. Jason's room, however, is completely unchanged. It is the same now as the day he left for the final time for Afghanistan. Carl volunteered to go in and box his stuff up, but I am not ready yet. Jason was not only my brother, but my twin brother. He was one minute and fifteen seconds older than me; a fact he took great pleasure of reminding me about as often as he could. It nearly killed me when he joined the service, as ever since our parents' deaths, we were never apart. I cried every day of his basic training. When he died, a part of me died with him.

Fumbling with the keys as I unlock the door, I can hear Bo barking. It sounds intimidating and a good deterrent for anyone deciding to break in. Carl installed motion lights around the house and had an alarm company install a system. He hates me living out here alone. I kindly remind him I am not alone, I have Bo. He is my protector. I haven't seen Bo be aggressive, and the officer that handed him over assured me that Bo would not show aggression toward me. It is nice to come home to him, instead of an empty, quiet house.

As I open the door, he is there wagging his tail and looking as handsome as ever as he greets me. He starts barking at the alarm system beeping so I quickly punch in the code to get it to stop. After locking the door, I kick off my shoes and go curl up on the comfy couch. I call Bo over to me for his daily dose of loving. He immediately starts with the doggie kisses.

"Whew, Bo, I appreciate the kisses but your breath ... yuck." He just sits there panting as I speak to him like he is a human instead of a dog. "We need to get you some doggie mints. So how was your day, boy?" He gives a quick and sharp bark and puts his paw on my knee.

"My day? Well, let's see. I decorated the Christmas tree at the diner today. It looks beautiful by the way, and I even included an ornament that has a picture of you." I rub his ears as I continue "Then, I had to clean up vomit in one of the booths where some kid threw up." I did not enjoy that. His parents were nice and gave me a huge tip, though. Bo nudges my hand, wanting more petting. Then I remember the highlight of my day.

"Oh, and I helped a homeless man today. He is a Marine, just like you." I stare up at the fireplace where my brother's flag is sitting on the mantel beside his picture. I still haven't bought a frame for the flag that was given to me at Jason's funeral. I just haven't found the right one. I can't believe that in a few days it will be a year. It seems like only yesterday that Carl and the Marine officers came to my door to tell me the news. I didn't even hear the words, because once I saw them, I knew.

Thank God for Carl, who went with me to receive Jason's body a few days later. He took care of all the arrangements to give him a proper military funeral and bury him next to my parents and Aunt Gina. I feel the lump in my throat and the tears building in my eyes, causing my vision to be blurry now. I lean down, hugging Bo to me as the memories start playing in my head.

My parents were killed in a car accident sixteen

years ago. Jason and I were seven when Aunt Gina came to live with us. She was my dad's sister and didn't hesitate to adopt and raise us. She was awesome and I felt like she was my mother more than my aunt, but she insisted we call her Aunt Gina in respect to our mother and father. Jason left for the Marines right after high school, so for a while it was just me and Aunt Gina. Then she started dating her boss, Carl, who after a year's courtship moved in with us and we became a family. I loved the times when Jason could come home, and with all of us living here, it felt like a family again.

It was short lived, though, because three years ago Aunt Gina was diagnosed with terminal lung cancer and died the following year. Carl moved out, not feeling right staying since he wasn't married to my Aunt Gina. Then last year we lost Jason. Needless to say, I am no stranger to death. It is the reason I am having a hard time wanting to celebrate Christmas.

Bo lays his head on my lap. He must feel my sadness and I know he feels sad at times too. I remember the first day I actually met Bo. I was so touched when the Marines brought him to Jason's funeral. I remember seeing Bo dressed up with his medals as the Marine walked him up to the front. Bo sat there as the Marine laid down his leash and stepped away. Bo had laid by Jason's coffin with his head on his paws and looked so sad. He would look at me as I sat in the front row at the funeral home and then back at the coffin.

I finally got up during the service and sat next to him on the floor. I didn't care if anyone thought it was wrong or not proper etiquette. Who cares about those things when you are mourning those you love? I knew at that moment that Bo and I were kindred spirits sharing the same loss. I was grateful that the Marine didn't try to stop me; he even offered his gloved hand to me to help me up before taking Bo's leash and leaving.

"I know, boy; I miss him too." I look around the living room. Today would have been the day that we would decorate. The tree would already be up and the stockings hanging on the fireplace. Jason and I would be arguing about who put the lights away last year in a tangled mess. One year when Jason couldn't be home for the holidays, I made a video of me decorating the tree. I was worried it would make him sad, but he called me to tell me how much he loved it. He also reminded me that after Christmas, to not to just put away the lights in a bunch but to use the holder he bought. The memory has me smiling. That was Jason's brotherly way of saying he loved me.

I look at the clock. In a few hours I will need to get ready for a night out with Holly, Mike, and Ryan, who I have yet to meet. I agreed to dinner and bowling, because it sounds like a safe non-date evening, and who knows, maybe it will be fun. Holly keeps telling me how cute Ryan is. She says he has beautiful eyes. Thinking of beautiful eyes, my thoughts return to Ben. I wonder if I will be as interested in Ryan as I am in Ben.

My mind tells me that I am crazy for continuing to think of this homeless man. I meet many unfortunate people when I volunteer for all the charitable events that I do. There is something about Ben, though. He is not some ordinary person down on his luck. I wish he would have let me help him more. Living on the streets, especially during this time of year, is dangerous. He seems so young, and I wonder why. Doesn't he have family that cares? If he is a veteran, why is he out on the streets? Don't we take care of our soldiers anymore? I wonder if he will be there again tomorrow. I guess I will have to wait and see.

"So, do you have plans to go back to school?" Ryan sits next to me as we slide on our bowling shoes. Holly was right, he is cute. I am sure there are many girls that would love his sandy blond hair, warm brown eyes, and bright smile. I find him appealing also, except when he talks. In fact, Ryan is kind of irritating me. He has an opinion on everything, and all through dinner, he did most of the talking. Sure I am shy, but it would have been nice to have been asked about myself. After all, he is the one that had been bugging Mike to set us up, ever since he supposedly saw me with Holly one day. I don't remember seeing him, but he swears I smiled at him. I don't correct him as I am trying to be polite.

Meeting him tonight wasn't too awkward. Holly sat in the back of the car with me so it made it easier on the drive to the restaurant. He has polite manners but talks excessively about his education and new job as a retail buyer. He has talked so much about himself, that I am shocked when he finally wants to know something about me. After tying my laces, I finally answer him, simple and to the point. "No." I smile getting up and walk over to rack to find a bowling ball.

He follows me, chuckling. "No? Don't you want to do something better one day than wait on tables?"

I give him a look, hopefully my face showing my displeasure with his comment. I don't see anything wrong with waitressing. "I don't know, Ryan, right now it pays the bills and most of the time I enjoy it." I walk back to our lane, rolling my eyes at Holly as she looks over at me. I hope she is using her best friend ESP, and knows that I am not having the best time with Ryan.

"But with a college education you could do so much more." He sets his ball down beside mine as we both check the bowling order on the overhead monitor. Mike goes first, then Holly, then Ryan, and me.

"Yes, I suppose. I could also have student loan debt that I don't need right now, especially if I am not sure what I want to do."

Ryan stands next to me; he has been trying to get closer and closer to me, and now our arms are touching each other. I am not interested and when I feel the moment getting too much, I step away to sit on the chairs, waiting my turn. He must get the hint not to join me as he continues to stand there.

I watch as Mike gets a strike, and Holly goes next, knocking over three pins. She gutter balls the next one and walks over to sit next to me, as it is Mr. Higher Education's turn.

"Not going so well, huh?" Holly whispers so Ryan can't hear us.

"No, not really, Holly. I don't think he wants to be stuck dating a waitress, anyhow," I whisper back.

She is more disappointed than I am about it. "I am so sorry, Julie. Mike feels bad; he says he doesn't act like this at work." As if on cue, Mike looks over at us and shrugs apologetically.

"Not your fault. I am still glad to get out of the house. You were right, I was hiding at home. But I think this will be the last night for Ryan and me."

First shot and Ryan gutter balls it. I can't help but smile as he looks over at me. I can see his embarrassment, as it seems his degree doesn't help his bowling.

"I am not giving up. I will find you a great guy, just like my Mike." Finding a guy like Mike would be nice. He has a muscular build, thanks in part to his daily workouts at the gym. Holly complains about all the time he spends there, but she obviously loves the results. I have always found Mike attractive, but would never admit that to Holly. It's not just his looks, although I find his brown wavy hair and blue eyes appealing. I love Mike's sense of humor and the way he takes care of Holly. Holly and Mike are too perfect for one other.

I smile knowing she won't give up until she sees me in a relationship. I don't have the heart to tell her that I am not sure if I am ready for that yet. I also didn't tell her about Ben. I know she would disapprove and I don't want to hear her lectures. Ryan tries again and manages to knock over one pin. I try not to laugh at his expense as I get up to get my ball. Now it is my turn.

"I think the lane has a warp or something, so don't be upset if you don't hit the pins, just have fun," Ryan says as he walks over to sit down.

I think something is warped all right, but it isn't the bowling lane. I square up and guide my arm back and come forward, rolling the ball straight to the center with good speed. All pins fall. A perfect strike. I smile looking back as Ryan's jaw opens.

"Dude, she is on her boss' bowling league; she is their best player," Mike says loud enough for Ryan to hear. He then smiles and winks at me. Mike has no problem laughing at Ryan's expense.

Holly rides in the back with me again when they drive me home. I wish Ryan all the best and I try not to act offended when he doesn't get out to walk me to my door or ask for my number. I guess it is safe to say, there will be no sparks between us. I give Holly a quick hug and head inside. They honk the car horn as they take off, and I bundle up as it is even colder than this morning.

Bo is there at the door waiting for me, whining. I

realize that this is the first time I have ever left him alone at night. The officer had warned me that Bo occasionally has PTSD issues, and being alone in the dark must be one of them.

"Oh, boy, I am so sorry. You are not sure what is going on, huh?" I kneel down, petting and hugging him. I feel bad that I left him alone at night, especially since my non-date with Ryan was a big-time failure. I get up, heading to the couch. I lay a blanket down on the cushions and invite Bo to get up on the couch with me. I know it's bad dog manners, but I feel so badly about leaving him alone.

Ryan's words about me waitressing still burn a little. I just see it as a job, and helping Carl out. I really don't know what my problem is about going to school. It's not that I found school hard. In fact, I did okay in school. I wasn't valedictorian or even an honor student, but I had my share of A's and B's and was never below a C. I had a great relationship with my teachers, as I was always respectful and helpful. When I graduated, I just wanted a break, so what if that break has lasted five years.

# CHAPTER
## *three*

It's a sunny Saturday morning and I have a hard time holding in my excitement. It is almost break time, and I am hoping I will get to see Ben again. I had a dream about him last night. He was clean-cut with a short haircut and not a trace of facial hair as he walked into the diner. He was in his military dress uniform and looked so handsome and proud. He didn't say a word as he took the coffee pot out of my hand and set it down on the counter. He then knelt and swept me up in his arms before giving me a kiss. It was like a scene out of An Officer and a Gentleman. It was most likely prompted by the fact I fell asleep on the couch watching that movie with Bo last night. It was a great dream, and I wanted to go back to sleep and dream some more.

It is time, so I go to the back and grab my sweater. A few minutes before my break, I asked Carl to make me a breakfast burrito. He was so excited to see me eat, that he didn't even question it. In the last few days, Carl has been watching me like a mother hen, knowing that the day is fast approaching. I wish he would stop worrying about me. I have done my best to show him I will be okay.

I grab the burrito and a coffee in a to go cup, before heading out. It is still chilly outside, but not as bad as yesterday and thankfully the garbage service emptied the dumpster. I go ahead and sit on the crates, but as I look around, I don't see Ben anywhere. He must have decided to move on, and the disappointment I am feeling almost has me on the verge of tears. Maybe I am losing it. Why does this upset me so? I go ahead and pull out my phone, checking the social sites again. I just hope he is okay wherever he is.

After a few moments of checking out Facebook, I look up and scan the parking lot again. I spot someone walking this way from the gas station, and as he gets closer, I realize it is Ben. I try to hold back my excitement over seeing him. When he finally gets close enough so I can see his face, he is smiling.

"Good morning, Ben." I smile, making room and inviting him to sit next to me.

"Mornin', Julie." He goes ahead and joins me on the crates.

The fact he doesn't hesitate to sit next to me thrills me. Then I remember the gifts I have for him. "Here you go, hot coffee." I hold out the cup for him.

"Thank ya." He eagerly accepts the large cup, and starts sipping it slowly. He closes his eyes and savors the sip. He must be a coffee lover like me.

"Good?" I continue to watch him, enjoying the brew.

"You've no idea." He sighs before taking another sip. As I watch the steam come off the cup, I realize that the warm coffee has to be a luxury for him. Something so simple that I take for granted every morning.

"Well, if you like that then hopefully you will like this too." I hold out the foil wrapped burrito. "Carl's famous big breakfast burrito. It's his specialty."

He smiles, accepting the wrapped burrito, not hesitating as he did yesterday when I offered my sandwich to him. I frown when he sticks it in his jacket pocket though.

He must have caught on to my disappointment. "Thank ya, but I'll save it for later." He pats the pocket. "Right now this coffee is heaven." He takes another sip.

We sit in silence for a few moments, as I allow him to enjoy the warm brew. I don't want to interrogate him as he is enjoying the coffee, so I sit watching the traffic go in and out of the truck stop.

"How long ya been workin' here?" he asks and I can hardly contain the thrill inside me for his interest.

"Let's see, I started here right after graduation in June, so almost five and half years now."

"So, whatcha doin' when ya ain't workin' or feedin' homeless bums like me?" When I glance his way, I notice his playful smile, and even with his bushy beard, his face lights up, especially those eyes. Like his laughter yesterday, his smile is contagious.

"Well, I usually stay home and read, watch TV, and crochet." As I hear my words, I can't help but think that sounds pretty pathetic to say out loud.

His face grows more serious now. "Hmmm, seems kinda ..." He narrows his eyes and hesitates, but I already know what he is going to say, because Holly says it all the time, so I finish for him.

"Boring?" I offer. I have to admit, it really does.

"Yeah, sorry, none of my business." He sips, looking over at the truck stop again.

"I suppose it is boring, but I like it." I shrug, acting like I don't mind, when in fact I do.

"Well, I ain't got no room to talk, it ain't like I'm livin' an excitin' life myself lately." I look at him expecting to see him joking, but his face is still serious. "Are you in college?"

A surge of irritation washes over me as I remember my disaster non-date with Ryan last night. I shouldn't have let him get to me, but he did. "Oh, not you too? Jeez what is with everyone and higher education?" I say a little too loudly in defense. Ryan's words from last night still sting, as if being a waitress is something to be ashamed of.

Ben looks at me in surprise at my outburst. "Ouch, darlin'. Seems I touched a nerve there." He smiles down at me.

He is right, I did overreact, but I wish people would just drop the college question. "No, it's okay, it's just this guy I went out with last night. He was giving me a hard time because I am not in school." Now I stare out to the parkway. "If I want to go to school, I will go. Right now I am happy doing what I am doing." Wow, that statement sounds familiar—I probably say it to everyone that asks the same question.

"You mean stayin' at home and knittin', right?" He chuckles as he says it.

"It's crochet. Oh, never mind." I am not sure why I am trying to explain myself, or acting so defensive.

"Doesn't your boyfriend take you out for fun?"

My eyes widen with that statement, the whole college thing forgotten. I look at him again. "Boyfriend?" I start laughing. The thought of Ryan the snob as my boyfriend? No thank you.

"What's so funny?" He looks at me strangely, obviously not in on my joke.

"He's not my boyfriend. I mean, I never ..." I stop right there, not wanting him to know that I have never had a serious boyfriend—ever. I shake my head. "He's not my boyfriend."

"So, no boyfriend, huh? Well that's interestin'." He takes another sip of his coffee, looking out at the parking lot again.

I stare at him again after that statement. "What is that supposed to mean?" Now it is me looking at him strangely.

"It makes sense now why you stay home and ... what was it? Oh yeah, crochet." The last part he says in a chuckle.

"And what is so wrong about that?" I ask, wondering why all of a sudden he is picking on me.

"You are too pretty to not have a boyfriend," he says, still looking away.

I suddenly blush at his compliment. I pull my sweater closed as if I am cold, but really I think I am trembling because he just called me pretty. "You think I am pretty?" I whisper. Are we seriously having this conversation? I think to myself.

"Does that surprise ya?" He looks back at me, with no smile on his face.

"I don't know, maybe." I shrug, looking away. I am suddenly uncomfortable with this topic. It is not the first time I have been complimented on my looks, but coming from Ben it feels different.

He starts laughing. "Oh, come on, I can't be the first guy that has ever told ya you're pretty."

Actually it is the first time a guy has come out and said it to me. Most of the time, it is secondhand from Holly or Mike.

We stare out at the parking lot again, in silence for a moment. He takes another sip of coffee before continuing. "Besides bein' pretty, you seem awfully young to want to just hang around home and crochet."

Oh, here we go on that subject again, and I am tired of hearing it. "Well, you seem awfully young to be on the streets homeless." I challenge back.

"Touché." He chuckles, amused by my quick comeback. "Your tongue is like a razor today, darlin'."

I smile. Our playful banter is fun, I suppose, but I feel we are avoiding the real problem here. He is homeless and why is that? I stop smiling and try to be more serious. I am worried for him. "I know it is rude to ask and none of my business, but why are you homeless, Ben?"

Our eyes connect and I feel that flutter in my stomach again. When he looks at me like that, it is like we are bonding on some level that I am unsure of. I watch as his smile fades, and his eyes once again show his pain. I understand pain and I know I just ended our conversation for today, by the look on his face.

"Long story, and your break is almost up. Another time, maybe." He smiles and then stands and faces me. I don't try to stop him from leaving this time. He is right, I need to head back inside.

"Thank ya for this, Julie." He holds up the coffee. "One day I'll pay ya back."

Hating that he is leaving, I stand up and face him. I see his hand and before I even think twice, I touch it softly as my fingers slowly caress his. He opens his hand and ever so gently grasps mine. I have never just held hands with someone before, not like this. I just need to touch him. He inhales deeply, smiling again, when he looks down at me.

"You're welcome, please be careful," I say, looking up at him

"Always," he replies as he gives me a wink and squeezes my hand one more time before releasing it.

He starts walking and heads back toward the truck stop, disappearing out of sight around the corner. Part of me wants to follow him but I know I have already embarrassed him so I go back inside the diner. Still in a daze from the hand holding, I run right into Holly.

"Oh, sorry, Holly."

"Whatcha doing?" she asks as she grabs my arms to keep me from stumbling. She is eying me suspiciously.

"Taking a break, what are you doing?" I remove her hands from my arms.

"Ughhh, your hands are ice cold. Well, I am doing what I always do."

"Being nosy?" I slide off my sweater and hang it back up.

"Yep. You have been acting funny today, like you are hiding something."

There are no windows in the back of the diner so the only way she could have seen me is to open the door, which I would have heard, or come around from the front in the parking lot. I have to be careful what I say since she knows me too well and she is good at knowing when I am lying. "Okay, you caught me. I was searching for what to get you for Christmas. I am so busted." Please buy it, Holly. I don't need this right now.

"You were searching for my gift outside? You are not going to make one of those recycled trash crafts again, are you?" She puts her hands on her hips, obviously not believing me.

"On my phone, silly." I pull my phone out of my pocket and hold it up. I hope like hell she believes me.

"Uh huh, fine." She smacks her gum for effect. "Keep your little secret, but I will be watching you." She points her finger at me as she walks back out to the front of the diner.

That was close. If Carl or Holly find out that I have been talking and flirting with a homeless guy, they will lock me up and throw away the key. Ben needs to remain a secret.

ON MY WAY HOME, I decide to stop at Walmart to pick up a few things. I stroll down the aisles looking at all the families shopping for Christmas. Christmas music is playing all throughout the store and there is a festive display everywhere you turn. I used to love all this. Aunt Gina and I would shop for hours, finding gifts for everyone. Christmas without her has not been the same. I try to get in the festive spirit, especially at the diner, as it is good for tips, but it's an act. Truth is, I wish the holidays would hurry up and be over with, so everyone will start acting normal again.

My thoughts turn to Ben again. Should I buy him a gift? After all, he is a friend now, right? Would it be inappropriate? What if it was something he could use? That would be okay, right? As I think of Ben, I start adding to my cart things he might like or appreciate having. I may be going overboard, but it makes me feel good getting these things for him. Suddenly, I find myself smiling just like the rest of the shoppers as I hope he likes what I get him. It makes me feel good to help, which is part of the reason I help Carl out with such things as the Operation Gratitude, where we send care packages to troops. I love crocheting hats and sending them out. Aunt Gina taught me how to crochet and we would sit talking and crocheting.

An hour later, I make it home and while Bo enjoys his dental chew treats, I arrange a care package for Ben. I checked out homeless care packages on Pinterest and bought the suggested items—wipes, toothbrush, toothpaste, sunscreen, lip balm, lotion, a phone card, beef jerky, bottled water, thermal mug, and a small first aid kit. I also got some travel size shampoo, shaving cream, soap, deodorant, and a razor, just in case he finds a place he can clean up.

Having the things in a bag, I start thinking and walk to my closet, pulling out an old coat that belonged to my dad. I occasionally like putting it on when I am feeling scared and lonely. Daddy used to put it on me when I was little to keep me warm while I watched him work outside. Ben looks like he is the same size my dad was and he could use the coat more than me.

I look on the hanger and see Jason's old backpack and grab it too. Might as well put it to good use. I smile as I remember the scarf I crocheted. It was supposed to be Jason's Christmas present last year. I used the Marine Corps colors. Ben was a Marine so it should be okay. I take all the toiletry items and put them in a large plastic freezer bag and place everything but the coat in the backpack. Hopefully he will be there again in the morning. I can't wait to give this all to him.

# CHAPTER
## *four*

It's Sunday morning and my day off. I turn over and stare at my alarm clock before shutting it off. I still plan on going to the diner today. Not to work, but to hopefully see Ben. The little breakfast I gave him the last two days might have been his only meal and I can't stand the thought of him being hungry. I hurry and take a shower. I decide to take a little extra time to look nice. Not wearing my usual wardrobe of a T-shirt and jeans, I put on a dress instead.

I don't have my hair up in a ponytail like I normally do, choosing instead to blow dry it straight. I have never been a fan of lots of makeup, so all I wear is a little light foundation and some lip gloss. I look in the mirror, thinking about how he said I was pretty. No guy has ever said that directly to me before. It may be a little conceited, but I liked it.

I look at the time on my phone. Damn, I spent so

much time grooming that I didn't leave time to make breakfast. I will have to stop for fast food somewhere. It's not the best choice but it will have to do. Bo watches me running around the house gathering my purse. "I will be back soon, boy. You be good, okay?"

The drive-through lane at the fast food place is crazy. It is almost time that I would normally take my break as I look at my phone again. I can't call or text him that I am going to be late. When I finally get my turn to order, I order enough food to make sure he is fed throughout the day, plus two large coffees. Nervous energy has me unconsciously tapping my fingers on the steering wheel, wishing these guys would hurry up.

When I finally get the food and head to the diner, it is already fifteen minutes past the time I should have been out there. I have been panicking, curious if Ben showed up and left when I wasn't there. Pulling in to the truck stop, I find a quick place to park. I grab the food and coffee and try my best to walk quickly to the back of the diner. The heels are not helping with this endeavor as I am trying to juggle the drink carrier and the bag of food, without falling and breaking my neck. I am relieved when I see him sitting on the milk crates waiting. He stands when he sees me coming toward him.

"Good morning." I pause, trying to catch my breath. "I am so sorry I am late," I say, taking another breath, "but am happy you waited."

He looks at me funny, as his eyes scan me over. He takes the coffee tray from me as it is about to spill over. He isn't smiling like he is happy to see me.

"What's wrong?"

"You scared me, when ya came around the corner so quickly. I thought maybe you were in trouble." He scowls at me.

"Oh, I'm sorry, it's just today is my day off, and I was

running late." My breathing starts to slow down now.

"Why didn't ya tell me yesterday? You didn't need to come all the way out here."

I notice he is wearing a different jacket today. It is gray and in better condition than the blue one. He has on a different flannel shirt today too. Instead of the unruly hair, he is wearing a black beanie, with his long hair hanging out the sides of it. He still has that ghastly beard but it really appears he took the time to groom today. He doesn't look so much like a homeless person as before. It has me hoping that maybe he took my advice and went to a shelter.

"But I wanted to. I wanted to see you and give you this." I hold out the food bag and smile, looking at him and wishing he would smile back. Right now he looks very intimidating as he stares at me.

He waits before speaking again, just shaking his head as he finally cracks a smile. He hands me my coffee and goes over to the dumpster to toss the carry tray. I go ahead and sit down as he walks back over to join me. As soon as he sits I hand him the bag. I watch him as he looks inside the bag and looks back at me.

"Damn, Julie were ya plannin' on feedin' an army?" His tone is more cheerful now, so I hope he is just teasing me, and not serious.

I start blushing, not really knowing what to say. "I just wanted to make sure you had enough for the whole day." I am embarrassed by the fact that maybe I did overdo it.

"Whole day or whole week?" he laughs.

I feel better now knowing he is just teasing me again. He is so much like Jason, when it comes to picking on me. Whatever. I turn my head to look out at the street. Out of the corner of my eye, I see him grab one of the many breakfast sandwiches I bought before folding the bag up and setting it next to him.

He sits and enjoys his coffee and sandwich and I let him eat in peace as I people watch the folks going in and out of the truck stop.

"It's Sunday," he says between bites. "Don't ya need to head off to church?"

"Oh, I don't go to church." As I say that, I think to myself, Well, at least not anymore.

"Really? Why's that? You believe in God, don't ya?" He is finished eating now and wads up the wrapper, stuffing it in his pocket.

"Well, yeah, but ..." I stall, thinking to myself is there ever a good answer to this question? This conversation is getting too deep for this early in the morning.

"But what?" He presses me to answer.

"I don't want to talk about this right now. Besides, why would you think I was heading off to church?"

"Well, look at ya—you're all dressed up." He fans his hands out at me, like I am a showcase prize on a game show. "I just assumed it was to go to church. I mean isn't that what you do gooders do? Go to church, raise money, help out the less fortunate?"

I sit and stare at him, waiting for the punch line, but I see he is serious. I want to be angry with him, for the do gooder remark. Does he really think I see him as a charity case? One thing is certain, I will not admit to him that I dressed up for him. I try to act nonchalant. "Oh, well I have plans later so ..."

"Ah, a date." He says with a huge grin on his face.

"Nooo ..." I immediately respond. "I mean, not a date, date." Well, so much for dressing up to impress him. Now he thinks I am a do gooder, going out with someone else.

"Hey, it's none of my business. You don't have to tell me."

"Umm, there's nothing to tell. I was just going to hang

with friends, is all." Wow, that's a lie.

"So ya do have friends, that's good." I cut him a dirty look for that remark and he finally loses the teasing grin. Maybe he finally realizes he is pushing it. "All I am sayin', is that ya look very nice today, Julie."

"Thank you." I pause for a second, enjoying the fact he just paid me a compliment when I remembered the first part. "What do you mean by, so I do have friends?"

He starts laughing again; obviously I am amusing him today. "Well, I was afraid ya didn't, seein' how for the last few days you have been hangin' around with me. I just figured ya must be lonely to make friends with a bum." He stretches his legs out, with his hands in his pockets.

"I am not lonely." That's lie number two. "Stop calling yourself a bum. You're not a bum. You're just ..." Damn, great going, Julie, what do you say now?

"I'm just what?" He is looking at me, with no humor on his face now, waiting for me to respond. I look into his eyes, that today, look grayish, with hints of gold. What color are they?

"Down on your luck, is all." I look down at the ground, not knowing what more to say.

"That's puttin' it mildly," he responds, but neither one of us are joking anymore.

I wonder if he is ready to listen to my advice. "Ben, my friend can help."

"No," he snaps quickly.

"But if you would just talk to him." I plead with him, trying to make him see reason.

"I said no, Julie. I got myself in this mess I will get myself out when I am ready."

So he is in trouble. I am not sure if he even caught what he said. He is also stubborn as hell. I know Carl and I could help him if he would just let us. I look away from him, crossing my arms as I try to think of some way to get him to be reasonable.

"Hey, don't pout now, it is too nice of a mornin' to be poutin'."

"I'm not pouting."

"Oh, really? Then what's this?" He crosses his arms, copying me and then he squints his eyes and puffs out his cheeks. That is very extreme to what I would be doing if I was pouting, of course.

He looks so damn silly that I can't help but start laughing. "Stop it!" I continue to laugh. "You look ridiculous. I don't look like that."

He finally stops. "Maybe not, but I gotcha to laugh again." He takes a deep breath, staring off into the horizon. "It looks like you picked a good day to go hang with your friends."

I look up, enjoying the blue sky. "Yeah, it is a pretty day. The sky is so blue today, not a cloud in it."

"Yeah, real pretty." Out of the corner of my eye, I can see he is no longer looking at the sky, but at me. I act like I don't notice.

"So, what about you?" I suddenly turn my head. "What are your plans today? What do you normally do after I see you in the morning?"

"Oh, I have a few friends that I met here and there, and I go and talk with them, and you know, help 'em out."

"Oh, you mean like a do gooder?" I throw his remark from earlier back at him.

"Yeah, I suppose." He seems amused by my snappy comeback. "Sometimes I just find a quiet place and read, like the library or just under a nice tree somewhere."

"Read? I love to read. What do you like to read?" This is exciting as we have found a common bond now.

"Oh, anything I guess."

"What are you reading now?"

He reaches into his backpack and pulls out a Stephen King novel and shows me.

"Stephen King—I have never read his books. I just have seen the movies."

"Ah, but the books are so much better. You should give him a try sometime. Who do you like to read? No wait, let me guess. You like them sweet little romance books, right?"

"No, not always."

"Oh, are you one of those naughty girls that like that book ... what's it called? You know that book all you girls are crazy about?"

"What book?" I wonder where he is going with this now.

"Come on, you know the one with the tie or something on the front cover. I forget what it's called but women are so funny at the library when they ask to check it out. Like it is a sin to read it or something. Must be pretty hot. You know what I'm talkin' about, right?"

"No, I don't think I do." There is lie number three today. I have read it twice, secretly on my e-reader. It is cool today, but my face is getting hot.

"You little liar, ya do too or ya wouldn't be blushin' right now." He starts laughing.

I can't think of any snappy comeback for this so I decide to fess up. "Okay, fine. I was curious what the fuss was all about."

"Uh huh, was it good?" He continues laughing and giving me the eyebrow wiggle.

I don't say a word, deciding it is better to just let him have his laugh and move on.

"Never mind, ya don't have to answer that. I can tell ya kind of liked it. Never go to Vegas, baby. You, my dear, do not have a poker face."

I look at him and smile, not because of the gambling

crack, that I already knew. Both Carl and Jason told me that numerous times, I am smiling because he just called me baby and not like he meant little kid. He doesn't react. Maybe he didn't realize what he said.

"Maybe ya should go to church today, darlin', and confess your sins to your preacher. Shame on you for readin' such dirty things." He continues to laugh as he is in no hurry to let this one go. Enough is enough.

"Maybe you should read it since you seem so interested in it." I softly punch his upper arm, giving him a clue that it is time to drop it.

"Maybe I will, especially since it made ya blush so."

I shake my head as we both start laughing now. This little banter between us reminds me of Jason and me, with the teasing just to the point of us both laughing but not going too far to hurt each other's feelings. Thinking of Jason, I stop laughing suddenly as a wave of grief hits me. Why am I laughing? My brother is dead. I shouldn't be laughing. Oh no, don't you dare cry right now, Julie. If Ben notices my quick shift in emotions, he is kind enough to not ask. I sit there silently until Ben gets up.

"I best be goin', so ya can go meet with your friends. Thank ya for the breakfast, and dinner and supper, for the next three days." He smiles as he holds up the bag.

"Sorry." I look at him quickly, trying to hold back the tears.

"Nah, don't, I am just bein' an ass. Really, Julie, thank ya, it was very thoughtful of ya. I just …" He doesn't finish his sentence and looks down at his feet.

"Just what?" I wonder what he was going to say.

"Nothin'. Come on, let me walk ya to the car."

I get up and start following him to the parking lot. He then follows me to my car as I click the key fob, unlocking the doors. He opens the door for me, and waits for me to get in before closing it. I crank it up and roll down my window as he stands there.

"Can I give you a lift somewhere?" I take a chance even though I am sure he will say no. He surprises me when he doesn't answer quickly, as if he is considering my offer. I sit patiently waiting and hoping.

"No, I'm good. Thanks though." He smiles. I try not to frown in disappointment. For a moment I thought maybe he would be logical. I need to back off and not push him.

"Will I see you tomorrow?" I ask, hoping I didn't run him off by my sudden distance.

"I guess. You're workin' tomorrow, right?" He gives me a stern look. He must still be unhappy I came here on my day off.

"Yes, I promise."

"Okay." He smiles. "I guess I'll see ya then." That smile of his, makes me want to stay and spend the day with him instead, even if we just sit on the crates and talk. I know he will not have it though.

"Be careful, Ben."

"Always and you drive safely home now."

I nod and start driving away slowly. I can see in the rearview mirror that he is standing there watching me. When I pull onto the street, leaving the parking lot, I look up again and he is gone.

# CHAPTER
*five*

MONDAY MORNING AT THE DINER is crazy busy for some reason, probably because people are back to work after the Thanksgiving weekend. I keep watching the clock; my break was supposed to be twenty minutes ago, but we have been too busy. When I finally fill all the cups and help all the customers in my area, I alert Holly that I am going on break. She waves me on as I rush, grabbing a to go cup of coffee a breakfast sandwich.

When I open the door I am so afraid he is not going to be there, thinking I stood him up or something. A wave of relief washes over me when I see him sitting on the crates and watching out over the parking lot. He must have heard the door open because he turns to look at me. He rewards me with his handsome smile as I close the door and walk over to him.

"I am so sorry, it is crazy in there this morning. I

couldn't take a break until now. Here." I hand him the coffee and sandwich. "It's not a breakfast burrito but it is pretty good." I go ahead and sit down next to him.

"Thank ya, and don't apologize, you are helpin' me, remember? Not the other way around." His voice sounds funny. Before I can ask him what's wrong, he suddenly starts coughing. He turns his head and covers his mouth to avoid coughing on me.

"What's wrong? Are you okay? Are you sick?" He coughs and nods, unable to speak. At first I thought he choked but I realize by listening to him, he is coming down with something. I rub his back on instinct, to help him. He finally stops and looks at me.

"It's fine. I think I picked up some bug." His voice is nasally. He is stuffed up, that's why he sounds so strange. My heart sinks as I start to worry. The weather is colder today and if he is staying out here all night it is no wonder he is getting sick.

"Are you doing okay out here? I mean, where do you sleep? Is it warm enough?" I can't help myself, but my mother hen side is coming out as I am spewing out questions and not giving him a chance to answer them.

"Hey, slow down, darlin', I need coffee if you're gonna start twenty questionin' me." He manages to strangle the words out. His coughing has stopped for a moment at least. He takes another sip of coffee and tucks the sandwich away in his pocket again. As much as I like seeing him every morning, this can't continue. The weather is getting colder and now he is sick.

"Ben, what if I took you somewhere, find you some help, and maybe a job? Carl is looking for a dishwasher; it doesn't pay a lot but it is something."

He starts shaking his head and stands up as if he is ready to leave. "I don't want ya to do that. I manage, Julie. I appreciate the food and your company." He holds up his coffee for emphasis. "Look, if this is too hard for ya, just say so. I will quit hangin' around."

What the hell is his problem this morning, besides being sick? He seems angry at me as I am suddenly hit with the sting of his words. What is wrong with showing some concern? Is he saying these things because I am aggravating him and he doesn't feel well? I hate confrontation so I back down like I normally do. "Fine, I won't pressure you, but if you change your mind, please let me help you."

He nods, but refuses to sit back down. He starts coughing again. He can be stubborn all he wants but we have to get to somewhere warmer. This is ridiculous.

"Come on, follow me." I get up and start heading to the parking lot.

"Julie, wait, where ya goin'?" Now he is the one that is acting like he doesn't want me to leave.

I walk back over, grabbing up his arm and noticing how muscular it is under the sweat shirt. I start to pull him and he resists at first. I look up at him and the smirk on his face. He is finding my attempt to move him humorous. Not amused, I tug at his arm again and he starts walking with me, showing no resistance this time.

I reach in my apron pocket, retrieving my car keys, and unlocking the doors to my car. I open the passenger door, nodding my head for him to get in. "Get in, you need to get warm."

He stands there, as if he is ready to bolt at any minute. "Julie, I told ya I don't want to go anywhere."

"Fine, we won't, but we can sit in the car and get warm at least," I spit out as I motion with my head again for him to get in. I am very irritated and no longer feel like playing games.

Again he doesn't argue as he sits down in the passenger seat and I am happy he is allowing me to help him just a little. I go around and get into the driver's seat, starting the engine and turning the heater on high.

"I just got here a few hours ago, so it shouldn't take long to warm up." I begin rubbing my hands and enjoy the warm heat myself. Looking over, Ben is shivering more than me. It is so cold today, and then I remember the blanket in the trunk that I keep for emergencies.

"I am going to get a blanket out of the trunk, I will be right back." Before he has a chance to protest, I quickly get out, and open the trunk, grabbing the blanket. I see the backpack and coat there that I wanted to give to him and grab it too. Closing the trunk, I open the back door, throwing the coat and backpack in the back before opening his door to wrap the blanket around him. I take my time, tucking it in as if he was a small child instead of a grown man.

I look up to see him watching me with a strange look on his face. Our faces are so close, closer than I have been to a man in quite some time. A funny feeling comes over me. The cold wind reminds me that I don't have time to analyze this strange feeling, as I quickly finish and close his door. I hurry back to my side and get in.

As the car quickly warms up, we both sit quietly except for his coughing fits, which seem to be slowing down. I stare out the window, deep in my thoughts. I am still a little hurt by his reaction to me wanting to get him help earlier. I just don't understand why he will let me help him like this but not get him real help. He starts sipping on his coffee again. The silence is almost deafening. I finally cave.

"You can eat your sandwich in the car if you like," I say very quietly. I am churning with many emotions right now, and I don't have a clue why.

"It's okay. I'll rather save it for later," he responds and out of the corner of my eye, I can see him looking at me now. "What's wrong?" he asks.

"Nothing," I quickly bite out, still not looking at him as I look out the windshield.

"Julie, look at me." His voice is demanding. I continue to avoid him, afraid that if I look at him I will start crying. "Please look at me." He softens his tone, and now I can't help but to look over at him, hoping like hell that the tears won't fall. His expression seems apologetic.

"Julie, I'm sorry if I hurt your feelins, darlin'. I really do appreciate everythin', but I just don't get why ya bother?" He starts coughing again.

I was ready to accept his apology until the "why bother?" remark. All he manages to do is piss me off. "Just stop talking, okay? When you talk, you cough." I turn away again. Damn stubborn man. He leaves me alone and relaxes in his seat. At least he isn't getting ready to bolt out of the car. He needs help, and I have to think of some way to get him the help he needs. I may have to tell Carl anyway. No sooner than that thought leaves my head, I see a charter bus pull up in the parking lot and they look like they are stopping at the diner. Well, my day just got busier.

"Oh, no!" I mumble as I stare out the windshield

"What's up?" Ben asks as he sits up.

"A tour bus, and I think they are going into the diner." Ben and I watch as the bus parks and the people start unloading. Teenagers—just great—lots of food, no tips. I have to get back inside, otherwise Carl will come looking for me to help and he will have a coronary if he sees me in a car with Ben. I turn to finally look at him, no longer angry.

"Ben, I'm sorry, I have to go back inside. You are welcome to stay in the car and keep warm for as long as you like. Just bring the keys back to me when you leave."

"No, turn it off and take the keys with ya. I'll be fine,

Julie." Great here we go again.

"No, really, it's okay if you want to stay here and get warm. I trust you, Ben."

He hesitates a split second, his expression unreadable. "No, it's not." He shakes his head as he reaches over, shutting the car off, and handing me the keys. I reluctantly take them, putting them back in my pocket. My hands still cold, I rub them together. His mind is set, no sense in arguing about it.

"Well, stay in here for as long as you like, and in the back is a coat and backpack I put together for you. Be sure to take them and the blanket too."

I go to get out but he grabs my hand, holding it very gently in his. He holds out his other hand, and I take it as an invitation to place my other hand in his. I place my small hand in his and he holds them tight and rubs them. He is warming my hands as well as my heart. The contact is so innocent but yet so intimate. We both look at our hands, my small ones inside his large ones, while he continues to rub and warm my hands.

He looks up into my eyes again. "Thank ya, Julie, for everythin'. You are a true angel, darlin'." He smiles and continues rubbing my hands, quickly warming them. I am touched as he tries to make me comfortable, but the way he is thanking me, has me worried. My heart sinks, thinking that he is somehow saying goodbye. I know I can't force him to stay. I can only hope he will take my advice and get some help.

"Stay in here for as long as you like. I hope you feel better soon. If I don't see you later, please take care of yourself."

He nods at me again, not correcting me on my insight. I was right, he is going to leave. He finally releases my hands as I watch him lean back in the seat. At least he will stay in here for awhile out of the cold wind. He looks so tired as he closes his eyes. How do I ask him to stay? I have done all I can. Maybe he will take my suggestion and go to a shelter.

As much as I would like to see him more, I can't keep him from taking care of himself. I glance at him one more time, to take a mental photograph of him. He must sense it as he opens his eyes briefly. It's as if he is doing the same to me. I give him a smile, and I am rewarded with one back as I quickly get out of the car. I rush to the diner, not looking back.

Through the rest of my busy shift, I steal moments to look out into the parking lot to see if I can still see Ben. My car is too far to tell if he is still in there or not, and I didn't see him leave. I see Carl watching me as I keep looking into the parking lot and I quickly get busy so he doesn't question me. If he had any idea of what I had done, he would throttle me and probably run Ben out of here. Soon my shift is over. I say my goodbyes to Carl as I walk out to my car. It is empty, which I suspected, but I also notice he took the coat, backpack, and blanket, which makes me feel a little better. I look around outside, hoping just maybe he is out there, but I don't see him. Wherever he is, I hope he is safe.

Bo and I settle in for the evening after supper. My thoughts all day have been on Ben and where he could be right now. I just pray he went to a shelter. I invite Bo on the couch again to lie next to me. It is definitely getting colder outside by the second. As I channel surf to find something for us to watch, I stop at the local news channel as they are talking about the weather. I listen as they announce very frigid temperatures for tonight and the early morning—record lows they say and it isn't even officially winter yet.

My thoughts immediately turn to Ben again. What if he is still out there? He will freeze tonight, especially with him being sick. If only I could just get him to go to shelter at least. This is ridiculous—no way can I sit here in a warm house knowing he is out there probably freezing somewhere. I don't care anymore if he is stubborn, I am going to insist he lets me help him find shelter at least. I look over at Bo, who is watching me as if he knows what I am thinking. "Hey, boy, do feel like taking a little ride?"

# CHAPTER *six*

I PULL INTO THE TRUCK stop parking lot and I am thankful there is adequate lighting. Driving very slowly, I look at the sides and behind the store and diner, but I don't see Ben or any other homeless person lurking around. It is almost eleven o'clock, so hopefully he went to a shelter to sleep and stay warm. It is his protest earlier today about going to the shelter that has me worried for him as I park behind the diner. Bo sticks his nose to me as if he knows my plan. I grab the leash sitting on the seat and hook it to Bo.

"Want to go for a little walk, boy?" I get out and open the backdoor to let him out. I don't expect him to sniff Ben out. I just want him more for protection than anything. Using Ben's comment from today, I must be nuts for being out here looking for him. We walk over to where I first saw Ben when I was taking my break. I stand and turn completely around, looking for any sign of him.

Bo begins whining, capturing my attention.

"I know, boy, we should just go home and be in our nice warm bed, but I had to try." I look around again but it is no use. No one is out in this cold weather but stupid me. I exhale my frustration and can see the fog of my breath. Bo whines again. "Yes you're right, this is nuts. Let's go home." I start to walk to the car but the tension on the leash has me stopping suddenly. Bo just sits there, and gives one sharp bark, so I walk back to him.

"What's wrong, boy? Come on, let's go home where it is nice and warm." But Bo still sits there and keeps looking toward the dumpster and whining. I am not sure I understand what he is doing. I know he has training, but I don't know all the military commands my brother used with him. I just know the basics: sit, stay, lie down, and shake. My brother said they used Bo to sniff out explosives and the enemy. He was very loyal to my brother. In fact, the day my brother was killed, they had to find another dog handler to remove Bo from my brother's side. Bo had laid on top of him, protecting him, even though he had died instantly from the bullet.

With Bo insisting to stay put, I go ahead and carefully approach the dumpster to investigate. I am hoping it's not a bomb he smells. Bo now follows me. I give him a look, figuring he is sending me on a wild goose chase, or more likely a wild cat chase. "If this turns out to be a cat, no treats for you when we get home."

There is a gap between the dumpster and the concrete wall. It is narrow, but a person could fit back there if they needed to. I point my flashlight, prepared for a cat or something worse to come scrambling out at any second. At first I only see a large piece of cardboard, but as I shine the light down, I see a familiar pair of military boots sticking out and then I hear the unmistakable coughing.

I carefully remove the piece of cardboard, and there is Ben, huddled up and shivering with his eyes closed. He is wearing the coat I gave him and wrapped in the blanket. He doesn't even realize I am here. Kneeling down, I call out to him before touching him, in hopes that I don't startle him.

"Ben. Ben, can you hear me?" I still get no response, so I finally touch his arm and he opens his eyes wide in shock as his body jerks away from me.

"Go away." He starts coughing, turning his head as to not cough in my face.

"No. I have to get you out of here. You will die out here."

"Leave me be, Julie." He coughs again, closing his eyes as if he is blocking me out.

"Ben, you can't stay out here; it is freezing."

"Pl-please ... Jul-ie ... just ... just ... go." He can barely get the words out, he is shivering so much.

"I can't. I have been worried about you all day. Please let me take you to the hospital or the shelter."

"No hospital. No shelter," he whispers before coughing again.

"Ben, please, please don't do this. Whatever the problem is, dying out here is not the answer."

He stares at me, not speaking, and suddenly Bo squeezes in and makes an appearance beside me. "Is that your dog?" he whispers before starting another coughing fit.

"Yes, this is Bo. He is the one that found you." I pet my fluffy roommate, deciding he will get a nice reward for finding Ben. Ben stares at Bo as Bo walks up to him, nudging his hand with his nose. I figure it's Bo's way of telling him the same thing.

"Come on, Ben. See? Even Bo wants you to come with me. Let's get out of here, please."

"Bo?" Ben looks at me, then looks at Bo, a questioning look on his face.

"Now is not the time to ask about my dog's name. Come on, please." I grab at his coat sleeve but Ben makes no move to come with me. It is just like earlier today, but I am not in the mood to play his game anymore. I know he has said no to the hospital and the shelter, so I try another tactic. "Fine, if you won't go to the hospital or the shelter, then come back to my home. It is warm there. I have an extra room you can sleep in."

He just stares at me, not moving, but Bo squeezes in further and lies down, placing his head on Ben's lap. Ben stares down at him, and slowly reaches out to touch him, rubbing the top of his head. I am amazed at how quickly Bo is acting friendly toward Ben. It took Carl many weeks to get Bo to come up to him.

"See? Bo wants you to go with us too." Ben is still not budging, but he doesn't say no. I must be breaking him down. I decide to get sneaky now and use my fem fatale. He always seems to feel protective and concerned for me. I wonder ... "Ben, please, it is so cold out here. I am freezing. Please, let's get somewhere warm. I won't go unless you go with me." I start shivering as the cold is in fact starting to get to me.

He coughs again and gives me a look. I hold my ground and continue to shiver as I wrap my arms around myself. I got a feeling I am winning this argument.

"Fine, ya win, your place, no hospital." He starts standing, going slowly and is shaky, so I help him, not taking the time to gloat in my victory.

As I did this morning, I help him to my car, but this time with Bo walking carefully behind. Opening the passenger side door, he ducks down and sits inside. He has the blanket I gave him wrapped around his head and shoulders. I hurry to the driver's side, holding the door open for Bo who jumps into the back without being told. Ben turns, looking at Bo as if he was amazed by him or something. He must be a dog lover. It's another reason to like him. I start the car and crank the heater on full blast, pointing most of the vents on Ben.

"I better get you home. Are you sure you won't go to the hospital?" I ask as I buckle up.

Ben turns to face forward again, and at first I think he will buckle up but he reaches for the door handle. "No hospital, Julie, or I will get out right now." He starts coughing again. The warmth of the car must be giving him a little strength as he tries challenging me again. Realizing I have already got him to agree to come home with me, I decide to not push my luck.

"Okay, fine. I will stop about the hospital. And you call me stubborn," I mumble under my breath. Ben nods and releases his hand from the door and buckles up.

After getting Bo settled in the back, I start the drive home. I look up in the rearview mirror and see Bo keeping his eyes on Ben. I look over at Ben several times in concern. When he catches me, he immediately misunderstands why I keep looking at him.

"I won't hurt ya, Julie, I promise." He starts coughing again. Bo starts whining again.

I am appalled by his statement. I wasn't even thinking that, although, if I was smart I should be. After all, I am inviting an almost stranger to my home. But I trust my gut, and it tells me that Ben would not hurt me. I am angry he would even consider I was thinking that.

"Shhh, every time you talk, you start coughing and it is upsetting Bo." I look up in the rearview mirror to check on Bo again before looking back at the road. "Besides, I know you won't hurt me."

I look over at him again and he is laying his head on the seat, slightly reclined, and is staring intensely at me.

Sometimes I wish I was gifted with mindreading so I would know what he was thinking right now. His coughing slows down and his shivering has completely stopped and soon all is quiet. I take one more glance and notice his eyes are closed; he must be exhausted. The desire to reach out and touch his face has me gripping the steering wheel harder.

We arrive back at my house just before midnight. It is a good thing I am off tomorrow as the long day and night starts to wear on me too. I look over at Ben, who is awake now. He rubs at his face, looking around as if he has no idea what has happened. I turn off the car, resting my hands on the wheel.

"Well, this is it, home sweet home." Ben looks out the window, the expression on his face is hard to judge, but deep down, I hope he likes it.

I get out and open the door to let Bo out as I walk over to make sure Ben gets out okay. He is steadier now; the warmth of the car bringing back his strength, but the moment we hit the cold air, his coughing begins again.

"Let's hurry and get you inside and get you warm." I open the front door and Bo runs in and I wait for my guest to walk in first. He still has the blanket around him as he walks into my home. The house is warm and welcoming; the lamp is still on, giving a soft glow to my living room. If I had a fire going in the fireplace, it would be downright cozy.

He looks around, taking in his surroundings, and again I wonder what he is thinking. Something else is puzzling about my homeless guest. I noticed on the drive home that he didn't smell. I would expect someone who has been on the streets to have an unpleasant odor but Ben doesn't. I mean I didn't stick my nose to him, but we were close in a car together; it would make sense that if he stunk, I would smell it.

But he has to be homeless. I caught him sleeping behind the dumpster in the freezing cold. A person who had a home wouldn't do that. Maybe he got clean at the shelter, but if that is the case, why didn't he spend the night there? I have many questions, but I am also tired and so is he. I will save the interrogation for tomorrow. He continues looking around as Bo sits right next to him.

"Are you hungry? I have some leftovers in the fridge."

"No, thank you." He starts coughing again, covering his mouth and holding his side. He is looking worse. Since he refuses to go to the hospital, I am running out of ideas on how to help.

"Let's get you into bed." He stands back up straight. His eyebrows shoot up, making me realize how that sounds. Well, at least his dirty mind is working.

Before he gets the chance to tease me, I say, "The spare room is down the hall, follow me." I start walking down the hallway and Ben follows slowly. I hesitate a moment at Jason's door before opening it. I have to wonder if I am betraying my brother by letting someone sleep here. It takes but a moment to remember that my brother considered all Marines his brothers, and by that, he would not mind.

"Is there a problem?" Ben asks, probably wondering about my hesitation.

"No, not at all. Come on in." Turning on the light to my brother's room, it is just like he left it the last time he was home. I refuse to pack up his things. I am just not ready to say goodbye, and in fact, except to dust once in a while, I haven't been in here. Ben looks around and I can tell he isn't sure what he should do. I start walking around giving him the tour.

"This door is to the joining bathroom. Just make sure to lock and unlock both doors, as I use this bathroom too sometimes. There are towels in there if you need one, and shampoo and soap in there too. You know, in case you want to take a shower or bath." "Why, do I smell?"

Suddenly I turn red with embarrassment, thinking about my thoughts earlier. "No, I didn't mean ... I just thought, just in case ..." I shake my head in mortification. Ben smiles and holds up his hands.

"Julie, it's fine. I'm just messin' with ya." He takes the blanket off and sets it down on the chair by the desk. He looks around the room as if he is taking it all in. "This is a nice room."

I start to get uncomfortable, not wanting any questions to be asked. I quickly go over to the dresser and find a pair of lounge pants and a T-shirt. I walk over to Ben and hand them to him. "Here you go. These should fit you, they are my brother's." "Won't he be mad?" That look of concern returns to Ben's face.
"No, he won't ..." I don't elaborate and turn quickly away to avoid further discussion. "Anyway, I will leave you alone and let you get settled." I start heading to the door, thinking I can't handle watching Ben get undressed.

"Julie." His voice is sweet and sounds concerned.

I turn back to face him. "Yeah?" I wait, as he seems deep in thought before speaking again.

"Thank you," is all he manages to say, but it is more than enough.
"You're welcome." I give him a smile and turn and leave, closing the door. I look down at Bo who hasn't left my side since Ben walked in. He has a look about him, a look of judgment or at least that's how I interrupt it.

"What? Don't look at me like that. What was I supposed to do, leave him out there to freeze to death?" I whisper so Ben can't hear me. Bo starts panting. "Yeah, that's what I thought. I had no choice. Come on, boy, you deserve a treat." We walk to the kitchen, leaving our guest to get settled in.

# CHAPTER
## *seven*

I ROLL OVER ON MY other side. Every time I am about to doze off, the sounds from Jason's room wake me up. Ben's coughing is keeping me awake and Bo keeps whining at the door, wanting to investigate as well. This is ridiculous. He is sounding worse, not better at all. I give up and turn on the lamp. In my zombie state, I go into my bathroom and look through the medicine cabinet. I don't normally get sick, but I did have a cold around Halloween. Maybe, aha, yes. I take out the cough syrup. If this doesn't help, he will be going to the hospital whether he likes it or not.

I quietly open the bedroom door, hoping not to surprise or scare him. It is very dark. It is a good thing I know my way around. I will need light to see so I walk over to the desk and turn on the lamp.

Through his coughing fits he sits up and manages to speak. "What's wrong?" He squints, looking over at me. I come over to the bed to check on him. He is bundled up like he is freezing, but the room is warm. He turns his head, coughing again before looking at me and sitting up as I sit on the bed next to him. Not a minute later, Bo jumps on the bed to join us. I take the dosage cup and start pouring the syrup into it, filling it to the top.

"What the hell is that?" he says, leaning back and trying not to cough, but he fails and has another coughing fit.

"This is to help with that," I say after he finally stops coughing. I hold the cup out to him. "Here you go, drink up."

"No fuckin' way," he says, turning his head.

I am tired and not in the mood for a grown man to be acting like a child. "Excuse me? Now listen to me." My tone causes him to turn back to look at me. "I am tired and I don't feel like arguing with you anymore. First, you wouldn't let me take you to the hospital, then I had to practically beg you to come here with me.

Secondly, I am tired and I need sleep. When I don't sleep, I get grumpy. So, yes, you will take the medicine, even if I have to sit on you and pour it down your throat myself." I raise my eyebrows at him as I hold the cup out to him, giving him the clue to just try me mister.

He looks at Bo and then at me. A huge smile comes over his face, and even though it is covered with that horrible beard, it is still a beautiful smile. He takes the cup and quickly swallows the medicine, making a disgusted face and smacking his lips. He looks at Bo again. "Is she always so bossy?"

I am suddenly taken aback by the way he talks to Bo. He talks to Bo like I talk to him, as if he was a person and not just a dog. I like that.

He is still bundled up and I have my suspensions, so I reach up, touching his forehead, and then I start touching his cheeks. "Ben, you're burning up. You have a fever."

"I guess so, but it will be fine, Julie, don't worry."

I jump up, going back in the bathroom to get the ibuprofen and a glass of water and bring it back to him. "Here, take these, it will help." I sit back down at the edge of the bed

He looks at me like he is about to argue but quickly decides against it and takes the pills, swallowing them down with the water. "Ya satisfied now?"

"Yes."

"May I go back to sleep then?" He settles back down, punching his pillows and getting comfortable again.

I get up off the bed. "Sure, hopefully it will kick in soon." He is lying back down, but is staring at me. His eyes trail me up and down. I am wearing my long pink T-shirt nightgown with a kitten on the front that says "purrfect." The nightgown covers everything and is not sexy by any means, so I am not sure what he is staring at.

"Do you need anything else?" I ask before turning off the light.

"No, unless you are gonna sing me a lullaby." He smiles at me as he closes his eyes.

"I better not. I can't carry a tune in a bucket. Bo could probably sing better than me."

"Doubt that, kitten," he mumbles and I am not sure if I heard him correctly. Did he just call me kitten?

"What did you say?"

"Good night, Julie," he mumbles into his pillow, dismissing me for the night.

"Okay, good night, Ben," I whisper as I shut off the light and tiptoe out.

The next morning, I am up early and I sneak in to check on Ben ... again. Last night I snuck in to notice he was still warm, so I placed a cold washcloth on his forehead. If he was awake, he didn't flinch and allowed me to take care of him. He is still sleeping and I touch his face, finding that once again, he is running a fever. He opens his eyes, watching me.

"Good morning." I smile down at him.

He hesitates before saying anything. "Good morning." He smiles back. Even sick, his smile still gets to me.

"You're still running a temperature. I am going to go get more medicine. How do you feel?"

He sits up, and the sheet rolls down but the T-shirt he is wearing has ridden up slightly and his flat stomach with a light patch of hair is exposed. I try not to stare, but it is hard not to.

"Not so hot. My head is killing me and this cough ..." As if on cue, he starts coughing again. He winces, so I know the constant coughing is making him sore. "This cough," he continues, "isn't making it feel any better. My ribs are sore too." He sits up a little more before stopping. Feeling a little strange for sitting next to him on the bed, especially because I can't stop staring at his naked stomach, I quickly get up.

"I am going to make you something quick to eat and bring you more medicine, so just relax and watch TV." I get up, walking out of the room, only stopping when he responds.

"Yes, ma'am." He mock salutes me. "I wouldn't want you getting mad at me again, like last night." Even sick, his sense of humor is still there. I am not sure if I want to smile or frown at him, so I just give him an eye roll and walk out.

I called the diner this morning before I checked on Ben. Carl worries so I like to check in. I told Carl I had some business to take care of today when he asked me my plans. If I told him I was sick, he would have been over here in a flash and I can't have that. If he saw Ben here he would kill him, veteran or not. All right, maybe not kill but he would kick him out. Carl didn't ask about what business I needed to do. He knows I volunteer for everything, so it is not out of the ordinary for me to spend my days off this way. I stand at the stove, an unexplainable smile on my face as I prepare a quick ham, egg, and cheese scramble. It is nice to cook for someone else for a change.

I gaze out my kitchen window. Bo is running around the backyard, doing his usual walking the fence line he does every morning. It is like he is inspecting the parameter, making sure everything is safe. It's a good feeling. Even though Ben is sick, I feel happy. I guess I was lonelier than I thought. I place the plate of eggs with two slices of buttered toast on a tray. A small glass of orange juice and a cup of coffee are the final touches as I head to Jason's room.

I peek in, just in case he fell back asleep, only finding him watching TV. He glances over at me as I walk in. "Here, sit up. I have some medicine for you, but first you need to eat something." I set the tray down on his lap, thanking God that he has covered up. He looks at the plate, picks up the fork, and takes a bite of the cheesy egg scramble. He closes his eyes and swallows before opening them and looking at me, smiling.

"What? It tastes okay, doesn't it?" I am unsure of the expression on his face.

"Purty and a good cook." He winks, giving me his flirtatious smile.

My face warms at his compliment as I watch him, making sure he eats as much as he can and takes the medicine. When he is done, I take the tray, handing him a box of tissues and the TV remote. I touch his forehead again, noticing he is still warm. If he doesn't break this fever soon, I will have no choice but to get him medical help.

"What's the verdict nurse? I'm gonna live?"

Normally I would laugh, but fear that he is really sick has my sense of humor on hold. "I wish you would let me take you to the doctor." I frown. He gently takes my hand, removing it from his forehead but not releasing it. The simple delight I feel when he holds my hand is indescribable.

"Nah, you're cuter and the food is better here." He tries again to get me to smile, but it's not working this time. He frowns, as he releases my hand. He must have decided to give up trying to get me to make light of this. "Look, don't worry, it's just a cold. I am a Marine, I have handled a lot worse." He starts coughing again.

Right now, I don't know much about him and I want to know what more has he had to handle. I don't get the chance to ask, however.

"Go, do what you normally do. I am just going to chill and finish watching this movie and sleep."

I start walking to the door slowly, as if I am still debating on what to do. I decide he is right, sleep is what he needs. "Okay, I will check on you in a little while." I turn at the doorway.

"I know you will," he responds, staring at the TV.

I go into my craft room and start working on some gifts I want to make for Christmas. I smile remembering that Ben was wearing the scarf I made. I wonder if he knew I crocheted it. I work for a little while crocheting, but then I put it away to work on my other project. Starting up the computer, I begin working on my story. This is my secret no one knows. I love to write. I have been writing for many years now. It is relaxing dreaming up stories.

I escape into the story as I imagine myself as the

female character being romanced by the hero. I get lost in my writing, not even paying attention to the time. When I finally remember to check, I see it has been a few hours since I gave Ben the cold medicine. I haven't heard any coughing so hopefully he is resting. I go ahead and put away my writing. Just when I decide to get up and go check on him, a soft knock comes from the door.

"Yes?"

"Can I come in?"

I quickly finish putting my laptop away and try to look busy crocheting. "Yes."

Ben slowly opens the door. He doesn't open it all the way, but peeks in.

"Oh, hi, why are you out of bed? Are you feeling better?" Knock it off, Julie, I think to myself. You sound guilty of something.

"Yeah, a little. What are ya doin'?" He opens the door a little more. I knew I sounded guilty of something.

"Come in. This is my craft room, sorry it's a bit messy." I apologize but I haven't had a chance to organize it. He walks in, still looking groggy, so he obviously slept some. He looks around, probably noting the lavender colored walls. It is still the same color it was when I was a little girl, with the purple flower curtains my mother made still on the window. I still have the matching bedding on the small twin bed. I never had the heart to change it, much less organize it. I am a little embarrassed, though, as I have many things sitting on top of stuff. It isn't as bad as an episode of Hoarders but I wish it was more organized.

"You have a lot of stuff in here." He looks around before looking at me.

"Yeah, I guess I do. One day I will get some shelves and organize it all." I feel a little strange having him in my old bedroom. My dad is probably rolling over in his grave right now. I never let a boy in here, not to mention a grown man. Ben looks at the scarf I am working on in my hands.

"So did you make the red scarf?" he asks.

"Yes." I try toning down my excitement at his question. I was wondering if he would ever notice.

"Thought so, it's nice. You're very talented." He looks around my room again. I don't know why I am embarrassed about the condition of the room. I mean after all, Ben has been living on the streets, this is so much better than that.

"Thanks." I watch as he continues looking around before looking at me again. Every time he looks my way, it's like I am just hit with a wave of energy. It is the only way to describe it. Now with him in sweats and a T-shirt, he doesn't appear to me like a homeless person. Just a guy talking to me.

"Do you sell any of them?"

I snap out of my daydream as his question surprises me. It has never really occurred to me to sell them. "Oh, no, I just do it for fun, gifts, and such. I would never ask money for them." Why I had the need to let him know that, I have no idea. I guess it was out of fear that he thinks that he owes me.

"I see." He seems as uncomfortable as I do as we stand in awkward silence.

"Did you need something?" I ask, wondering why all of a sudden he came to find me.

"I hate to bug ya, since you are busy, but I was kind of hungry."

"Oh my gosh, I bet you are. I am so sorry. I get in here and forget all about the time." I set my crochet work down on the desk and start walking to the door. "Come on. I made homemade soup. It's in the Crock-Pot on the counter in the kitchen."

"I thought I smelled somethin' cookin'. It smells good, and it's makin' my stomach growl. I guess my nose is clearin' up, since I can smell now."

"That's good. As soon as you eat, I will give you more medicine. It seems to be doing the trick." I head to the kitchen as he follows. In the hallway I could have sworn I heard him mumble, "I was afraid of that." I just smile to myself, not asking him to repeat himself.

We walk into the kitchen and Ben sits down as I dish out two bowls of homemade chicken noodle soup. I set a bowl in front of Ben, along with a spoon and crackers.

"Thank ya." He smiles as the inhales the aroma of the broth and the steam coming off of it.

"You're welcome." I smile as I set my bowl down. I don't sit down immediately, as first I have to feed the other current man in my life, Bo. He sits patiently by his bowl, waiting his turn. I pour a cup of dog food and he begins munching down. I quickly wash my hands and join Ben at the table. We sit in silence, eating our soup. I know he still doesn't feel well and I don't want to bore him with idle chitchat, even though I am dying to know more about him.

"Ya have a nice home here, Julie, have ya been here long?" he asks before taking a spoonful of soup.

"All my life," I respond, pausing to take a sip of tea.

"Really?" I am not sure if he believes me or is surprised.

"Yes, it was my parents' home." I am suddenly not liking the direction of this conversation. I am giving him info about me instead of the other way around. I take bite of a cracker, hoping he will drop it.

"Ya said was, do they live somewhere else now?" he asks.

So much for dropping it. I decide to be honest. Maybe if I give a little, he will give a little in return. I swallow the cracker in my mouth, and what I am about to say, makes it feel like it is stuck in my throat.

"Actually, they died when I was seven." I take another sip of tea, hoping to wash down the cracker before I start to choke. Ben stares at me, and I avoid his eyes. I don't want to see the pity look. Every time someone gives me the pity look, I start bawling like a baby.

He must sense my emotions as he looks back at his soup. "I'm sorry," he says very quietly as he takes another spoonful of soup.

I shrug, still avoiding looking at him as I stare at the pattern in the tablecloth. I trace my finger around the pattern, trying to keep my emotions in check. I hate crying in front of people.

We both are silent for I have no idea how long. I glance up long enough to see he is done with his soup. I am better now, as I remember my manners as hostess.

"Would you like more?" I ask. I feel brave enough to look at him now. He looks at me and I am scared of what he might say next.

"No, thank you. I'm tired. If you don't mind, I am going back to bed."

I almost want to sigh in relief as he asks no more questions about my family. He gets up, and picks up his bowl.

"Leave it. I will take care of it. You should go to bed." He doesn't argue or comment, he just quietly leaves the room. I stand, taking the empty bowls to the sink. I wash them up quickly, as I wallow in my own self-pity.

# CHAPTER
## *eight*

PERIODICALLY THE REST OF THE day, I check on him and as he said, he is sleeping. He ends up sleeping through the night, and I don't bother waking him for supper. Early in the morning, I sneak in to check on his fever, which has me worried. Fever usually means infection or at least that is what Aunt Gina used to say. I turn on the desk lamp, hoping I don't wake him. Walking over to the bed, I gently touch his forehead, and am relieved to feel it isn't as warm as before.

He looks so vulnerable lying there. There is a sadness about him that I wished I knew what it was all about. Something compels me, and before I can stop myself, I reach down and gently kiss his forehead. I would prefer his cheek but with that big burly beard, how would I find it? I touch his forehead with my hand one more time. Before I can remove it he grabs my hand hard and opens his eyes wide.

"Ow," I exclaim, more surprised than hurt, but it is too late as Ben quickly releases my hand and sits up.

"Dammit, Julie, ya shouldn't sneak up on me like that." He covers his face with his hands. He is angry, and for the first time I am a little frightened and hurt by his anger. He starts coughing again. As I back up to the safety of the other side of the room, I recall Jason warning me one time when he was home on leave to never surprise him. He explained it was nothing personal, just a reaction of always being on guard, waiting for someone to hurt or kill you. I should have known better.

"I am sorry. I only wanted to see if you were better." My eyes tear up under no control of my own. I stand there with my hand on my chest, rubbing it.

Ben finally removes his hands from his face. He squints in the dim light looking over at me. His angry face is now replaced with a look of horror. He immediately jumps out of bed, coming straight to me. On instinct, I take a step back but I feel the desk behind me. I am backed into a corner.

"God, kitten, I am sorry, ya just scared me is all, let me see your hand." He goes to take my hand, just like he has on a few occasions. Only this time, I don't let him take it.

"It's fine, really." I still continue to rub it. "You just startled me, that's all. I shouldn't have snuck up on you like that. I only wanted to see if your fever was gone." Oh shit, I couldn't get the words out without choking up. Damn my timing. I didn't want him to see me crying.

"No, let me see it, please." He holds his hand out gently, and the look of shame on his face is breaking my heart. I know he didn't mean to react so violently. I let him take my hand. He examines it as he holds it gently, soothing the pain he caused it moments ago. When he releases it, I can't help another tear falling down my cheek. He touches it with this finger, collecting it like it is his to take. The next thing I know I am in his arms and he is holding me. It was so quick, I didn't have time to object, not that I would have. One hand is at the small of my back holding me to him, while the other is on the back of my head as he is kissing the top of it.

"Ah, kitten, I am so sorry, please don't cry. I was havin' a dream, and when ya touched me ... shit, it doesn't matter. I hurt ya and I am so, so sorry." He kisses my head again, squeezing me tighter. My face is against the soft Marine Corps T-shirt he's wearing, and I am enjoying being in his arms. "Is your hand okay?" He eases me away from him as he looks at me. The pain in my hand is long gone as well as my tears. He takes my hand again, holding it, and caressing it.

"Yes, I am sorry. I wasn't thinking. I was going to make some coffee and cook breakfast. Would you like to join me?"

"Don't apologize. I am the one actin' like a fuckin' jerk. Shit, I mean shoot. I am sorry about the swearin'."

I smile at his attempt not to curse. I used to get onto Jason too. Cursing for Marines is as natural as breathing, he used to say. I smile at the memory, forgetting all about my hand.

"You're amazing, ya know that?" I look at Ben as he continues to massage my hand, not sure I understand what he means. "I yell at ya and almost break your hand and here ya are smilin' and wantin' to cook me breakfast. I never believed in angels before, but they must exist 'cause here ya are."

I blush at the compliment. From any other guy, I might think it is a cheesy line, but coming from Ben, it is different. "Your fever is gone and you don't sound as stuffy. Are you feeling better?" As if on cue, he starts coughing again.

"Yeah, I still can't shake the cough though." He lets go of my hand so he can cover his mouth.

"Well, you should eat first and then take more cough syrup."

"Yuck, I was afraid you were going to say that." He smiles as I walk to the doorway.

"I better get started. See you in the kitchen?" I return his smile, as I am still in a daze from being in his embrace.

"Sure, I will be in there in a few minutes. Let me clean up." I nod and head to the kitchen.

I am busy getting the coffee ready when I hear him walk in. I turn, finding him in his old clothes and boots and jacket over his arm. He doesn't look like he is ready for coffee. "Going somewhere?" I jokingly ask, but his expression is far from joking.

He clears his throat and coughs again, turning and covering his mouth. "Yeah, I appreciate ya lettin' me crash here the last few nights, but I should get going now." I stand there in shock. What the hell happened in the few minutes he was getting dressed to change his mind? I don't want him to go and I am desperate to think of anything to make him stay.

"But I have coffee brewing, and I was about to fix you some breakfast." I look at myself, in an apron over my night shirt. Maybe if I had fixed myself up this morning he wouldn't be in such a hurry to leave.

"I'm fine. I really should get goin'."

I pretend that he is teasing. If I do that maybe he will change his mind. I turn and continue to prepare breakfast. "You can't go yet. It is still very cold outside, and you need to eat, so I can give you some more cough syrup." I am rambling, feeling desperate to not have him leave. I don't know why I am acting this way, but I just don't want him to go. On cue, Bo goes up to him, jumping up, wanting his attention. Ben smiles and starts petting him.

"See? Even Bo wants you to stay, so come sit down. Coffee should be ready any second now." I start getting busy, avoiding looking at him, and not giving him the opportunity to argue with me. He could still walk out and I can't stop him, but I am so relieved when I hear the kitchen chair scraping the tile floor.

I open the fridge and pull out the ground sausage and can of biscuits in there, still avoiding looking over at him. "I hope you like biscuits and gravy." He doesn't respond so I keep busy cooking up the sausage and getting the biscuits ready for the oven. Looking over, I notice the coffee is ready so I grab two mugs out of the cupboard and pour us each a cup. When I finally look at him to bring it over, he is still petting Bo as he is thumbing through a hunting magazine I left on the table.

"I never asked, do you take anything with your coffee?" I ask as I place the mug in front of him.

He finally looks up at me, and smiles. "No, black is perfect, thank ya."

I grab my coffee, adding creamer and go back to cooking. I finish the gravy, and set it on simmer and join him at the table. He is still reading the magazine, but when he looks up to see me sitting down, he closes it, holding it up for my viewing.

"Huntin' magazine?" His eyebrow raises in question.

"My brother's." I take a sip of coffee, hiding my expression behind the huge mug.

"Does he still live here with ya?" He presses further.

"Not anymore." I get up quickly. If I don't talk about it, the pain won't be as bad … "I think the biscuits are almost done." I open the oven door to check. I turn back and lean into the counter. He keeps staring at me, making me feel like I am under a microscope, and I don't like the feeling. "Would you like more coffee?"

"Yes, please."

I nod, turning to get the pot and refresh his mug.

"So your last name is Walsh?"

"Yes, how did you know that?" Again he holds up the magazine. "Oh, yeah." I shrug.

"So where is Jason now?" he asks as he takes another sip from his mug.

"He died." I don't add that it was exactly a year ago today. I know he will ask how, so I go ahead and get it out. "He was in the Marines and was killed in Afghanistan. He was shot and died instantly."

The room is silent except for the sounds I make getting the pan of biscuits out of the oven and setting it down on the top of the stove. I turn to look at him, wondering why he is so silent. I can read the sympathy in his eyes, a look I get a lot from friends and coworkers when I discuss my brother.

"I'm sorry," he says and I nod, turning, not wanting to show my vulnerability as I grab some plates, setting the table. Everything is done and on the table as I finally take a seat next to him.

"Go on, help yourself, there is plenty." I dig in, watching as he takes his time cutting his biscuits in half on his plate and spooning the gravy on top. Even though I know he must be starving, he shows impeccable manners as he takes a bite of his food like a gentleman. It is strange to watch a man dressed the way he is being so polite.

"So you now know my last name, what is yours?" I ask before taking a bite off my fork.

He takes a paper napkin and wipes his mouth before responding. "Parker."

He doesn't add anything and he keeps looking at my hand. He must think he really hurt me bad. When he finishes, he looks at the food and then to me. "Go ahead and have the rest. I am full and I am not a fan of leftovers," I say, encouraging him.

"This is good." He goes ahead and fills his plate again. My biscuits and gravy are always a winner. Aunt Gina gave me the recipe and when Jason was home on leave, he would beg me to make him some. I sit and watch him enjoy each and every bite. When I finish my coffee, I get up, hoping the taste of a home-cooked meal will change his mind about leaving. I start cleaning the dishes, only to be joined by him at the sink.

"Let me clean up; you cooked the meal." He tries taking my plate, which I in turn refuse to give it to him.

"And you are my guest, so you sit down and finish your coffee. I will do the dishes."

He shakes his head and sits back down. "I won't argue with ya because I know I can't win."

"Now you are getting it." I look over my shoulder at him and smile. "You can go out there and watch TV or stay here and keep me company."

"Keep you company?"

I turn, grabbing his plate and walking back to the sink. "Yeah, you know, I talk and you talk." I have so many questions for him.

"What do ya want to talk about?" Yes, finally I will maybe get some answers.

"Well, let's see." I think for a moment as I take a towel and dry a plate. "What did you do in the Marines?"

He stares blankly at me. "I don't want to talk about that," he says. No reason why but his tone is firm, so I don't push.

"You know Bo is a veteran too." He looks up, interested again. "He was my brother's dog, and they served together. He worked with my brother, helping to find explosives." I take another sip of coffee before setting my mug down on the table. He looks at Bo as I continue. "They told me that Bo wouldn't leave my brother's side until they sent for another handler."

Ben looks back up at me, his expression strange.

"What?" I wonder what I said to upset him. He stares at me a moment, and I can't figure out why. What did I say? Before I can ask out loud, he asks another question.

"Nothing. So how did you end up with Bo?"

"Well Carl is also a veteran and he has some friends and well, I guess he inquired and the next thing I know, they are asking me to come to a leashing ceremony where they retired Bo and awarded me custody of him. He has medals and certificates just like any other war hero." I smile remembering the ceremony.

"Who's Carl?"

"Carl is my boss and dear friend. He has helped me through some very tough times."

Ben gets up and strolls into the living room. I follow him as he walks to the fireplace. He stands there a moment, looking at the pictures. There is a picture of my mom and my dad and a family portrait taken just before they died. There is also a picture of Aunt Gina, Carl, and me. Then there is Jason's military portrait right next to his flag.

"Your brother's?" he asks, nodding his head to the flag.

"Yes, I still need to find a case for it. I feel bad I haven't done that yet."

"First your parents and then your brother," he says quietly as if he is whispering. "Damn, Julie, ya poor kid."

I try not to look offended by the kid remark. I was hoping he didn't see me as a kid. Maybe that is why he is in a hurry to leave. If I was sexier maybe he would stay. Maybe if I gave him an option. I walk up to him, touching his arm.

"You know, I was thinking, the holidays are coming

very quickly and the weather is extremely cold right now. You could stay in Jason's room until you got back on your feet. We could be roommates and share the holiday together." His eyes grow wide and he frowns, but I continue.

"Carl could help you contact some veteran services to help you find work. There is no hurry, I don't really use the room." I squeeze his arm a little, hoping it helps to coax him. "What do you say, Ben? Would you like to spend the holiday with me?" He walks away from me quickly, going to the side of the room near the front door. Geez, did I come on too strong?

"Julie, I appreciate it, I really do, but I need to go." He picks up his jacket and slides it on. My heart sinks, what did I say? Why is he leaving?

"Why? I know you are feeling better but you are still sick. At least stay a few more days."

He continues to gather his things, as if it doesn't faze him that I am almost begging him to stay. I stare at the ground, trying to think of anything I could say to change his mind. He must see the sadness in my eyes, though, as he steps toward me. He touches my chin with his finger tip, tilting it up so I will look up at him.

"I don't think that is a good idea, kitten. I appreciate the help, but it is time to go." He caresses my cheek and gives me a very slight smile as he starts toward the door.

But I don't understand. He doesn't try to explain but keeps getting ready to walk out. The wheels in my head are spinning, but then I remember about this morning. I grab his arm, making him stop and turn to me.

"If it is about this morning when I woke you, listen, you didn't hurt me, Ben. Honestly, you just scared me a little, that's all, I swear. I should have known better than to do that. Jason warned me several times about it. Please don't let what happened make you leave."

He will no longer look at me, and he stares at the floor. His hand touches my hand holding his arm. He gently removes it, but holds it for just a moment. "I'm sorry, Julie, but I have to go." He reaches over and kisses the top of my head before releasing my hand and opening the door.

Something inside me explodes. Damn, why is he being so stubborn on letting me help him? "Go where? Back to the streets or your cozy little cardboard place behind the dumpster?" He pauses, his hand on the knob before turning back to me, and the angry look has returned. "One minute you let me help you and the next minute you are pushing me away, wanting to leave."

"Dammit, Julie, I can't stay here with ya!" he shouts, causing Bo to start barking. He looks at Bo and holds his hand up, to keep him from coming near him, I suppose. Bo stops barking.

I am angry now too at his stubbornness and walk up to him in challenge. "Why not?" I raise my voice now and put my hands on my hips, as I stand my ground, Bo standing right next to me.

"Look, I am sorry about your brother, but I am not him, okay? Your brother is dead; he isn't comin' back, so fuckin' stop tryin' to save me!" he shouts back.

My heart just drops, and I am beginning to feel my breakfast wanting to come back up as his hurtful words sink in and hit their target. Now I am angry and we glare at each other. I just wanted to help but I won't let anyone talk to me about my brother like that. I take a deep breath and my vision starts blurring with unshed tears. I will not give him the satisfaction of watching me cry.

He must sense it. "Julie, I'm ..." He reaches out to me, but I don't let him finish.

"Fine, I'm done. Suit yourself." I say through gritted teeth, trying my best to fight back the tears. "You want to sleep on the streets and feel sorry for yourself, that's fine, but I have to say, for a Marine you sure are taking a coward's way out." That remark probably pissed him off, but I no longer care. I turn and head for the hallway, trying to make it to my room before the meltdown occurs. "It was nice knowing you. Be sure to lock the door on your way out," I shout back as Bo and I go into my bedroom, slamming and then locking my door.

"Julie, wait." I heard him say as I was going to my room, but that is all I hear. I sit on the bed, letting my silent tears fall. After a few minutes, when I hear my front door close, I lie down and cry. I was really hoping he would knock on my door and fight back. Bo jumps on the bed, lying next to me and starts licking my hand.

I am not sure how long I laid there crying and getting it all out, but I sit up, determined that I will not let Ben's painful words bring me down. A part of me regrets the mean words I said. It is never cool to call a Marine a coward, especially when they risk their lives for us, but his refusal to stay here and try to get better, ticked me off. Even if I was helping him because of my brother, it did not make me a bad person. He has no idea about me, and he obviously doesn't care to.

"Oh, Bo, I guess some people don't want to be helped. We are not going to let this ruin our Christmas. We still have each other right?" I get up and go back to the living room, and it is confirmed that he has left. I don't see the coat or backpack so at least he took them. I suppose I should be happy that he at least got a few good nights of sleep and some hot meals.

I walk over to my brother's picture next to his flag and dog tags. I take the dog tags into my hand, feeling the cold metal and punched letters. These once hung on my brother's chest, near his heart. What about his heart? Was he happy? Did he have someone he loved? He never really told me much, just about the lives he saved and his Marine buddies. We talked about the old times and our parents, and while I knew Jason Walsh, my big brother, I didn't know Sgt Walsh the soldier, or Jason the man.

# CHAPTER
## *nine*

THE DOORBELL RINGS—COULD IT be Ben coming back to apologize? Feeling hopeful, I quickly walk over to open the door only to find Carl standing there with a red, white, and blue memorial wreath. I try not to look disappointed as I remember that Carl was going to pick me up to go to the cemetery.

"You're not dressed?" He looks at his watch as he walks in. "You did say you wanted to leave at ten o'clock, right?" I am now somewhat relieved that Ben's gone. I will not have to explain him to Carl. Until now, I totally forgot he was coming over today.

"I'm sorry, I slept late. Come in out of the cold." Carl walks in, looking me over as I yawn, pulling my robe tighter.

"Yeah, and you look like you barely slept at all. Is Bo giving you trouble?" He places the wreath and poinsettias down, and slides off his coat.

"He's fine, Carl. Have a seat and watch some TV. I will go get dressed and be ready in a few minutes. Bo, you keep Carl company." I head for my bedroom, hoping that Carl doesn't ask any more questions.

A half an hour later, we are headed to the cemetery in Carl's truck with the flowers and Bo in tow. Carl volunteered to drive today, and I am glad. My head is pounding from my crying jag earlier and my stomach is in knots. My biscuits and gravy ended up coming back up after Ben left. I am not sure what has upset me more, his leaving or what day it is. I stare out the window, the weather matching my mood, with gray clouds and a bitter chill in the air.

"You are awfully quiet this morning. Are you okay, kiddo?" I turn to him, trying to give him a smile, but it isn't working. Today is not about smiles. "You were crying this morning before I arrived, weren't you?" I simply nod and bite at my lip before turning my head to look out my window again. "I know today isn't easy, sweetie."

I continue to stare out the window. "Yeah, I'll be okay. You know Christmas was Jason's favorite holiday. He even pretended to believe in Santa Claus, telling me if I didn't believe he would never come." I can't help but smile remembering the Christmas mornings we would sneak into the living room and see what Santa had brought us. Also, we would go and wake Mommy and Daddy, and it would be like four o'clock in the morning. Mommy would make monkey bread and cocoa for us to enjoy as we opened presents. Then my Aunt Gina would come over and we would have a big Christmas dinner and even more presents.

Carl reaches and grabs my hand, and I look over at him again and finally smile. The words that Ben said earlier are still haunting me—was I really trying to replace Jason with him? Not exactly, but I will admit having Ben at the house, even if it was only a few days was helping with my loneliness. Ben's mistake is that I wasn't looking for a brother in him, I was looking for a friend, and to be honest, maybe something a little more. I did want to change him, but not into someone else, but back to who he was before whatever happened that changed him.

We pull into the driveway through the gates of Clover Cemetery. I have been to this cemetery more times in my twenty-three years than any person my age should. Carl parks in the drive, and I can see the graves in the distance near the large oak tree. We get out, and with Bo on his leash, we begin the march up the hill.

We place one set of poinsettias on my parents' grave and I leave Carl alone at Aunt Gina's grave after we put a beautiful poinsettia bouquet at hers. Christmas was her favorite holiday too. I walk over to Jason's tombstone, touching the marble as if I was touching him. I place the wreath in front, and kneel there staring at it. When we arrived, Bo immediately went to Jason's grave and laid down. He knows who is there and he mourns him too. I don't care what people say, dogs know more than you think. I pet Bo, giving him the comfort he has been giving me all these days.

"Hey, Jason, it's me your kid sister. It's almost Christmas time again. I got a nice bouquet of poinsettias for Mom and Dad's gravestone, like you always did. I got one for Aunt Gina too." The tears start falling as I touch the engraved letters on the smooth and very cold granite. I trace his name with my fingertip. This is the only way I can touch my brother now, letters on a tombstone. No more hugs, no more nuggies, no more high fives. I take a deep breath, trying to hold back the tears. I stare at the gravestone.

Jason Andrew Walsh
Sgt
US Marine Corps
Afghanistan
June 19, 1993
Dec 3, 2015

I taste the salty tears, running in my mouth as I speak. "I miss you, brother, so much. Please give Mommy and Daddy and Aunt Gee Gee a hug and kiss and tell them Merry Christmas for me, and that I love and miss them. I love and miss you too, Jason." I kiss my fingertips and place the kiss on his tombstone.

Carl comes over, offering me his hand to help me up. We both take one more look at our loved ones. Once again, my thoughts turn to Ben. I wonder where he is and if he is warm enough. Since our fight, I am assuming he hitched a ride out of town. It serves me right for wanting to help someone who obviously doesn't want help. I think of telling Carl, but decide not to. He doesn't need to worry about me being naïve and allowing strangers into my home. He has worried about me too much over the last few years.

"Come on, Bo, let's go." Bo gets up and walks to me and we leave the cemetery.

The next morning when I arrive at work, Carl and Holly are waiting for me in the back stockroom, and by the looks on their faces, it is not to wish me a good morning. If both are here to talk to me, this can't be good. I got a feeling they know something by the way they are looking at me, so I just try to play it off. I chuckle at Carl's outfit—he almost looks like Santa Claus, minus the beard, in his red shirt and pot belly. "Good morning, Carl. You are looking very festive. Holly, how's it going?"

"Lenny says he saw you the other night driving

around and putting some strange guy in your car. What the hell were you thinking?" Holly scolds as Carl just fumes in silence.

Just great. I forgot about Lenny, the cook. I am surprised he didn't call Carl right away when he saw what I was doing.

"I am thinking that Lenny needs to mind his own business," I say as I take off my jacket and tie my apron on.

"Julie, you have no idea who that guy is. That was really stupid. Where is this guy now?" Holly crosses her arms, watching me.

"Well, I am not sure. He left my house yesterday morning."

"HE WHAT?" They both say in unison. Carl finally speaks as his face turns as red as his shirt. "Girl, have you lost your mind?"

"Guys, I appreciate that you are worried about me. The guy was a homeless veteran that I gave a warm place to sleep and a hot meal to, that is all, and he is gone now so you don't need to worry about it." I am going to kill Lenny for this.

"You seriously let some strange guy off the streets stay at your house? What if he ...? Ughhh, I don't even want to think about it." Holly turns away from me. I am sure she is needing a second to calm down, she looks like she is about to strangle me.

Carl seems to have calmed down a little. "A veteran, huh? Why didn't you come to me? I would have tried to help."

"He doesn't want our help." I feel so sad admitting that.

"He on drugs? Drunk?" Carl interrogates.

"No, I wouldn't have let him come home with me if he was into that. Look, he was angry when he left so I doubt I will ever see him again, so you both can stop worrying, all right?"

"Angry, why? He didn't try to hurt you, did he?" Carl is getting angry again.

"No, Carl, he was just mad because I told him that maybe he should seek help."

Holly turns back now, grabbing my shoulders. "Julie, you can't keep doing stuff like this. This wasn't a stray dog or a lost kitten. This was a man. A man living on the streets. Do you have any idea how dangerous that is, inviting him to your home? You could have …" And then she starts tearing up. I reach out and hug her.

"Holly, you have to trust me, I knew what I was doing. I was in no danger with him, I promise."

Holly pushes away gently from my embrace and wipes her eyes, dismissing my words of comfort. "We aren't done talking about this. I will be watching you." She points to me in her sassy Holly fashion and walks back to the dining area.

I look at Carl, hoping for a bit more understanding.

"Sorry, sweetie, but I agree with Holly. That was a stupid thing to do. Promise me you won't do anything like that again, and if this guy comes back around, you have to tell me, okay?"

"Okay, I promise I will." I nod.

Carl makes no attempts to give me his normal bear hug. He must really be pissed with me. "Fine, but I will be watching you too. You better get out there and help Holly, we are busy this morning." He walks past me, heading back to the kitchen.

It seems everyone is upset with me. Maybe I should just go home. No, I won't play the poor me card. Like Aunt Gina used to say, "Suck it up, buttercup." I grab the order form pad and a pen and head out to the dining area.

Carl is right; we are very busy this morning and

when I finally take a break, I go outside. It is not as cold today as it was a few days ago, but I can't help but look around, hoping to see Ben. I even go as far as looking behind the dumpster, but he is not there. I wonder where he went. The rest of the day, I periodically check, but no Ben. He is gone as quickly as he came.

# CHAPTER *ten*

A FEW MORE DAYS PASS and I still don't see Ben. I have accepted the fact that he is gone, and I am sad. I thought we were friends, and even though we said some ugly things to each other, I thought for sure he would come by the diner and we would forgive each other.

I stare out of the diner window and every time I see someone that looks like him, I get hopeful.

"Still pining for your homeless guy?" Carl comes and stands beside me as I look out the window. He has calmed down the past few days and has even asked me more questions about Ben. He said he would keep an eye out for him and try to help him if he wants it. I appreciate him understanding finally.

"Hey, Carl."

"He's a grown man, sweetheart, and if he is a Marine like you said, he has been through worse, trust me." He places his hand on my shoulder.

"I just thought he would stay, that's all. I thought he would let me help. I thought he was my friend."

"Well, he obviously has a lot to work through, and maybe it is best he does it alone. Sweetie, those boys have seen horrible things over there. I am not so sure you should be around someone that is having those issues."

I touch his hand and turn to him, giving him the smile I know he is looking for. "You're probably right. I just wanted to help. Maybe he was right, maybe I was looking to him to fill the void of losing Jason." I shrug.

"And there is nothing wrong with that. You are a caring and kind person. I am sure he appreciated all you did for him, but a man has to work things out on his own sometimes."

Carl is right, I know this, but it doesn't help me missing Ben. I give Carl a hug, hoping he will drop this discussion now. "Thanks for the pep talk. So, what are the plans for Christmas?"

Carl's face looks surprised by my quick recovery from sadness to joy. "Well, the Legion Hall's Christmas party for the needy families in the area is next weekend."

"Are you going to play Santa again?" Every year he does, and he makes a wonderful Santa, seeing how he already has his own stuffing.

"You know it!" He slaps at his stomach, knowing exactly what I was thinking.

"What can I do to help? Oh, I made lots of mittens and beanies for the children already. We can use those, I am sure. I will make a list of games we can play, and I will ask the local retailers to donate some gifts. I better get busy." I walk past Carl, with pen and pad in hand. This is what I do best—I find something to make me so busy, that I have no time to be sad or miss anyone.

I am in the mall doing some Christmas shopping. I try to enjoy myself as I walk past the stores, but as I pass couples holding hands and sneaking kisses when they think no one is looking, I can't help but feel like the loneliest person in the world. I miss Ben so much. I stop at the center of the mall, where Santa is taking pictures with the kids and babies. The excitement in the little kids' eyes as they get ready to tell Santa their wishes always puts me in a better mood. I love children, and one day I hope to have several of my own. One of my favorite Christmas carols, "I'll be Home for Christmas" is playing. As I get lost in the words to the song, I see a man approaching me. He is tall, wearing a leather jacket and dark jeans. He is wearing mirrored shades, and as he starts getting closer, I can see he is handsome. He is heading this way, he must be meeting up with his wife and kids—what a lucky woman she is. As he continues walking toward me, he takes off his shades. I can see his eyes now. I turn away at first, but then I turn back. I recognize him—it's Ben. He smiles when he gets closer; he is cleaned up and mostly clean shaven with just a scruff of a beard left. I don't mind, because he is looking very sexy. He is in front of me now, and reaches his hand out to me.

"What?" I ask.

"Come on, Julie, let's go home." Those words, this man. I give him my hand and he gently pulls me to him. On instinct, I wrap my arms around his neck as he pulls me closer next to him. "I missed you," he says, as he leans down to kiss me.

"I missed you too," I try to tell him, but the ringing is so loud, I am not sure he heard me.

The loud ringing of my cell phone finally wakes me up. Looking over at my alarm clock, I notice it is only eleven o'clock, and I barely went to bed a few hours ago. Grabbing my phone, I see the diner number on the display screen. They wouldn't call me this late unless it is important, so I go ahead and answer.

"Hello." I say as I mourn the loss of the wonderful dream I was having.

'Hey, Julie, it's Lenny. Marcy called in sick, and no one else is answering. Can you come in and work her shift?" I look at the clock again, eleven o'clock on a Friday night. I just bet she is sick, probably at some bar somewhere, hanging all over some guy. Carl really needs to get rid of her and find someone else as this isn't the first time she has done this. The last time, Holly had the pleasure of filling in, but now it's my turn.

"Yeah, give me an hour to get ready and wake up."

"You're an angel. See you in an hour." Lenny hangs up. Just as well, I wanted to talk to him about telling on me to Carl and Holly.

Bo looks up at me from the foot of my bed. "Sorry, boy, but duty calls." I get up and get dressed.

The night shift brings a whole different clientele and I can't wait for this night to be over. One guy in particular keeps making comments to me that are making me uncomfortable. He is a truck driver, and most of the time, truck drivers are polite and respectful, but this guy must have missed that memo. He keeps trying to get me to go out with him after my shift is up this morning. I keep trying to politely let him know that I am not interested.

I had to stress the point a little more, earlier, when I went to refill his coffee and he took the opportunity to play grab ass. That is crossing the line and I gave him his tab and told him to pay the cashier before he leaves and that if he touched me again, he would be asked to leave. I don't even care if he leaves a tip as long as he leaves.

I should tell Lenny. He is Carl's assistant manager and good friend. He is as gentle as a pussycat, until you piss him off. This jerk's behavior would definitely piss him off, but the shift is almost over, and I just want to go home and forget about it. Now I can understand why Marcy hates working nights. I head to the back and make Lenny ring the weirdo up. If I never see the guy again, it will be too soon. I try to look busy when I spot a few bags of garbage. Deciding I will help Marcus the night cook out, I take them outside in case Mr. Touchy Feely tries waiting for me to show up out front again.

"Hey, Marcus, I am going to take these to the dumpster. I will be right back." I am not sure if he heard me or not, because I didn't wait for his response as I go outside. I walk over to the dumpster and remember the other night when I discovered Ben sleeping there. I lift the bags up and throw them into the dumpster, and when I turn around, I see something sitting on top of the milk crates. I walk over to see what it is, expecting it to be some trash that just needs to be thrown away.

I am shocked when I notice it is a red scarf. In fact, it is the same red scarf I gave to Ben. I look around but there is no one in sight. Was he here? If he was, why didn't he come see me? I pick the scarf up and hold it next to me, wishing it was on the man I gave it to. I wish I knew where he was.

"We are alone at last." The familiar voice of the creep from the diner startles me. I turn to see him walking toward me from around the corner. He must have been watching me more than I thought. I spy the door, wondering if I have time to make a run for it, but before I can decide, he is next to me now. I am not liking the fact he came back here to find me; this guy just doesn't understand the meaning of the word no. Jason taught me to not show fear in the face of danger. I decide to play cool and maybe he will go away.

"I need to get back inside." I try to walk past him to the door, but he grabs my arm, stopping me. His grip is hard and he quickly releases me. It is the second time he has touched me, and if I have anything to say about it, it will also be the last. This guy has pushed it and now it is time to get Lenny and Marcus involved. I don't like how this guy is looking at me and I need to get back inside as soon as possible.

"Now, don't be like that now. I paid the bill and I want to leave you a tip." He is so dirty and unkempt, even his hands have dirt under the nails, or at least I hope it was just dirt. Either way, I will be cleaning up. Ben is homeless but he still looks cleaner and better than this guy. His stained gray shirt barely covers his beer gut. He is wearing sweats, too, that look like they haven't been washed in a week. Don't these guys have a dress code to follow?

"Don't worry about it, it's okay, really." I try to pass him and make it for the door, but he grabs my arm harder this time. This time, he is not letting go.

"Come on, let's go back to my truck and have some fun. I have a nice comfy bed in there."

I try pulling my arm back but he squeezes harder. "You're hurting me. Let go." I start to panic, looking around, but it is very early and still dark and there is no one in sight.

"Come on, let's go. I will be quick, I promise." He starts pulling me along with him as we walk to his truck. If I don't get away soon, this is going to be very bad. I start hitting him and kicking him. He is so out of shape, if I could just get him to release me, I could outrun him with no problem. Unfortunately, my hits and kicks are not even fazing this dude, so I do the next best thing and scream. He immediately puts his disgusting hand over my mouth, and without a moment's hesitation, I bite him hard.

"Ow! You stupid bitch." He releases me but I don't have time to run as he hauls off and hits me in the face, knocking me to the ground. My head hits the asphalt causing me to bite my tongue, and for a second I am wondering if I will pass out, but immediately I feel sharp pain in my ankle. I must have injured it when I fell. I have no time to worry about it now as he is standing over me very angry as he holds his hand.

"I was going to take you back to my truck where it was private and comfortable, but since you want to be a fucking bitch …" He grabs me by the arm and drags me up to him and I scream out once again, but this time in pain as my ankle is jarred. I know it is hurt bad as I can't stand. He grabs me, pulling me toward the dumpster, his hand over my mouth and nose to where I can't breathe and am dragging my injured ankle. My mouth is filling with the metallic taste of my own blood. He throws me to the ground again and is immediately on top of me. He finally lifts his hand off so I can breathe, but his hands are around my throat now as he squeezes.

"I should kill you, you stupid bitch. What? You think you are too good for me or something?" I try to remove his hands but I am not strong enough. He stops squeezing long enough to tell me, "If you scream, I will strangle you. Do you understand me?"

I nod as I am crying in agony from the pain in my ankle and face. I keep choking on the blood as I feel it dripping down the side of my face too. He starts tearing at my buttoned blouse, the buttons flying as he rips it open. He continues as he rips the front of my bra, exposing me to his view. I stare up at the night sky. I see no stars, just darkness. I try to escape in my mind. He is going to kill me, I know it. I just pray he does it quickly or maybe God will take me before he rapes me.

At least I will be able to join my family. I close my eyes hoping that if I play dead maybe he will get scared and leave, but no such luck as I feel him unbuttoning my jeans. Oh my God, I realize whether I am dead or alive he plans to rape me. Now I really want to die. I have to think of something to stop this. He must realize I am playing dead as he grabs for my throat again. My eyes are open wide now as I claw at his hands to get him to let go. My air is running out—this is it, he is going to kill me.

Suddenly, I feel the weight of him lift off of me and the sounds of grunting and hitting. I roll to my side, coughing and gasping, trying to get air in my lungs. I don't know why he is off of me and I don't care. Hopefully it is Lenny and Marcus and they are beating him to a bloody pulp. My worry for my friends has me rolling onto my back and looking toward the sounds of the struggle. My vision is blurred but I can see only two men.

It can't be Lenny, because if he was out here, Marcus would be right behind him. I recognize the coat, it's my dad's, the one I loved having wrapped around me, and I wish was around me now. My brain finally registers that it is Ben fighting my attacker. He is here, it's him. The attacker is at his mercy as Ben keeps pounding him in the head. The guy is not even trying to defend himself anymore.

If Ben doesn't stop he will kill him, and there is a part of me that would have no problem with that. But, I need him here beside me, in case this is it and I die soon. I don't want to leave things where we left them. I want to apologize for the things I said. I want him to hold me, so I can erase this and die peacefully in his arms. I gather up as much strength as possible to call out to him. "Ben!!" It is a weak cry, but he must have heard me because he stops suddenly, looking my way.

"Julie?" He lets go of my attacker and the son of a bitch falls to the ground, not even trying to break his own fall. I hope he is hurt really bad, but really all I want is Ben. I reach my hand out, wanting to touch him and pull him near. Ben rushes over to me and immediately drops to his knees. He quickly removes his coat and gently wraps it around me as he pulls me into his arms. He pulls the coat to cover my exposed skin as he holds me close, rocking me in his arms. This is just where I want to be.

"Oh, Julie, sweetheart, what are ya doin' here? Hold on, help is comin', angel." He moves the hair off my face and places his hand on my forehead and presses down. I just stare at him in silence as he shouts for help. He shouts again and then looks at me. "Julie, can you hear me? Just hold on, sweetie, help is comin'." He continues holding me close to his body, doing his best to shield me from the cold.

I think I hear the diner back door slam open as Lenny and Marcus are outside, standing over us. Lenny is on his phone as Marcus stands holding a butcher knife, ready to take on the world. They look at me and Ben but then look over at the guy on the ground. Marcus heads toward the guy as Lenny stays by us calling 911.

I hear mumbling but I can't make out the words. Lenny left only to come back with a blanket that Ben places around me. I am feeling warmer now as I look into the eyes of my hero. I notice his beard is shorter now and his hair is too. He is still wearing the beanie but his hair is no longer sticking out of it. He looks so handsome, even if he still has the beard. He is talking to me but I can't understand.

His face changes now. It's my daddy. Daddy is holding me and talking to me. Now it's Jason, my big brother coming to save the day. I am so happy to see him; I miss him so much. They are still trying to talk to me, but I can't understand. It doesn't matter. I am safe now, safe in the arms of my loved ones.

I hear Ben's voice one more time and I look at him. We are so close now that I can finally make out his eye color. "Hazel," I whisper before darkness takes over.

# CHAPTER
## *eleven*

THE FIRST THING I SEE when I open my eyes is a TV on the wall with some war history documentary playing on it. Next to it is a white board with the room number 303. My nurse's name is Sarah and my doctor is Carson. I am in the hospital, but why am I here? I slowly turn my head to look over and see Carl sitting in a chair, struggling with the remote. I look at my arm and see that I am hooked up to an IV and wearing a hospital bracelet. Everything is fuzzy. How did I get here? I must have said it out loud instead of thinking it, because Carl turns to look at me.

"It's about time you woke up." He stands, coming to the side of my bed. "How are you feeling, kiddo?"

The memories start flashing back at me like scenes in a movie. The sirens, the lights, people talking, the diner, the attack, the guy on top of me trying to rape me, the pain—everything comes back to me in a rush. I start crying not knowing what to say.

"It's okay. You are going to be okay." Carl leans down, carefully taking me in his arms as I cry. "They got the bastard. He is in jail and I will kill him if he ever comes near you again." Carl stands there and holds me as he has more than a few times in my life, from a scrape on the knee, when we lost Aunt Gina, and when we lost Jason. Knowing Carl's back issues, I let go so he can stand straight again.

"The doctors said you have a slight concussion and they had to operate on your ankle. It was banged up pretty bad. They put pins in it just like my knee." He rubs my forehead but he can't hide the concern on his face. "Holly and Mike were here for a few hours, but he needed to get back to work. She told me to tell you she loves you and will call you later."

I remember Holly barking orders to someone when they brought me to the room. There is no telling who she was going on to about it. I go over all the events in my mind; how did they get the guy? I then remember—it was Ben. Ben fought my attacker and saved me. I look around the room to see if he is here too. The room is empty with just Carl and me. Ben helped me but where is he?

"What's wrong, sweetie?" Carl asks as he sees me scanning the room.

"Ben. Where's Ben?"

Carl looks at me as if at first he doesn't know what I am talking about, but realization must have kicked in. "Ben? Oh, you mean your homeless guy? He is out in the waiting room."

Why is he out there? Doesn't he want to see me? Is he still angry about what I said? "Doesn't he want to see me?" I whisper.

"Oh, I am sure he does. He has been out there all day

and most of the night. When he finally got here that is."

"What do you mean, when he finally got here? Where was he?" My mind is scrambling for answers. Ben was with me after the attack, why did he not stay with me? Is he that mad at me?

"Well, the police took him into custody."

"What? Why?" I sit up straighter, lifting my bed upright.

"Listen, calm down. They just wanted to question him. It's okay now."

"No, that's not right. Ben saved me. Why would the police be questioning him?" I struggle to think of a way to get out of this bed and find out what the hell is going on. Visions of the police cuffing and manhandling Ben have me worried for him. He was the hero, they had to know that.

Carl sees me getting upset and places his hands on my shoulders, easing me back down. "Now, in their defense, they only saw a girl hurt and a guy unconscious. They had no idea what happened, nor could they know for sure which one of them did it."

"He didn't hurt me, he saved me. Carl, you have to tell them that." I try sitting up again, but the pain in my head stops me short.

"Easy, they know that after they spoke to Lenny and Marcus. They got his story and let him go. He is in the waiting room, I swear. Holly made him stay out there. She is still not convinced he is harmless. I am not even sure how he got here from the police station but he has been out there ever since."

I look out the window; it is dark just like when I was attacked. "How long have I been asleep?"

Carl finally releases me as he glances at the clock on the wall. "You have been in and out for hours. You have been here all day since they brought you in early this morning."

Knowing that Ben is not in trouble, I settle down. I stare at my ankle, the thrashing around causing it to throb with the motion of the sling. It is bandaged and elevated. Carl gently stops the swinging motion to give me relief, being so careful not to touch my foot.

"Can I see him?"

Carl frowns. I know he isn't a huge fan of Ben's, but he has to realize he saved my life. "Maybe you should rest. I will go out there and tell him you are doing better. You can see him first thing in the morning maybe. I don't want you getting upset."

"Carl, please, I want to see him now. He saved my life. I have to thank him. Please."

He sighs as he finds it hard to ever say no to me, especially if I sound like I am begging. "Okay, I will go get him. But if you get upset in the slightest, he is out of here, whether he saved your life or not." Carl nods his head after every word in his speech, his way of showing me he is serious. I smile a little knowing that Carl is quite serious. He is protective of me, and even a large man like Ben would find my bulldog uncle a bit of a challenge if tested. He steps out, and not even a minute later, Ben walks in. He cautiously approaches my bed, Carl right behind him.

"I am going to get something from the cafeteria. I will leave you two alone, but I will be back." He starts to leave but stops. "Soon!" he adds in his fatherly voice, causing both of us to look at him. Carl closes the door and Ben turns to me again and gives me a small smile.

"They say you are goin' to be all right?" His tone makes me feel that he is unsure.

"I suppose. I don't remember seeing the doctor, or anything about getting here, but Carl says I will be okay."

"He cares a lot about ya. He has been here since they

brought ya in." He stares down at my bedrail, running his hand up and down it. He has barely looked me in the eyes since he walked in.

"Yeah, he is a dear friend and very protective of me."

"He's not the only one. Your friend Holly cares a lot about ya too." I can see him smiling but he still is not looking at me. It is not like Ben to be shy.

"Well, Holly is Holly. She takes a while to get to know you. Don't take it personally."

He nods, finally looking up and all around the room, but still avoiding eye contact with me. What is his problem? He reminds me of a stray animal, wanting to be near, but ready to bolt at any second. I can't stand it any longer.

"Please sit down, you are making me nervous standing there. I keep thinking you are going to run out at any moment."

He finally looks at me, puzzled by my statement no doubt. Frowning, he lowers himself to the chair. "I'm not goin' anywhere." Well at least he is looking at me now.

"Good. That makes me feel better. I am so sorry about the police; I wish I could have told them that you were just helping me."

"Don't worry about that, it is all sorted out." He continues to look around, eying my IV and things around my bed. He definitely is acting uncomfortable. Maybe he didn't really want to see me. Maybe Carl insisted he come in. All these doubts are running through my mind.

"I thought you had left for good."

He stares at me a moment, before looking away again, not responding to my statement. I feel he is hiding something from me by his odd behavior. I am curious why he was at the diner last night, but he has been interrogated enough by the police. I am just so glad he was there. "Thank you for saving me. He was going to kill me."

He shakes his head, his lips in a tight line as he puts his elbows on his knees and holds his head down. "I am sorry. I didn't get to ya sooner before he hurt you." He hangs his head, pulling at his hair, refusing to look up. I am not sure if he is crying or what is going on. I reach my hand out to him. He looks at it strangely but finally takes it and holds it gently in his strong hand. I once again feel the comfort of being safe.

"Ben, I am sorry for what I said to you the other day, you're not a coward. I was just mad that you wouldn't stay and it was wrong of me to call you that." I have been wanting to apologize for days now. It feels good to finally do it.

He looks up at me now. He wasn't crying but he is definitely upset. "You were right, though, I have been a coward."

I shake my head in disagreement, but it causes the pain in my head to return. He continues holding my hand, petting it in a way that is comforting to me. His touch is so soothing. I feel too weak to argue with him. I continue watching him; he looks so tired. I would tell him to go home if he had one. Suddenly my thoughts of my home have me tensing up. He must feel my tension as he looks up at me, concerned.

"What's wrong? Are you in pain? Should I get the nurse?" he asks as I squeeze his hand harder.

"No. I forgot about Bo. He has been home alone all night and day. He doesn't like being alone that long. Please, you have to go check on him."

Ben looks around, obviously uncomfortable with my request. "Don't you want Carl to do it?"

"Carl to do what?" At that moment, Carl walks back into the room. I look at Ben again, who is staring at my hand and avoiding Carl's disapproving eyes. I don't have time to play referee for these two.

"Carl, Bo is home alone. Someone needs to check on him." Carl looks at me, and then at Ben with curiosity before looking at me again.

"Well, I was headed back to the diner after I leave here. Let me think ... maybe I can call Holly?"

"No," I interrupt. "Bo is still trying to adapt to living with me. Holly would want to take him to her parents' house and I am unsure how he would act. He doesn't know Holly that well yet; she can't comfort him." I again look over at Ben and suddenly I have a brilliant idea.

"Ben, you can do it. Please go and stay with Bo. I don't like leaving him alone for long periods of time." Both Ben and Carl just stare at me in silence, before looking at each other.

"Julie, I am sure Bo will be fine. I will check on him in the morning," Carl says and I can tell he is not liking what I am suggesting. From the look on Ben's face, neither is he.

I shake my head. "No, I want someone to go now. He is probably already frightened." I continue to thrash around, wanting to get up and leave on my own.

Both men stay frozen in place.

"Fine, I will go myself then." I start to get up. Carl starts to head for my bed, but Ben stands up, releasing my hand and gently eases me back again.

"Whoa, right there, little lady. You aren't going anywhere. The doctor says you are staying the night," Carl says as he comes around to the other side of my bed.

Ben gently takes my hand again and is looking into my eyes. I am comforted by his touch and begin to relax again.

"I'll do it. That is if ya are sure ya want me to," Ben offers.

"Yes, please, Ben. He knows you and likes you. Thank

you." I squeeze his hand when I feel he is wanting to let go, not allowing him to break contact with me.

Ben nods silently, giving me a small smile. He glances up at Carl, waiting to hear his disapproval. I look over at Carl, who is frowning at Ben. I know he is not happy with my request.

"Carl, where is my purse and my car?"

Carl breaks his glaring at Ben to look at me in question. "Both are still at the diner, why?"

"Please take Ben to the diner and give him my keys so he can use my car to check on Bo."

Carl's eyes widen with shock. "Julie, are you sure you want to do that?" I can check on Bo later. I am sure he is fine."

Ben continues to look at me and then at Carl, as if he is unsure what to say.

"Please, Carl, I want Ben to do it." I look at Ben with pleading eyes. "Ben, please go take care of Bo for me." I begin to sit up again, bringing his hand to my chest. I wince from the sudden movement as it brings attention to the pain in my head and ankle.

"Sure, I will do it, if ya promise to relax." Ben releases my hand to help ease me back down. He surprises me by taking my hand again.

Carl must realize he is defeated. He has known me long enough to know that when my mind is set, it's set. He sighs, leaning over and kissing my cheek. "Well, let's go, I need to get back to the diner. I will drop by to check on you in the morning." He starts heading for the door.

"Thanks, Carl. Can you give Ben and me a moment alone, please?"

Carl frowns at me again, before looking toward Ben. "Yeah, sure, I will be outside." He steps out but not before cutting another nasty look at Ben.

Once we are alone, I look over at Ben. He watches

Carl exit the room, before focusing on me again. "He's really a nice guy, you just have to get to know him," I whisper.

Ben nods as he sits back down in the chair. He looks better, since the days ago when he was staying with me.

"You cut your hair and trimmed your beard." This makes him smile. "Does this mean you found a shelter?" I say, hoping I am right.

"No, just a cheap barber." He finally speaks, but he is avoiding eye contact with me again as he focuses on my hand. He is holding it in both of his and caressing it. It feels nice and it feels right.

"Ben, when you go and check on Bo, I want you to stay and spend the night at my place. There is food in the fridge, just help yourself, and Bo's food is in the cabinet in the kitchen. Just make yourself at home."

"Julie, I don't think I should." He starts shaking his head and tries to release my hand but I squeeze tight, not wanting our newfound connection broken. I can't bear to think of him on the streets any longer.

"Ben, please, I am insisting this time. Visiting hours are almost up and I won't sleep well knowing you are back out on the streets. Please, stay there so I don't worry about you and Bo." I know it's a cheap shot, but after what has happened, I will do anything to keep him safe.

He takes a deep breath in and exhales slowly. "Ya always have to have your way, don't ya?" He smiles, shaking his head before finally looking at me. "Fine, I will crash at your place tonight if it makes ya feel better."

"Thank you. The security code is one, zero, zero, nine." I squeeze his hand one more time before finally releasing it. He gets up out of the chair and stretches. When he reaches the door, he turns to look at me one more time, before exiting.

I don't get a chance to sleep. After Carl and Ben leave,

the police show up. They ask me questions about the attack and have me confirm Ben's involvement in the situation. They bring a photo of six men and make me point out my attacker. I point him out right away. It isn't difficult, that disgusting man's image will be cemented in my mind for a very long time. Before they leave, they assure me that my attacker will go away for a long time. They say his name, but I quickly forget it. I am not going to give this asshole notoriety in my brain. It is bad enough, I have his disgusting image imbedded there.

# CHAPTER
## *twelve*

I TRY TO RELAX AND sleep after they leave, but the pain in my ankle and the memories of what happened cause me to be restless. I am alone in my room and scared. Now I wish I would have asked someone to stay with me. I turn on the TV, just for the noise. The silence scares me, as well as the darkness. Awhile later, when the nurse comes in to check on me, she brings me something for the pain and says it should make me very sleepy. After she checks my vitals and puts medicine in my IV, she begins to leave until I call out.

"Something's wrong." I keep grabbing at the front of my hospital gown, pulling it away from my skin. I feel like it is choking me. I feel a tightness in my chest and I am shaking all over.

She comes back over to me, checking my chart and the medicine she gave me. "You had this medicine a while ago, so you are not allergic to it. Just relax, Miss Walsh, you're going to be fine. Just control your breathing."

No, I am not. I want to get out of bed. I want to run out of here. She tries getting me to lie back, but I push her hands away.

"Just take deeps breaths now and try to relax and the medicine will help in a minute."

"Please, help me. Don't leave me."

"Is there someone I can call for you?" My mind can't think, but all of a sudden, as quickly as it came on, it slows down, and I am sleepy. I stare at the TV screen until I finally close my eyes. Sleep feels good as suddenly I feel safe in my dreams. I feel like I am floating on a soft pillow or maybe it's a cloud. Maybe I died and this is heaven. I see the silhouette of a man coming toward me.

I am not sure—is it Daddy, is it Jason, or is it Ben? He takes my hand. I still can't see his face, but I am safe now. I feel someone is with me but I don't have the strength or the desire to open my eyes to see who it is. It is a man because he whispers for me to go to sleep and that everything will be all right, that I am safe now. The voice changes from my dad, to Carl, to Jason, and finally turning to Ben. Whoever it is, I feel safe and I finally drift off to sleep.

I awake when the morning charge nurse comes in to start his shift. I look over to the chair to find it empty. That surprises me because I could have sworn someone was with me last night. I don't have too much time to ask questions before my doctor comes in.

"Good morning, Julie, I am Dr. Carson."

"Good morning," I respond as she walks in and stands by my bed, reading over my chart. She is a younger doctor, who I would guess to be in her mid to late thirties. If it wasn't for the white lab coat and stethoscope around her neck, I would say she looks more like a secretary or librarian with her hair in a neat bun and black rimmed glasses. She closes my chart and smiles at me.

"How are you feeling this morning?"

"Tired and sore." I reach up and touch my face; it feels puffy where I feel the pain.

"Yes, the swelling and bruising in your face should go away soon." She comes over and touches my forehead. "The laceration on your head looks better. The liquid bandage seems to be holding up. Any headaches or nausea?"

"No."

She then starts looking at my ankle. "Your ankle is broken, and we had to do surgery to place it back with a plate and pins. The swelling looks like it has gone down, so we will go ahead and cast it this morning. If you keep it elevated and stay off it until it heals, you should have a full recovery. You may need physical therapy to help you, but we will evaluate that in the next few weeks."

"Can I go home today, then?"

"Well, I don't see why you can't go home later this afternoon, as long as you have someone to help you for the next few days. You are going to be very sore and the pain meds will make you sleepy. It will be important that you rest and take it easy and stay off the ankle."

"I am sure I can get help."

"All right, I will have the nurse draw up the release forms and get your prescriptions ready. I want to see you back in my office next week for a follow-up."

"Yes, Doctor, thank you."

She closes my chart and looks at me. "Julie, I have a question. Have you ever been diagnosed with an anxiety disorder?"

I look at her strangely. What the hell? "No, ma'am."

"Hmm, have you experienced any other episodes like you did last night?" It figures that nurse would say something to the doctor about my panic attack last night. "Yes, I have had them before, but not quite as bad, though." That is not exactly true, but I don't want her thinking I am losing it.

"I would like you to make an appointment to talk to a therapist. I can prescribe you something for the anxiety in the meantime. With everything you have been through, I think speaking to someone could be beneficial. I can also recommend some counseling for you with victim services. I am going to go ahead and put a few names of some counselors that I recommend on your release papers."

"Okay." I nod to her, but the thought of talking to some stranger about this is nothing I want to do right now. All the therapy I need is in the comfort of my home. If I get home, I will be fine.

"They should be ready to release you after lunch. I want you to take it easy, no unnecessary standing or walking, and keep that ankle elevated as much as possible."

"I will." I sit up as the orderly brings in my breakfast tray and the doctor leaves. I look at the tray of food, an omelet and toast. It looks okay, but I am just not feeling hungry. I eye the cup of coffee on the tray. Now there is something I do crave. I load it up with the cream and sugar packs. I savor the first sip, which reminds me of Ben and the day I first brought him a coffee. It's not the best coffee, but it's coffee!!!

As I lie in bed enjoying my cup of java, Carl and Holly walk in carrying a huge display of balloons.

"What is this?" I smile, setting my cup down on the tray. The balloons nearly fill the small hospital room. There are all different colors and styles of get well messages on the Mylar bouquet. The funny face with the Band-Aid is my favorite.

"Just a little something from us girls at the diner. How are you feeling?" Holly comes over to kiss my cheek. Carl takes the balloons and sets them down near the window.

"Better, but tired. The doctor just left. She says I can go home today if someone is willing to stay with me while I heal up."

"Damn, I just let Lenny take a vacation so he could go back to New York and visit his family. He won't be back until the first of the year. I can help you a few hours a day; maybe Holly and I can juggle shifts."

"Oh, babe, you know I will help you as much as I can. Maybe I can ask my mom to move you into our house for a few weeks until you are better. We have lots of people to help and watch you."

My eyes grow wide. I love Holly's family but that is way too much family, all the time, for my taste. Besides, I think it would upset Bo. "Holly, I appreciate it but I really want to go home and be in my own bed. I am sure I can manage for the most part."

"Well, if the doctor wants you to have around the clock care, I guess we could hire someone." Carl looks at me, smiling.

The thought of having a stranger being with me is unsettling, especially after what happened. Besides, Ben has returned and I really want to try to talk him into staying with me again. He saved my life, the least I can do is offer him a place to stay to get back on his feet. He was so wonderful last night. Holly and Carl may not like the idea, however.

"No, Carl, really, you don't have to do that." I sit up, getting ready to argue my point.

"I'll watch her."

We all turn to the sultry southern voice of the man walking into my room. He is very handsome wearing a black leather jacket and blue jeans, with his dark hair trimmed short on the sides, but long and styled on top. With no more moustache and no more beard, he looks like he just walked off the cover of fashion magazine. But I then see his eyes and I know those eyes, the bright hazel eyes of Ben. My Ben.

"Ben?" My eyes widen with surprise and delight. Wow, I can't believe how good he looks. Holly moves to the other side of the room next to Carl as he sets a bag down on the floor and walks up to my bed, smiling with one hand behind his back.

"How are ya feelin'?"

I have to pick up my jaw before I can speak. "Better. You look so ... so ..." I can't even find the words.

"Clean?" he answers for me, with a large grin, reminding me of our embarrassing conversation the other day.

"Yeah, that too." I laugh and I am having a hard time removing the smile off my face. I want to jump around because I was sure of it. Ben is HOT!!!

"Here, these are for you. Bo sends his love and says to hurry home." He hands me a beautiful bouquet of pink roses.

"Oh, Ben, they are beautiful." I sniff them. "Bo is okay then?"

"He is just fine, but he misses ya." Ben looks down at my hardly touched breakfast before looking at me again. Ben and I keep staring at each other, until Carl clears his throat, reminding us that he and Holly are still in the room.

"So, where did you get the money for the roses, Mr. Homeless guy?" Holly spouts off and I give her a dirty look.

"Holly Winston, that is rude." But in the back of my mind I am wondering the same thing.

Ben touches my arm and I look up at him. He smiles down at me, before looking at Holly. I take it as his way of letting me know he is ready to fight his own battle.

"I would have been here sooner but when I drove up, one of the docs here had a flat tire. I helped him change it and he gave me twenty bucks. I tried to refuse it but he insisted, so I got them at the gift shop."

I smile at him and give Holly a shoulder shrug, like, See you were wrong about him.

"So, you will be able to stay with her? What about Christmas? Now that you seem to have ... cleaned up, don't you want to go to wherever you came from and see your family?" Carl starts in on the interrogation now too. You just wait until I am alone with these two.

"No, sir, I don't think I am ready to do that just yet. I need to get some things sorted out first. Besides, I think I'd rather be with my friend this year." He looks back down at me. "She invited me the other day, but I was rude to her. Hopefully the invitation is still open."

"Absolutely," I whisper, not believing what is happening right now.

"That's good to know." He smiles, taking my hand and bringing it to his lips for a soft kiss and giving me a wink.

"Oh, brother," Holly moans.

Carl has an unexplainable smirk on his face as he starts walking toward me. "Okay, I guess you are all set then." He leans down, giving me a kiss on the cheek and heads to the door. "We need to get back to the diner, Holly."

Holly looks at me and then at Carl and then back to me again. Knowing her as well as I do, she can't believe that Carl is fine with this arrangement. Actually I am surprised myself. "Fine. But I will be checking on you often." She kisses me on the cheek.

"I will see you later too, kiddo, and you better take care of our girl, Ben, understand?"

For the first time since entering the room, Ben looks over at Carl, taking his eyes off me. I am in a state of awe that I can't seem to shake and only nod at Carl and Holly as they leave. "Yes, sir, will do."

Holly and Carl leave, and now it's just Ben and me. He sits down in the chair next to me, still holding my hand. He looks so different, nothing at all like when we first met. To see him now, no one would ever think he was living on the streets only yesterday.

"Wow, you clean up pretty nice, Mr. Parker."

"Well, I made use of those toiletries ya left for me." He takes his hand, feeling his chin. "Does it really look okay?"

I nod, wanting to say, Okay? Are you kidding me, you look gorgeous? I recognize the clothes right away. Jason was in love with that jacket. I spent my whole paycheck on buying it for his birthday several years ago. It's funny. I should be mad that Ben is wearing it, but I am not. It feels right somehow.

He must have read my mind when he says, "I hope ya don't mind about the clothes. I found them in a box in the closet."

"No, I am glad you found them and that they fit. Jason's jacket looks good on you."

He smiles, finally releasing my hand as he sits back in the chair. He is relaxed and I haven't seen him ever act that way. I also haven't felt this way before. I have a nervous energy running through my body. I hold my flowers, sniffing their sweet fragrance. No guy has ever bought me flowers before, but of course, only I know that.

"So, when are they releasin' ya?" Ben asks, bringing me out of my daydream.

"Today, as soon as the nurse gets the forms ready."

"Good. I brought ya some clothes and things from home, just in case." I blush thinking of Ben going through my clothes, finding things like panties and a bra. He smirks at me, once again acting like he read my mind. I am sure it is my normal paranoia.

"I just realized you are not coughing anymore." I quickly change the subject.

"Yeah, I took some more of that nasty, awful cough syrup of yours last night, and this morning it was completely gone."

"See? I told you it would work." I sit up straight, relishing in the glory of being right.

"Yeah, ya did." He smiles but then his face turns serious. He leans forward, putting his hands together, his elbows on his jean clad knees. "Julie, about the other day, I am sorry about what I said to ya. I was way out of line. You were so kind to me, playin' nursemaid and all. I was a complete assho—sorry, jerk." He looks up, and I smile at his attempt to not curse.

"It's okay, I was pushing you too far, and you were partly right, having you there was helping me not think of Jason."

"I still shouldn't have said that." He shakes his head.

"And I shouldn't have said the things I said, either. I should have never called you a coward like that. You risked your life protecting our country and if you hadn't been there the other night ..." I stop as I feel the lump in my throat growing.

We both sit quietly, reflecting on our mistakes. I don't want to sit here and be in bad mood. Ben is here, I get to go home, he is staying with me, and he is looking very handsome. I smile over at him as he is still sitting there deep in thought.

"So," I say, causing him to sit up and look at me.

"Moving forward now, you are going to be spending Christmas with me then?"

He relaxes back into the chair. "I guess so. I'm not sure how great of a Christmas it will be with ya stuck in bed restin', but I will keep ya company while I get my life back in order."

"That sounds good to me." I am thinking it is going to be a wonderful Christmas after all.

# CHAPTER
## *thirteen*

BEN AND I WAIT PATIENTLY for the nurse to remove my IV and bring my release forms. Earlier, the nurse helped me shower and get dressed and then wheeled me into a room for an intern to put on my cast. I chose neon pink. They also gave me an awkward boot to wear and a set of crutches to use in a few days.

The nurse wheels me out to the front of the hospital, where Ben has pulled my car up to the front and is opening the doors. It is cold and rainy out. He carefully and quickly helps the nurse get me inside the car. He gets a blanket out of the back and covers and tucks it in around me. We both smile as we share the déjà vu moment where I did the same thing for him the other day.

We both are quiet on the way home as the radio softy plays. I normally listen to pop or country but Ben has it on a classic rock station and the soft tune of a familiar rock ballad is so soothing and relaxing. I close my eyes for just a second.

"Hey, kitten, wake up, you're home," Ben softly whispers as he touches my shoulder, giving it a small shake.

So much for just closing my eyes, it appears I passed out. The drive from the hospital to my house is at least thirty minutes. "I'm sorry, I had trouble sleeping last night." I yawn as I stretch my arms out before unlocking my seatbelt.

"I know," he says as he unbuckles his seat belt.

I stop mid-stretch at his statement. "How do you know?" When I look at him, he is staring at me, looking very guilty for some reason.

"I mean, I have been in the hospital before, the nurses never leave ya alone to sleep." He recovers.

"Oh." I realize he just gave me a tidbit of personal information. "When were you in the hospital?" I ask, hoping he might open up.

He smiles, knowing what I am doing. "We will discuss it another time. We need to get you inside and in bed. Besides, Bo is waiting to see you." He touches my nose, like I am a kid or something. It's cute, as long as he doesn't think of me as a kid.

"Okay, another time then. I can't wait to see him." I take the blanket off, maneuvering my way to get out.

"Stop," he demands

"What's wrong?" I look at him as if he has lost his mind.

"Ya need to stay put until I get around and help ya. The doc said no weight on your ankle at all. So sit tight for a sec." I roll my eyes, feeling a little too babied right now.

Ben gets out, hurries to my side and opens the door and very slowly I stand and let him lift me and carry me into the house. Bo is waiting for me and is very excited that I am home, as he is jumping around.

"Bo, heel!" Bo immediately stops and sits at Ben's loud and commanding voice. Bo stays put as Ben helps me sit down on the couch, adjusting the pillows and picking up my legs and feet to place them on the couch.

I keep staring over at Bo. He is wagging his tail furiously but refuses to move. He is a good dog and minds well, but I have never seen him mind this good.

When Ben is satisfied that I am good, he sits down in the chair next to me as I just stare at him.

"What?" He looks at me perplexed.

"What do you mean what? You yelled at my dog, that's what."

"I didn't yell at him, I commanded him. There's a difference."

I look over at poor Bo. He is still sitting by the door, not moving from his command. Ben smiles at me and then looks over at Bo. "Bo, come." Bo walks over to sit beside both Ben and me, allowing me to finally pet my dog.

"Bo is a Marine service dog. He is used to commands. He wasn't upset by it, if that's what ya are worried about."

"How did you know which commands he knew?"

"Because that was my job, I was a dog handler."

I blink at him in shock at what he just said. "Like my brother?"

"Not exactly. I was military police and we worked with dogs, but we teach them all the basic commands."

"You were a cop?"

He nods, petting Bo.

The wheels in my brain start turning. As I remember the day we met and he was laughing about what I said about donuts. Now I get the joke. "Tell me about your time there."

"We will talk more later, but first things first. I noticed ya didn't eat much at the hospital, so what would ya like?"

Man this guy is good at changing topics fast. He is also observant, and possibly a mind reader. I am hungry. "I don't know, what do I have?"

"Not much. A frozen burrito, a package of ramen noodles, both of those are horrible for ya, by the way. I could make ya a grilled cheese and then we could make a grocery list and I will go shoppin'."

"You can make grilled cheese?" My mouth is salivating at the thought. "I would love a grilled cheese sandwich."

He stands up. "One Ben's famous grilled cheese, comin' right up." He hands me the TV remote. "Now relax and I will be back soon."

★

WE SIT IN THE KITCHEN, enjoying our lunch of delicious grilled cheese sandwiches. The best grilled cheese sandwiches in the world, by the way, with lots of sharp cheddar cheese oozing out the sides.

"Do ya want another?" he asks as he eyes my empty plate.

"That was so good, better than hospital food any day."

"Glad ya liked it." He takes my plate to the sink, quickly washing up the dishes. Walking over to the refrigerator, he pulls my grocery list pad from the front.

"Ya have some things on here, do ya want to add to it and I can go out and get the stuff?"

"Yes, let me have it and we can get ready to go." I hold my hand out for the pad but he pulls it to him.

"Correction, kitten, you are stayin' put while I run out and get the items. Doctor said rest, not run around a store."

I sigh, but realize there will be no winning this conversation. "All right, you win, can I have the list now, please?" I hold out my hand, a little irritated about being treated like a child. He smiles, handing it back to me.

I grab the pen sitting on the table, and looking over the list, I immediately get embarrassed about some of the items on it. Pads and tampons, just great. I can't have him get those but I will need them soon. I cross them off, and I will text Holly and have her get them for me.

I write down some simple foods that we can make it on for a few days, and I grab my wallet, taking my ATM card out. I write the PIN at the top of the list. "Here you go."

He looks over the list, and takes the ATM card, putting it in an old leather wallet he is carrying.

"Okay, well this shouldn't take long." He smiles looking at the list and gives a little chuckle.

"Why are you laughing?"

He looks at me, his eyes so mischievous. "Ya think I can't handle gettin' your girly things?" He raises his eyebrows in question.

My face turns hot from embarrassment. If I was close to a rock, I swear I would crawl under it. The thought of Ben getting me female hygiene products—I just want to die. "Well, I didn't want you to have to worry about it."

"Julie, if ya need these I don't mind gettin' them, and if it makes ya feel any better, I have bought them before and survived the embarrassment."

I jolt my head up in shock. "You have? For whom?" I can't hide my curiosity with an added note of jealously.

"Tell ya about it later." He takes the list, folding it and placing it in his jacket pocket.

"You keep saying that. It seems it is going to be a long story," I say, still a little stung by the shopping confession.

"Ya have no idea," he says quietly to himself before changing the subject. "Let's get ya back into bed before I leave. Once I give ya these pills, ya will be in la-la land."

Ben lifts me up, and I have to admit, I love the fact he has to carry me. I take advantage of the situation and I lay my head on his chest, enjoying the fact I am in his arms. I pretend that he is holding me as a lover and not just as a friend.

He lays me gently on the bed and helps me get comfortable, before going into the bathroom and getting my medicines and a glass of water. "Here ya go."

I take the mix of pills, some antibiotics and pain meds, but I decided not to fill the anxiety medicine. I hid the prescription order from them earlier when we stopped by the pharmacy. I swallow the pills without protest and drink the water. I am reminded of the role reversal from a few days back when I took care of him.

"Attagirl." He sets the glass down on my nightstand. I go ahead and lie down, turning on my side to watch him. "Here is your phone. Do ya need anythin' else before I go?"

Remembering what he said to me when I asked the very same question a few days ago, I decide to tease him. "If I asked you to sing me a lullaby, would you do that too?" I start laughing, expecting him to start laughing too. Joke is on me however, when he sits down on the side of the bed next to me and starts singing.

I am in awe; his voice is so beautiful. There is no way he hasn't done this before, he is too good. I lie there smiling, hugging my pillow, and listening to him sing. I think I recognize the song. I am pretty sure I have heard it on country music stations.

He only sings a verse and the chorus, when he stops. "Is that better?"

"Wow, Ben, that was beautiful." I don't know what else to say. It seems like with every moment, I am learning something new about him.

"Nah, I'm rusty. It's been awhile."

"Could have fooled me. Did you used to sing professionally before?"

"No, just with my friends in the garage, when I was a kid."

"Do you play an instrument?"

"Yes, the guitar." I want to ask him more, but I yawn and he catches me.

"No more questions, we will talk later, I promise." He gets up off the bed. I close my eyes, too tired to watch him leave the room.

# CHAPTER
## *fourteen*

I AM AT THE DINER. Everyone has left for home and we are closing for the night because it is Christmas Eve. I have no family so I volunteered to lock up. I walk to the door to lock it and flip the open sign over to show we're closed, but before I get to it, the trucker walks in. He is grinning at me, with his disgusting teeth that have most likely never seen a toothbrush. He locks the door behind him, coming toward me. I back up until I feel the counter behind me, and he keeps coming. He has his arms out now, and his hands are positioned to go around my neck. I scream ...

"Julie, wake up. Hey, Julie, come on, wake up, angel, it's a dream. It's just a dream."

I sit up, trying to catch my breath and look around. It is dark and I can't see. I touch my neck, no hands there, but someone is touching me. My airway is closing up. I can't breathe. I feel the hands on my arms and I push them off of me. I see faint light coming from the hallway. I feel something warm in my lap, and when I touch it, I feel fur. It's Bo. My bedside lamp comes on and I see Ben now sitting on my bed as he finishes turning on the light.

"You okay? Ya were havin' a bad dream. It's okay now, you are home and safe."

I push my hair out of my face, trying to make sense of where I am. I recognize the light blue wall and the Thomas Kinkade painting on it. My bedroom, it's my bedroom. I am home. Thank God, I am home.

"Julie, do ya need anythin'? Can I help?" He touches my hand, but I quickly pull it back. The comfort I usually feel with his touch is now replaced by a fear still holding me in its wake. "NO! Don't touch me." It is out of my mouth before I can think better of it, and the sad part is I don't mean it. I long for his touch. I stay silent, though.

"Why don't ya come out to the livin' room and watch TV with me and Bo? I made some supper; you probably should eat somethin'."

The best he gets out of me is a nod, as I pull the covers off of me. I am still dressed in the sweats and T-shirt I was wearing when I came home from the hospital, minus the bra I took off after he left for the store. I am a little embarrassed by that now. I draw my arms to my front, hoping to hide that fact, as I gently move my legs to the side of the bed. My ankle is throbbing like crazy, and the movement doesn't help.

"Do ya want me to pick ya up, or would ya rather use the crutches?"

The fact he is now asking for permission to hold me, is breaking my heart. What did I expect? I pushed him away. "You can pick me up." I hear the tremble in my voice. I am really trying to hold it together, but I feel I will crack at any moment.

He leans down in front of me. "Wrap your arms

around my neck."

I do and he gently lifts me in his arms and carries me out to the living room. He is very cautious of my ankle as he avoids the doorway, and is going very slow to turn. I watch him as he is carrying me, as if I was precious cargo. His smooth face is showing signs of stubble and I ache to touch it. I have never been with someone whose hair grows so quickly. I like it, it is very manly. We make it into the living room with Bo right behind us. Gently, he lowers me down on to the couch, but I refuse to let go, in fact, I hug him tighter to me.

"Julie?"

The concern in his voice is the final straw and I finally break and start crying. Everything is coming at me, the attack, the anniversary of Jason's death, another Christmas without my parents.

"I got ya, it's okay, I gotcha." He lifts me up again, but turns and sits down, holding me in his arms and rocking me like a small child. The soft flannel of his shirt feels good against my face as I feel my tears soaking the material.

I feel his lips on my head as he speaks. His strong arms are holding me close to him. "Get it out, cry it all out. Don't let it swallow ya up, get rid of it." The words he says as he holds me are different. Where most people would say things to get you to stop crying, he is encouraging me to continue. No shushing or pleading for me to stop.

"I got ya, no one is goin' to ever hurt ya again," he whispers. "Just get it all out, you are safe with me."

I hug him tighter. If I could crawl inside him, I would right now. My face is in his neck now, my lips touching his skin. I could kiss him, but I am too busy having my meltdown and trying to catch my breath. I do feel safe in his arms, and I realize it is the first time I have felt truly safe in a very long time. I hate that he is seeing me like this, though.

I have no idea how long we sit there. I am still cuddled in Ben's arms. Not once did he show a sign of protest. I haven't cried this long in a very long time and never in front of anyone if I could help it. Slowly, my crying starts to quiet down as I hiccup to get my breath. My trembling has stopped, but Ben continues to hold me tight. My head hurts and I am so tired that I could fall asleep like this, but the wetness of my bawling, that and my now stuffy and runny nose, have me sitting up.

Ben reaches over to the end table and hands me a tissue box, allowing me to clean my face. I look down at the floor to see Bo lying beside us, his head on his paws as his sad eyes look up at me. It is one thing for me to be sad, but to see it in his eyes is too much. I smile down at him, and the next thing you know, he is on the couch, lying next to me. Ben is about to say something but stops when I start petting and kissing Bo. I start rubbing Bo's ears and this is his favorite as he rolls onto his back. If I stop, he nudges me for more. I start laughing as he is acting like he is starving for attention.

"I think he is jealous." I look up at Ben. I am still sitting in his lap, but he has made no move to take me off.

"I think he needs more obedience trainin'." Ben gives him a look, but Bo couldn't care less.

"Cool your jets, Marine." I poke Ben in the chest, attempting to lighten the mood. "He is a retired war hero, you know? He deserves to break the rules now and then."

Ben gives me the strangest look, most likely because I have gone from bawling my eyes out to joking around in the matter of minutes. That is how I am though, once the crying jag is done, it's done. That is until next time.

"Cool my jets?" He raises his eyebrows and smiles. "You have definitely been hangin' with flyboy Carl for a while."

I start laughing because he is right, I did learn that from Carl. We both start laughing but as Ben keeps eyeing Bo on the couch, I can tell he doesn't like it. "All right, Bo, go lie down in your bed."

Bo hesitates until Ben repeats my command, only with a more authoritative voice. "Bo, down." Bo immediately jumps off the couch and heads for this pillow bed on the floor. He lies down, looking at Ben. "Good, boy." Ben gives him his praise and he pants and wags his tail. He is happy.

"I'm sorry, I have been letting him get up on the couch. I guess I have been spoiling him." Ben smiles at me, neither agreeing nor disagreeing with what I just said.

"Ya better?" Ben asks, rubbing my upper arm.

"Yes, thank you." I am starting to feel awkward now. I still barely know this man, and I am sitting on his lap. With my ankle, it is hard to just get up.

Ben must feel my anxiousness as he helps me off his lap and back onto the couch. He grabs a few pillows and places them under my foot to elevate my ankle. Even though he is very careful, I feel pain as I grit my teeth and inhale. He hears my distress. "Does it hurt?" He looks at me and removes his hands from my ankle.

"A little. It is throbbing a lot."

"Ya are overdue for your pain medicine, but ya shouldn't take it on an empty stomach. How about somethin' to eat and then ya take your pill?"

"Sounds good." I smile up at him as he heads to the kitchen. I am not used to anyone waiting on me like this. I think the last time it was Aunt Gina, when I came down with the flu. Ben comes back in holding a bowl, handing it to me. I look down and see it's ravioli with lots of cheese. It looks and smells delicious.

He sits in my dad's recliner and starts channel

surfing with the remote. "Tell me when ya see somethin' ya want to watch." He continues scrolling the channel guide.

"It doesn't matter to me, watch what you like. I don't watch much TV anyway."

"How about my classic go to show, Cops?"

"You like watching Cops? That's funny. It is actually one of my favorite shows too."

"It is? Why's that? Not a badge bunny are you?" He smirks.

I look at him, puzzled. "It was one of my dad's favorite shows. Mom would get so mad, because he would watch it all the time. She ended up putting a TV in the bedroom so she could watch her shows. So, what's a badge bunny?" I ask as I take another bite of ravioli.

"You know, have a thing for police officers."

What an interesting question—he is fishing. He knows that I know he was military police. I am not sure if Ben is just kidding around with me or going somewhere with this. I decide to turn the tables and see what he says.

"Maybe." I look over at him as I take a bite of the ravioli. I feel the warmness on my cheeks as I admit I might be attracted to police officers. Especially an ex-military police officer that is sitting in my dad's recliner, eating his food.

He pauses as he is about to take another bite, the fork not quite to his very sexy mouth. "Interestin'." He smiles before taking a bite. He doesn't say another word as we both sit and eat and watch the show.

I am glad we are back to the point where we can flirt with each other again. I missed it.

After I finish the delicious ravioli, he comes over and takes the bowl from me. "More?" he asks

"No, thank you. It was delicious, did you make it?"

"Nope, the chef did." He smiles as he starts to head to the kitchen.

"What chef? What did you do, order takeout?" I turn my head to see him stop and look at me.

"No. Ya know ... Chef Boyardee?" He grins. His witty comeback reminds me again of Jason.

I start laughing as he walks in the kitchen, putting away the dishes. He has a great sense of humor—jot that down as another thing I like about him. I remember that earlier today he promised we would talk more about him and his past. I want to know more and there is no time like now. He walks back in handing me my pill and a glass of water.

He sits back down as I take the pill and wash it down with the water before setting it on the table. He thinks he is going to be able to sit there and watch the show, but I have other ideas. I keep staring at him, waiting for him to look my way. He finally looks at me, doing a few double takes, just to see me continuing to stare at him.

"Yes?" He is acting coy now, as if he has no clue about what I am thinking. I seriously doubt that.

"We were going to talk, remember?"

Just as I thought, he sighs. He knows exactly where this is going. He frowns as he points the remote to the TV and shuts it off. "Okay. Ask away." He sits back, ready for his interrogation.

"Why are you homeless?"

"Wow, ya go straight for the jugular, don't ya, kitten? Why not ask my age first, or my favorite ice cream?"

I know what he is doing. He is trying to make light of the fact I want to know everything. It is time, whether he likes it or not, especially if I am going to continue to let him stay in my house. "Oh, I want to know that too."

"Twenty-eight and mint chocolate chip." He smiles.

"Mint chocolate chip? That tastes like toothpaste.

Yuck." I cringe, showing my disgust.

"Does not." He laughs at the face I am making at his horrible choice in ice cream flavor. "Okay, fine. So what's your age and favorite ice cream?"

"Twenty-three and butter pecan." I laugh but then stop, realizing that he is doing it again, and avoiding my main question. "Ben?" I put on my serious face, wanting us to get back on topic.

His smile fades as I am sure he realizes that it's time to get real, no more joking around. "It is simple. I am homeless because that is exactly what I am—homeless. I have no home to go to."

"I don't understand. Everyone has a home somewhere, right?"

"Not me." He takes a deep breath and begins his story.

As a kid, I remember watchin' the news on September 11, 2001. Everyone else was in school, but my mom kept me home because I had the flu. Watchin' all the horrible events on TV, I knew I wanted to join the military right then and there. When I was a senior in high school, I was already signed up to go into the Marines. I was just waitin' for graduation.

I also started datin' a girl named Renee. She had been after me for a while to go out with her, but I had a job and a car to pay for, so it made it tough to date. We hooked up one night at a party. I was drunk, she was drunk, and well ... ya know. It was a mistake and I chose to quit seein' her. Anyway, a month before graduation she comes to me and tells me she is pregnant and it is mine.

I didn't believe her at first, because she had quite a reputation, but there was no denyin' that the timin' matched and well, I felt I needed to do the right thin'. Ya see my dad left my mom to raise my sister and me alone. He took off shortly after I was born. I didn't want to take the chance of a kid of mine not knowin' his father, so I did the right thin' and married her right after graduation. We didn't have time for a fancy weddin' or honeymoon because I was due for basic trainin' two weeks after graduation.

Besides, just because I wanted to do the right thin' didn't mean I was madly in love with her. I thought maybe as we got older, we could build a relationship, but mostly, at least for me, it was about the baby. We would write each other and call when I was allowed. Just before my graduation from basic, she informed me she miscarried. I came home right after, missin' celebratin' graduation with my new brothers. I felt bad and mourned my child.

Renee was understandably upset and I did what any good husband would do and loved her and took care of her. I was committed to makin' our marriage, and hopefully one day our family, a success. Well, the Marines had other ideas. I was sent to Afghanistan for a long tour. I still continued to write to her and call her. I had a little money so I set her up with a nice house near her parents, so she wouldn't be too lonely. I would send almost all my money home so she didn't have to work.

Soon after, no letters came from her and no packages. She was never home when I had a chance to call, and her cell would go straight to voice mail. I would come home and she said she was busy. She would make it up to me and I would leave, thinkin' everythin' was fine. It would be a few weeks later and the same again. I had my sister check up on her and that was one of the only times she did call me, and it was mostly to scream at me for not trustin' her. I served two enlistments and was about to sign up for a third, until divorce papers came.

But I hated that my marriage was failin' and I blamed the Marines. So I didn't re-enlist. I packed my bags and came home. Unfortunately, I didn't get the welcome home I was wishin' for. My home was bein' foreclosed, my bank account was empty, and my car and all my belongings were gone. All that I had on me was what was in my duffle bag, and a set of divorce papers, with no Renee in sight. After talkin' with some neighbors, they informed me that she and her boyfriend took off for California, in my car. It seems my wife and her boyfriend were livin' the good life on my dime.

"Wait a sec, so you are saying that she was cheating on you from the very beginning?"

"It seems that way, maybe not before the miscarriage, but shortly after."

"Oh, Ben, I am so sorry." What a selfish bitch, I think to myself.

"Yeah, I should have not put that much trust in her. So, I found myself homeless."

"What about your family? Couldn't they help you?"

"Well, my sister is a single mom of three kids, so I couldn't burden her."

"What about your mom?"

"Mom died a few years ago."

"So you have been on the streets all this time? Isn't there any veteran services that could help you?

"Well, it sounds nice on paper but I wasn't wounded, I was just broke. And with no address it is hard to apply for a job. I have been doin' odd jobs here and there for some easy cash, but not enough for a home, car, or phone. I considered this my punishment for bein' a lousy husband."

"Ben, I am so sorry. No one deserves that. But now you can look for a job. You can use this address and we can get you a phone. You have a chance for a better life now."

"Hey, slow down, one day at a time, okay? I am still

not sure about this, Julie. I feel like I am takin' advantage of ya or somethin', and take it from me, no one should be done that way."

"You're not, though. I want you to stay for as long as you want or need."

"Let's just make it through Christmas and go from there, okay?"

Feeling a little rejected by his statement, I agree. I can't believe he was married. What woman in her right mind would cheat on such a handsome and kind man? The chick had to be a total loser, especially doing him dirty like that and leaving him with nothing, not even a home. Some welcome home.

Ben started talking again. "Now, last night I talked to Carl, and he is goin' to hire me to do some odd jobs and I am goin' to pay ya for food, rent, and bills ya have."

This statement brings me out of my thoughts. "Wait, you talked to Carl last night?" I begin to get irritated by Carl's interference.

Ben laughs. "Come on now, do ya really think he was just goin' to let me take your purse and car and not follow me here?"

Ben is right. Carl is protective and no way would he allow Ben to do this unless he gave his seal of approval. I wonder how that interrogation went. "I guess not." I smile.

"No worries, kitten, it was a good talk. He just wants to make sure I am not scammin' ya. I would do the same thin' if it was reversed. Hell, I might even be more aggressive."

I reflect on the fact he wants to pay me for staying here, which makes us sound like a business relationship instead of just a relationship. That doesn't sit well with me. "Well, you can help Carl for money but I don't want any of it."

Ben stares at me a second as if he is irritated by what I just said, before getting up and walking to the fireplace. "Come on, Julie. Look, ya are goin' to be out of work for weeks and I am sure ya have bills. I mean look at this place, it must cost a lot and on a waitress' salary, ya could use some help. Ya helped me out, now it's my turn to help ya."

Looking at my place, it would be understandable for someone to assume I pay a lot for it. It's a nice home, nicer than what a normal waitress trying to make ends meet could afford. Now it is time for me to confess a little fact. "Not really. I don't need to work."

Ben looks at me, his eyebrows raised as if he doesn't believe what I just said. "Huh? Like to run that by me again?"

I don't usually like talking about this and with the exception of Carl, Holly, and my financial advisor and tax guy, no one knows.

"I only work at the diner to help Carl out, but I really don't need to. I own this house, my car, everything. I am debt free and I have money."

Ben takes a moment to chew on what I just announced, but he doesn't ask the next question, which to me shows his character. He doesn't ask how much money. It makes me love him all the more. And with the fact that he is homeless and I am wealthy because of my family's misfortunate and untimely deaths, it is something I don't really want to talk about. So I am glad when he doesn't ask. Unfortunately, he does ask a question that tends to irritate me time and time again.

"Why aren't ya back in school then?"

Oh, great, here we go again with the college thing. "Why?" I try my best not to get too excited about the question as I did the last time he asked me.

"Why?" He chuckles, obviously amused by my

answer. "So ya can have a career, that's why."

"I am not looking for one," I respond, my face stoic.

"Well, what do ya want then?"

Talk about your loaded questions. I look at this handsome man and part of me wants to answer, I want you and I want to have a life with you, I want to marry you, have your babies, and grow old with you. I know it is not the modern approach of thinking for young women, but I want what was taken from me—a family. He continues to stare at me, waiting for my answer but I chicken out. I also decide that turnabout is fair play.

"We will discuss this another time." I try to play yawn, but it turns into the real thing. The crying, the warm meal, and the pain pill have me very sleepy. I yawn again, this time not on purpose.

Ben smirks at me. I am not sure if he is buying it or not. "Well played, kitten. I will let ya get away with that now, but this discussion is not over."

# CHAPTER *fifteen*

BEN HELPS ME BACK INTO bed, this time not asking to pick me up. I am so sleepy, I would probably fall down if he didn't help me. However, in the darkness, I fight the sleep. I toss and turn, worried that the nightmare will return. Then I start thinking about our earlier conversation. Ben's past, he was married? I wasn't expecting that and my own issues. What is everyone's hang up that I am not in college? I stare at the ceiling, my brain running ninety miles per hour. There is no way I am going to sleep. I get up and carefully grab my crutches. When I get into the hallway, I notice Jason's bedroom door is open and taking a quick peek, I see that Ben is not in there. I hobble to the living room and kitchen and they are both empty and dark. I start to panic, as being in the dark and alone gets to me, until I hear noise coming from the garage.

I open the door to the garage to see Bo standing

guard right in one of the very few open areas of the garage. There are mountains of boxes sitting on equipment so I can't see Ben anywhere. Bo looks at me and pants as he heads my way.

"Ben?" I call out as I carefully reach down to pet Bo.

"In here." He walks around a corner of boxes to come into my view. "Why are ya up?" he says, frowning at me. "And what the hell do ya think you're doin'? You are supposed to keep that ankle elevated."

I feel like I just got scolded from my dad. "I couldn't sleep. What are you doing?" I should have added, How come you're not sleeping?

He looks around and scratches his head. "Yeah, sorry, I guess I was snoopin' a little. Who in your family liked wood craftin'?" He looks over, resting his hands on his hips. He is standing there all brawny and sexy so that it takes me a second to remember he asked a question.

"My dad. We kept it because my brother tried to do a little but he didn't enjoy it. I just haven't wanted to get rid of Dad's equipment." Or anything else for that matter as I look around the garage, remembering how organized my Dad kept it.

"I had some woodworkin' tools once, but not as nice as this, but well, Renee took care of that." He continues to look around.

"Renee?" I ask as the name doesn't register with me.

"The ex," he spits out with a disgusted look on his face.

Definitely no love lost there when he mentions her name. That woman must be the stupidest woman on earth. Looking at Ben, how would someone cheat on that man? I watch as he looks at me, shaking his head as he walks toward me.

"What am I goin' to do with ya?" He stands in front of me with a disapproving look. He pulls a stool up to me and helps me sit down as he takes my crutches and sets them against the wall near the door.

"Ya know, I could help ya get this organized in here so ya can park your car in here again."

"Really? That would be great. I can't remember the last time I was able to park in here."

"Have you gone through all this stuff?"

"Some. Holly says I have enough to have quite the yard sale."

"She is right. Ya should, lots of good stuff here that others could use and it would give ya some extra money. Whatever ya don't sell, ya can donate for a tax write-off."

I don't really need the money, but I don't want to say that out loud. I am sure he already suspects now that I am financially well-off, but the last thing I want to do is rub that fact in his face. "It would be nice to park in here again. If you would help me I would let you have the woodworking stuff."

He continues exploring and doesn't respond to what I just said. At first I think he didn't hear me. "Julie, this stuff is worth a fortune, no way would I let ya give it to me." He continues his snooping around.

I can't help but feel a little hurt by his rejection of my gift. Again, it just reminds me that how I am feeling and what he is feeling are possibly two different things. After all, he was married and burned by a woman he was in love with, so he probably isn't looking to find himself in that situation again, anytime soon. I don't have the guts to tell him that I would love watching him working with my dad's tools and taking care of the garage just like Daddy did. But that is my illusion, not his. Maybe he is just waiting for me to heal and has plans to move on. That thought has crossed my mind.

"Well, we could work out a deal later. I am not using it and if you would help me get rid of some of this stuff, it would go toward trading for it. I have no idea what any of this stuff is worth." I am opening the door for him to stay longer. Looking around, it would take months for him to get rid of all this.

"Well, I will get workin' on this tomorrow after I help Carl. Speakin' of which, I better get some sleep and ya should be sleepin' too." He smiles at me, coming toward me again.

"Yeah, yeah, I feel like that is all I have done the last forty-eight hours." Sleeping is the last thing on my mind right now.

"Okay, grumpy, let's go." He bends down, and on cue, I wrap my arms around his neck as he lifts me up in his arms.

I enjoy this a little too much as thoughts of my ankle never healing run through my mind. Self-doubt has me opening my mouth again. "You know my crutches are just right there." I'm giving him an out to not feel like he needs to pick me up. That's me, my own worst enemy.

He just keeps smiling at me, not making one move to set me down. "This is quicker. I would like to get to sleep sometime tonight." He chuckles, amused by his jab.

"Ha ha, very funny." I make a face at him. Some of the things he says remind me of Jason so much.

"I'm a funny guy." He walks to the door as I help him open it and turn off the lights. "Come on, Bo, let's go," he calls out, as Bo sneaks by us. I try to act like the fact he carries me irritates me but I love it and once again I take advantage and hug him to me.

HE IS ON ME AGAIN, the weight of him crushing me as he pushes, trying to kiss me. My head hurts from the fall and all I can think is that I am going to be raped and then killed. Why me? No, stop, please stop. Please, God, don't do this. I am crying but it is doing no good, he won't stop. Ah, Julie, sweet virginal Julie, cry for me. Come on, Julie. Julie ...

"Julie, wake up! Come on, angel."

I open my eyes to see Ben sitting on the bed beside me. This time the room is lit up.

"Hey, it's me, kitten. Ya were havin' another nightmare."

"Uh huh." I sit up, wiping the wetness I feel off of my face. I was actually crying? Ben must think I am the biggest crybaby ever. I am embarrassed by my behavior and try to come up with some rationale on why I keep dreaming the shit I am dreaming.

"I am not taking those pain pills anymore; they make me have crazy dreams." That has to be the reason, I conclude. The pills make me sleep, and when I sleep, I dream.

"Wanna talk about it?" he asks, running his fingers up and down my arm to comfort me.

No, what I really want to do is pull you in here with me and snuggle away the bad demons, but no way am I saying that. "No, it is just dreams, no big deal." I smile, putting on my best brave face. "I am sorry I woke you. You should go back to bed. Carl will work you hard tomorrow." I fluff my pillow and lie back down, rolling to my side. I want to prove to him and maybe myself that I am not a little girl in need of comfort. I must be a great actress, because he gets up and reaches to turn off the lamp.

"Okay, try to get some rest. I am just down the hall, if ya need anythin'." He reaches over to click off the lamp, but the hall light has the room still illuminated.

"Uh huh," I say, pulling the covers up around me.

He gets up and turns off the light and I close my eyes to reassure him I will be okay, but when I hear the door close, I open them. I'm afraid to fall back asleep.

# CHAPTER
## *sixteen*

I LIE IN BED FOR hours, my comforter pulled up close to my chin. I know the house is chilly because I don't like it too warm at night and apparently neither does Ben. I glance at the clock, it is almost six o'clock. I suppose I can get up now and quit the pretending to sleep act. I need to do something to get busy. I am spending way too much time thinking and dreaming. If I stay busy, I won't think.

I gingerly stand, holding my hands out to the bed, in case I can't maneuver with this cast on my ankle. I hold onto the wall and hop to where my crutches are; Ben must have returned them to my room from the garage. I slowly make my way down the hallway and then to the kitchen. The crutches are awkward and take getting used to. I smell the odor of delicious and glorious coffee. It lets me know that I am not the first one up.

"Good morning," Ben says, not looking up from the

newspaper he is reading.

"Good morning. You made breakfast?"

He looks up from the paper to look at me. I don't get his usual happy face; instead, I get a frown as he folds the paper closed, laying it on the table. He then gets up and positions two of the kitchen chairs around before coming toward me.

"Don't get too excited. It's just two toaster waffles and some scrambled eggs, not as good as your biscuits and gravy." Maybe he is mad that I haven't cooked breakfast. I am being such a terrible hostess.

"I can make some biscuits and gravy if you like." I smile, hoping that might cheer him up. I don't like this grumpy version of Ben. Has he had coffee yet, I wonder.

"Nope, not today, ya need to rest. Come on, let's get ya set up and that ankle elevated."

"I rested yesterday," I whine as the irritation of being treated like a child again frustrates me.

"Yep and you are gonna rest today too. Remember what Doc said. Ya have to stay off that ankle. Now sit down, before ya fall down." The stern looks he is giving me has me sitting at his command and allowing him to carefully raise my leg and place it on the chair. His voice is strong and demanding, but his touch is gentle. When he looks at me again, he smiles but it's too late. His coldness earlier blew all my happy thoughts away. Now, I am just grumpy and in desperate need of caffeine so I just frown at him and remain silent.

His smile quickly fades as he gets up and heads to the stove. He places a plate in front of me, and puts the butter and syrup close so I don't have to reach too far. He then brings over a mug, placing it in front of me as he carefully pours the hot fresh coffee in. Finally, he places my favorite creamer and spoon next to it.

"Thank you," I say as I look up to see him smirk at

me.

"You're welcome." He winks as he takes the coffee pot back to the counter. Ben remains standing as he busies himself with cleaning and straightening up my kitchen. I give in and fix my coffee, allowing him to do the things that I should be doing.

"Where's Bo?" I ask as I take a sip of coffee. I sigh a little as the first sip is always the best.

Ben looks out the window as he is washing the few dishes. "He's outside investigatin' the perimeter." He chuckles to himself.

"Yeah, that's his morning routine. He started doing that the first day I brought him home."

Ben continues looking out the window as he rinses the dishes. "Old habits are hard to break," he whispers almost to himself.

Before I can ask him what he meant by that, Bo comes running in through the doggie door to greet me. "Hey, boy, good morning." I allow him to jump halfway on me, since I can't greet him the way I normally do. As I hug and love on him, I look over to see Ben watching us as he holds his cup of coffee. But it is unclear, if he is really watching us. His eyes are definitely locked onto Bo and me, but he seems lost in something as he continues to stare.

"Is something wrong?" I ask, as he finally snaps out of wherever his mind was at the moment. I kiss Bo on the head and make him get down as he heads off to the living room.

"No, everythin' is fine." He takes his final sip and turns to rinse his cup.

Feeling disappointed, I let it go and start eating my breakfast. I wish he would open up to me more, but I am one to talk. I shut him off last night when he tried to get me to talk about the nightmares.

"Carl is sending Holly over to hang with you today until I get back. Remember you need to stay off the foot, so it's couch city for you today, kitten."

"Okay." I stare down at my plate, not looking at him as I answer.

I am surprised when he comes over and kneels in front of me. If we were a couple, I would swear he was about to propose to me. That's just my romantic imagination playing tricks on me again. He smiles, looking at me and reaches out his hand to touch my cheek. I flinch and lean back a little. Why did I just do that?

Immediately my hand goes to my neck, as though to protect it. It is a knee-jerk reaction to having him too close that I did unconsciously, but I can't take it back. The damage is done. How do I explain it isn't him that bothers me? I hope he didn't notice but I am almost positive he did, by the fact he is no longer smiling at me.

He pulls his hand back away from my face and gently pats my knee. "Ya look exhausted. Should I call Carl? I am sure he would let me help him another day."

Dammit! What is wrong with me? I keep sending him the signals to stay away, which is the last thing I want. I am so tempted to ask him to stay, so I can fix the damage I am causing. I fear that in my state of mind, I am going to just make it worse. Maybe I need a few hours away from him, to work on my behavior. Time to pull out the fake and happy Julie. I take a deep breath and smile, placing my hand on his. "No, go, I'm okay. You go and help Carl. Holly will be here soon. I promise I will be good and stay off my ankle."

He turns his hand over to hold mine, caressing and squeezing it gently. "Promise me ya will try to get some sleep today."

"I promise, I will." I fake a smile, as I lie to him once

again.

He stares at me, and for a moment I imagine him leaning in once again and kissing me. It would be perfect, and if I hadn't blown it a few minutes ago, it might have happened. At least I hope it would have. He gently squeezes my hand again.

"Ya know I don't think I have said this enough, but thank ya for being so gracious and openin' your lovely home to me." I am so touched by his unexpected words that I feel like weeping. Not because of the words he said, but the tone in which he said it. He seems so sad that it is breaking my heart. He looks down as he stares at our hands. "Ya know the other day, when ya called me a coward—"

"Ben, ... I ..." I interrupt, wanting to stop this conversation, but he squeezes my hand and looks up at me.

"Shh, let me finish. I know ya didn't mean to hurt my feelins but it wasn't that, Julie, it was the truth. I have been actin' like a coward for a long time now. Ya made me see that I didn't want anyone to help me because I didn't feel like I deserved it." He continues to look at me as I feel the lump of emotions building in my throat.

"And then I was bein' an ass and pushed you away. I didn't feel like I deserved your help and friendship." He looks down again for a moment and then back at me.

"Anyway, I am lousy at this but what I am tryin' to say is that I appreciate everythin' ya have done and are doin' for me and thank ya for believing' in me." He smiles as my eyes are glossy with unshed tears.

I tighten my lips and nod. I am afraid to open my mouth because I know I will cry. Before I can react and pull away again, he leans in and kisses my forehead. He releases my hand and stands up. I am not sure what to say, so I just smile. This has been a bizarre morning.

"Well, I better get goin', see ya later tonight." He grabs the car keys and heads out of the room.

"See ya." I barely spit out the words as I hear the front door close.

What the hell just happened? I appreciate his words but now I am more confused than ever. Have I been reading this all wrong? Does he only see me as a friend? Even if he did, it wouldn't change anything. I would still help him but I thought for sure ....

Oh, who am I kidding? The guy has been married and burned big-time. The last thing he is going to want is another relationship. He is probably going to be one of those love 'em and leave 'em kind of guys, so he doesn't get burned again. The problem is, I am not that kind of girl.

Well, I guess that's that. It is most likely for the best anyway. But if that's the case, why do I feel so sad? No sooner does that thought cross my mind and Holly walks in. She is dressed all bright and cheery, in a red sweater dress and leggings. She walks in like it is her home, going straight to the cupboard, grabbing a coffee mug.

"Hey, girl, how's the ankle? I saw homeless guy driving off in your car, hope he brings it back." And that's Holly, speaking her mind again. She comes over and grabs the creamer, returning to the counter to fix her cup.

I love her but I really don't like her picking on Ben. "Holly, please cut it out. If he was going to steal it he's had plenty of opportunities already. Why do you dislike him so much?"

Holly turns to me, still stirring her cup, and then she takes the spoon out, putting it in her mouth before placing it in the sink. "Oh, my, someone is touchy this morning." She grins as she takes a sip from her mug.

This is not going to be an easy day. Maybe I should send her home and fend for myself today, but Ben would have a cow if I did that. I look over at her, not amused by her cheeriness.

"Don't give me that look, Julie Walsh." I continue to stare coldly at her. "Okay, I am sorry, geez!!" She walks over with the coffee pot, refreshing my cup, obviously a waitress habit. "Here, drink more coffee, grumpy pants." She sets the pot on the table as she sits down across from me. "Don't be all butt hurt. I don't dislike him personally, but you are my best friend and I don't want to see you get hurt."

"What makes you think he would hurt me?" I ask as I fix myself another cup.

She sits back and begins. "Well, let's state the obvious here, first. You barely know this guy, Julie, and you invited him to live with you?" She takes a sip of coffee and places it down on the table as she continues.

"I mean come on, just a day ago he was living on the streets. Then one day he lucks up and meets this girl who likes to take in strays and help people and BAM!! He has hit a gold mine." She slaps her hand down on the table for added effect.

It worked as I jump, hoping the coffee doesn't spill over. She just doesn't get it and I come to Ben's defense. "He saved my life, Holly. He is my friend and friends help one another. I would do the same for you or Mike."

"Yes, he saved your life and for that I will be eternally grateful. I just don't know, Julie. I still don't trust his motives." She shakes her head, taking another sip from her mug.

"I think you are being mean and unfair." I scold her as I grab my mug.

"Okay, I can see someone has pissed in your cornflakes, so let's start over, shall we?" She sets down her mug and leans over to me. Her face is animated with a fake smile. "Good morning, Julie ... oh, good morning,

Holly." I watch her and start smiling, as she continues. "It was so nice of you to take the whole day off to spend with me today."

"Stop it, goof ball." I wave her off as we both laugh. I never could stay mad at her for long.

She takes a deep breath and leans over toward me as she continues. "Julie, you are my best friend and I am going to say this as a best friend." I look at her concerned, wondering what she will say now. "You look like hell." She sits back, grasping her mug for another sip.

My hand self-consciously goes to my hair. I touch it, feeling the mattiness of it. I didn't even bother to brush it this morning. I am just not used to anyone being here to worry about how I look. Geez, no wonder Ben didn't want to kiss me. He even said I didn't look good today.

"Gee, thanks, you are only the second person to tell me that today." It's not like I can jump up and fix it now.

"Wait, he said you look like hell?" She sets her mug down again.

"No not in those words. It doesn't matter. What's the point? He doesn't think of me like that, anyway." Once again, I am feeling sorry for myself. I am pathetic.

"Think of you like what?"

"Never mind." Just great, I had to open my big mouth. She is not going to drop this now.

"Oh, no, you aren't getting away with that, so spill."

I was right. No sense in fighting it. "Like someone he would be attracted too," I shyly say as I tried to hide behind my mug.

"Excuse me?" Holly's eyebrows rise. "You're kidding right?"

Damn her, I am tired of being teased. I place the mug down and look over at her. No more hiding. "Holly, I know you don't like him, but I do. There I said it, okay?" I sit back defeated. "Oh, who cares? It doesn't really even matter. He is only being nice to me because I was helping him." Once again, pathetic Julie strikes out.

Holly doesn't respond right away, as I would expect her to. Maybe she agrees, finally. "You seriously believe that?" she asks very quietly—very un-Holly like.

"Sure, why else would he help me?" I shrug as I am glad that maybe we will end this discussion.

"Oh, girl, your head was hit harder than I thought if you truly believe that." She starts busting up in laughter.

I am not amused. "Whatever." I am so done with this conversation now.

She continues to laugh but slows down and finally stops when she realizes I am not joining her. "Wow, you really have fallen for this guy, haven't you?" Finally, she is serious as I cut my eyes to her.

Once again, I hide my face behind the safety of the coffee mug. "Does it matter?" I whisper. Going back to bed now sounds like a good idea.

Holly sighs and sets her mug down. "Look, I probably shouldn't tell you this and should let you go on believing that."

Now she has piqued my interest for the first time since walking in here this morning. "What are you talking about?" I peek over my mug at her.

"Never mind, bad idea, Holly," she mumbles as she leans back again.

I am at the end of my rope with her and Ben both. "Holly?" I put the safety of my mug down to stare at her.

She stares back in challenge. It is the stare down to beat all stare downs. I am usually the victor and today is no exception. She breaks the stare, shaking her head. "All right, all right! You win, but homeless guy is sure going to owe me for this one."

"I wish you would stop calling him that," I scold her.

"The morning of the attack, when they took you to

the hospital, I had a little talk with your homeless guy." I tilt my head and frown. "Sorry, Ben," she says as I smile at her.

"Yes, you were mean to him." I grab my mug again.

"Did he tell you that?" she asks, leaning toward me. It is obvious she is offended now.

"No, Carl did." I am amused as it doesn't take much to rile her up. "Carl told me that you were very protective of me and that you wouldn't let him see me."

"Oh, yeah." She relaxes once again. "Well anyhow, Lenny told me that the cops took him into custody because no one was sure what happened. Once he showed up at the hospital, it was all about you. Were you okay? How badly were you hurt? Was someone sitting with you? Were you awake?"

What she says doesn't surprise me. I know he cares about me, as a friend, anyway. "That doesn't mean anything, Holly. Like I said earlier, he was concerned like any friend would be."

"Nah, I am your friend and I was concerned. He on the other hand was obsessed. He kept blaming himself for leaving you alone. He was pacing the waiting room like a crazy man. That is why I wouldn't let him see you. He was acting weird." I cut her another dirty look for that jab. She just shrugs. "Well, sorry, but he was."

I set my mug down and grab my leg up and carefully place it down. I lean over, rubbing the circulation back in my leg. Holly is acting like this is big news. It doesn't change my mind on the subject. "None of that surprises me, Holly. He is a friend and was concerned." I continue rubbing my leg.

"And then that night he stayed in your room while you were asleep," she says casually as I look up at her.

Now she has my attention. "What?" I sit back up, the circulation in my leg long forgotten.

"Yep." She smiles, taking a sip of coffee before continuing. "I was coming back to check in on you, even if visiting hours were over. You know me, rules don't apply to me. So, I spoke to the nurse, wanting to know how you were and they said they had to give you something to help you sleep. I was about to head to your room but they said that your fiancé was in there and you were resting comfortably now. I didn't question them and started heading to room, ready to ... hell, I don't know what. Anyhow, I peeked in and I saw him ... Ben. He was in there holding you and comforting you. He didn't hear me I guess. That's when I heard him telling you how sorry he was and how much he was in love with you."

The last part about the love, she sort of mumbled to herself. But I heard her, or at least I think I did. "What was that last part?" It is important she confirms what I think I heard.

"Oh, stop pretending. You heard me. He was telling you he was in love with you."

"Seriously?" I sit back in shock. This is totally unexpected.

"Uh huh, no lie." She nods.

"He's in love with me?" I repeat it to myself, not believing it still. But Holly never lies, at least not to me, especially about something like this.

"Well, think about it. He did go and clean himself up and is trying to get a job. He acts like he is trying to straighten himself up. I still don't trust his motives, though."

"Why, Holly? You barely know him."

"Neither do you, Julie," she snaps at me. "What do you really know about him? One minute he's a drifter living on the streets, the next he is shacking up with you."

I sink down a little as she scolds me. She is still not happy about the night I found Ben and took him home with me. Then I remember what Ben told me last night. "That's not true. Ben told me his story last night."

"Really?" she says sarcastically. "Well, it's about damn time." She gets up and takes my plate to the sink. She grabs a couple of waffles from the freezer and pops them in the toaster before turning around and leaning on the counter, facing me. "So, out with it. What did he say?"

Holly sits down and I tell her everything Ben told me last night as she eats her waffles. She stops eating for a minute when I tell her how he was married and is now divorced. She is as disgusted with his ex as much as I was when Ben told me about her last night. When I am finished, she doesn't say much. Maybe she is rethinking her view on Ben. At least I hope so. We both sit silently, as I touch my hair again. I need a bath and my hair could use a good washing. The bad part is, I will need her to help me. I hate this. I don't want to ask for help, but I have no choice. I am usually the helper not the helpless.

"What's up?" Holly asks as she notices me squirming.

"Can you help me? I want to take a bath and wash my hair." I sigh in defeat.

"Sure thing, can you maneuver to the bathroom on these things?" She walks over, grabbing my crutches.

"Yeah, I can manage. Grab a trash bag out of the cupboard and the tape out of the junk drawer. I have to wrap my cast."

# CHAPTER seventeen

HOLLY HELPS ME TAKE A bath and wash my hair. I hop over to the mirror by the sink, my hair in a towel turban and my soft robe around me. When I look into the mirror, I gasp. I softly touch my face with my fingertips. It is bruised on one side where that asshole hit me. I see the discoloring around my neck. He even bruised me there when he was trying to choke me. Little bruises where his fingertips were. He is in jail, but the evidence of his touching me, is still on my body. It makes me feel violated all over again. I hide my face in my hands as I begin to cry. Holly immediately wraps her arms around me.

"Shhh, it will be okay, Julie," she says as she hugs me close to her. "I will fix you up, and after I am done, you won't even see them. Remember? Just like in high school when I hid the hickeys Mike gave me. I am an expert. It will be okay."

I smile through my tears. I am so lucky to have her in my life.

True to her word, Holly works her magic with the makeup and hides most of the bruises. She also brushes and fixes my hair, making it shiny and flowing again; not a rat's nest in sight. My wardrobe choices are few with this big cast on me. Since I am not going anywhere today, I decide on a long flannel nightgown.

A few hours before Ben is due home, Holly takes off after I insist that I will be fine. Bo and I lie on the couch watching more TV than I have in years. I have caught myself several times about to fall asleep, but the fear of having another nightmare has me drinking another cup of coffee. I have had an entire pot by myself today. It is only a temporary fix as I find myself drifting off again, this time with a cup of coffee in hand.

Bo's barks startle me alert, but thankfully I don't spill the cup on me. Someone has pulled up in the drive. It has to be Ben because Bo is pacing by door, waiting just as excitedly as I am. I could get used to this, waiting at home in the evening for my man to show up. But is he really my man? Is Holly sure she heard what she did? Maybe he just said he loved me, but is not in love with me. There are different types of love, after all.

I mean, I love Holly and Mike as friends. I love Carl as a friend and as a pseudo relative. I am so caught up in my thoughts, I don't even greet Ben as he walks in. I just sit there, staring at him as he is taking off his coat and hanging it on the coat rack in the entryway. He also removes his boots as Bo greets him and they exchange hellos. This is so unreal. Daddy used to do the same thing. Ben starts walking toward me, pulling me out of my memory.

"Hey, there, how ya doin'?" He greets me with a smile. His mood seems a lot better than this morning.

"Hey, yourself. I am doing okay." I smile back.

He looks so handsome in his flannel shirt and jeans. His sleeves are rolled up to his elbows, showing off his sculpted and slightly hairy arms. His beard is coming back, but more of a sexy scruff than the burly mess it was before. I watch as he starts sniffing the air. He looks around the room, before turning his eyes back to me. "Coffee? At night? Do ya have a caffeine addiction?" He laughs.

"Kinda." I confess, as I shrug my shoulders.

"If ya drink that ya will not be able to sleep tonight, and from the looks of ya, I would say ya need sleep more than coffee."

I become self-conscious and look myself over. Sure I am not dressed up, but I am clean and my hair is combed. I start touching my face; maybe Holly didn't do as well with the makeup as I had thought. "Do I really look that bad?"

He sits on the coffee table in front of me, with a smile. "No, you're cute as a button, but ya look tired." He tweaks my nose with his finger, giving me more indication that his love for me is childlike, a friendship. Not a passionate kind. He slaps his hands down on his knees before getting up. "So, anyway, I hope ya are hungry, because I brought dinner from the diner. Carl sure wants to make sure ya eat."

"Yeah, it's the Italian in him. Food makes everything and everyone better in his mind." I try to hide the fact that what he said a moment ago hurt my feelings. I knew it. Holly heard him wrong.

He pats at his stomach. "Between your good cookin' and his, I have managed to put back on the weight I lost, but I better be careful."

I remember seeing his abs before. I thought they were perfect, but he was awfully skinny. I wonder how they look now.

"Well, let me get cleaned up and I will heat up dinner." He reaches over and takes my cup from me.

"Hey," I protest as he continues walking to the kitchen with my wonderful, glorious coffee.

"No more, the caffeine is gonna to keep ya up and make the swellin' in your ankle go up."

I am a little irritated by his bossiness. I am not used to having so many people waiting on me and telling me what I can and cannot do. I go to get up, and follow him in the kitchen but he is already coming out.

"Stop!" He points at me and I halt, holding onto the arm of the couch. "Ya stay right there; supper is out there tonight so ya can keep that ankle up."

Defeated again, I flop back down as he heads back into the kitchen.

In a few minutes he returns, handing me the takeout plate container and a tall glass of water. "Here, imagine it's coffee and drink up." I give him a dirty look and take the glass of water. "Quit with the poutin'. Ya can have coffee in the mornin', grumpy." He smirks.

He goes back and grabs his tray, returning with his dinner and a cold bottle of beer. He places the cold brew on Mom's coffee table. It is déjà vu, when I clear my throat. He turns and looks at me.

"Yes?"

"Use a coaster, please," I tell him as I tilt my head toward his beer on the coffee table.

He smiles. "Oh, yeah, sorry." He sets down his food and gets a coaster out of the tray, lifting his beer to wipe up the wet circle it left on the wood. Taking a quick swig, he places it back down, but this time on the coaster. "Ahhh." He smiles again at me.

I am in my own little world right now, lost in a memory of my parents and this same incident.

"Hey, darlin'. Did ya want one? I can go get ya one," he says, misunderstanding my silence.

"No, I don't drink beer, but thanks, the water is fine." I snap out of my daydream to start eating my dinner.

"Ya don't mind me drinkin', do you? I'm sorry, I should have asked ya first if it is okay."

The worried look on his face has me wanting to quickly assure him that it is okay. "No, it's fine, Ben. I don't mind. I just don't like the taste of it, is all." I quickly recover.

"Oh, okay. Carl gave me a six-pack at the end of the day. A bonus he called it." He eyes me as he opens up his container to start eating. I can tell his protective guard is up again, so I change the subject.

"So, what did Carl have you do today?" I ask, setting down my water. The question does its trick and he relaxes again.

"Well, he had me do some work on an older home he is tryin' to fix up for a veteran and his family. They had some damage when the wind blew down a tree and hit the side of the house. It felt good to do some physical work again and help a fellow vet."

As he talks, I open the container to Carl's lasagna and garlic toast. It smells wonderful; the man knows his way around a lasagna. I dig in immediately.

"So, did ya have a nice visit with Holly?" he says before taking a bite of lasagna.

"Uh hmm," I mumble and nod, my mouth full of food. It is so cheesy that a cheesy string falls on my chin.

"So, what did ya girls do all day?" He glances over at me, handing me a napkin.

"Thanks. Nothing really, just hung out and talked." I start wiping my chin.

"So, what did ya girls talk about?" he asks, taking another bite of food.

"You know, stuff." I start twirling my fork in my food, and avoiding eye contact. He has a knack for reading my face. No way do I want him to know all that we talked about.

"Stuff, huh?" Oh, crap there is that tone of his. He isn't going to just let this go, I bet.

I try once again to just move forward. "Uh huh." I continue playing with my food.

"Care to elaborate a little?" he asks.

I knew he would. He and Holly have more in common than she realizes. Fine, he asked for it, time to get it out on the table. Besides, I am still pissed about the coffee. I look up at him with my best stoic expression. "She mentioned that you came and stayed in my hospital room the other night." I take another bite of lasagna, my eyes never leaving his.

He pauses with his fork not quite to his mouth, looking at me. Yeah, buddy, you weren't expecting me to say that. You are busted mister. Now he is the one, looking down at his food, avoiding eye contact. "She saw me, huh?"

"Yes."

He doesn't seem very happy about the news. Maybe this wasn't such a great idea, after all.

"What else did she say?" he asks as he still plays with his food.

"Nothing," I say, backtracking a little. Maybe I am not ready to clear the air, after all, but maybe just one more tidbit to see how this plays out, though. "Well, except that you told the nurse I was your fiancée so you could stay there after visiting hours." Well, no going back now.

"Are ya mad?" He looks up at me.

Now I am the one put on the spot and on the defensive. "No, of course not." I stare down at my food. "I just don't get why you came back, is all," I mumble to myself, but unfortunately a little too loud, as he heard me.

He sets down his fork and plate on the coffee table. I look up at him and he is frowning. He is studying me very carefully now. I may have just opened up a big can of worms.

"Why do ya think I came back, Julie?" He leans back, but refuses to look away.

Damn, I hate the way he turns it back on me. If I tell him what I think, and he doesn't feel the same, I am going to make a fool out of myself. I mean, seriously, the man is older and more experienced than me. He was married. Maybe all of this is just because he feels he owes me. I mean he did tell me that day that he would pay me back. Why can't I just keep my big mouth shut? He sits there waiting patiently. I am lousy at poker, but I decide to play the safe card. "You were worried about me."

"Yes, that is part of it, and …?" He continues staring at me. Damn.

"And …" Tell him the truth, Julie. Tell him what Holly heard him say. "I am your friend and friends worry and care about each other, so you came back to check on me." I chicken out and go back to eating, hoping he will drop the discussion. I eat a few bites, avoiding his gaze.

He is silent, so I finally look up, to find him sitting there staring at me, his expression blank.

"What's wrong?" I finally ask quietly like the timid little girl I am acting like right now.

"Friends? So, we are just friends?" Now I don't know if he is asking or confirming.

"Aren't we?" I try to act blasé about it.

He seems to be thinking before he finally answers. "Well, yeah, but I was hopin' …" He gets up, taking his tray. He smiles down at me, but not his normal bright smile. This smile seems forced and sad. "Never mind, I guess I was readin' us wrong, that's all." He walks away and into the kitchen as I sit here, my heart falling to my stomach.

I look at my lasagna. I'm no longer hungry so I close the container. I am in shock. Why am I screwing this up? Holly already told me that Ben confessed his feelings for me that night in the hospital even if I was asleep. I have been wanting him so bad. Now he is opening the door for us to confess our feelings and I just slammed it in his face. What do I do now? I don't go after him and spill my guts, although I should. I just sit here and remain quiet after he returns to get my tray. He doesn't say a word as he takes it and heads back to the kitchen.

When he returns, he goes ahead and puts on a movie for us, but I am so lost in my disappointment, I don't pay it any attention. I am fighting back the tears as I realize I have screwed up royally. This is me, Julie, this is what I do. I guard my heart so much, afraid of getting hurt, that I blow a good thing. I just took the spark and stomped my foot on it, and twisted it into the ground for added effect.

The tension in the air is so thick that I doubt a knife would even make a scratch. He just sits there, sipping his beer and watching the movie. It is up to me now to fix this. I have to remember that I am not the only one with a guarded heart here. I hear my brother's voice right now, with an expression he would use from time to time. It's time to nut up or shut up. As I stare at the TV, I take a deep breath and find the courage to say what's in my heart.

"You weren't reading us wrong," is all I manage to find the courage to say. From the corner of my eye, I see him turn and look at me.

Ever so slowly, a smile returns to his gorgeous face. I find more courage to finally look at him. He rewards me with an even bigger smile.

"I didn't think so, but it's nice to hear, all the same."

He gives me a wink and goes back to watching the movie.

While it was not a romantic scene out of a movie, with him coming to me on his knees and declaring his feelings, it is enough for now that the air is cleared. And that was it, no fanfare, but at least we are certain we are both on the same page. I smile again, and return to watching the movie. I look over one more time, to find him glancing my way. We smile and return our view to the TV. Baby steps, after all.

It is quiet and cozy, but as the movie continues, I find it hard to concentrate on it. My caffeine high is long gone and the lack of sleep is catching up to me and I beginning yawning.

"That's one," Ben says, still staring at the TV.

I turn to look at him, but he is focused on the movie. "One what?" I yawn again while I watch him.

"That's two." Yet again, he doesn't look at me.

"What are you talking about?" I turn to the movie we are watching. "Is there something going on that I ..." I don't finish as yet another yawn sneaks up, and I cover my mouth.

"And that's three." He points the remote to the TV, turning it off and he gets up, stretching. His T-shirt sneaks up, giving me another view of his abs. He steps over to me, his hands on his hips, staring down at me. I don't get a chance to ask him what's up. "Okay, time for bed."

I look up at him. "But the movie isn't over." I fight another yawn that is building.

"It is for you, kitten." He smiles.

"Seriously? I wanted to finish it."

"Sweetie, ya stopped watchin' that movie over a half an hour ago. You're dead tired. Time for bed."

Now, if this was an invitation to go to bed for other things, I would be a little more willing to go. I am scared if I go to sleep I will dream and not good dreams. He leans down, placing one arm under my knees and the other at my back. He lifts me up, effortlessly. The fear of sleep has me shaking, though. And Ben notices.

"Hey, you're shivering. Are ya cold? Ya should have said somethin'. I would have built a fire. Come on, let's get ya under the covers." He carries me down the hallway to my room. I don't tell him that I am not cold but scared, too scared to sleep.

He lays me down on the bed and places my ankle up on pillows again. Bo has followed us and he finds his usual spot on the carpet on the side of my bed. I watch them both, and I am so tired. But then it begins ...

The tightness starts in my chest again and the shaking. I can't lie here. If I lie here, I will die. Maybe he should call 911. I am sure it is a heart attack this time.

Ben must notice something is wrong. Hopefully he will call for help if I pass out. "Julie, sweetie, what's wrong?" He sits beside me on the bed. I grab his hand, squeezing tight. Now I can't breathe. When I try, it feels like I am suffocating. I start grabbing my throat.

"Sweetie, relax. Deep breaths, in through your nose and out through your mouth."

I shake my head. I can't speak.

He takes his hands and holds my face, making me watch him. "Julie, watch me. Do just like me. Deep breath in through your nose." He exaggerates the movement and inhales deeply as I follow his instructions. "Hold it and now blow it out through your mouth." He exhales loudly and once again I copy his movements.

He releases my face and holds my hands in his, keeping me concentrating on my breathing. We do the exercise several times and my shaking begins to subside. The deep breathing helps as I no longer feel like I am going to pass out. A tear falls and Ben finally releases my hands to wipe the tear off my cheek with his finger.

"Do ya feel better now?" he asks.

I look down at my hands, embarrassed by my panic episode. What do I say? No worries, you are just staying at the house of a crazy psycho woman. He runs his finger down my cheek to the bottom of my chin. He gently raises my chin to look at him. I pull my lips into my mouth, pressing them tightly. I am afraid if I say one word, I will be a bawling baby once again. He has no clue what he has fallen for.

He smiles, but it's not his usual one. This one shows the signs of his concern. "Ya wanna talk about it?"

I shake my head, causing his finger to release my chin. My lips are still tightly pressed. I try to swallow the lump down that is building in my throat. His voice is so soft, so loving. I am losing the battle not to cry very quickly.

My eyes betray me as a few more tears fall. My panic attack is over and done with, but not my crying that always follows. Ben frowns but takes me and pulls me into his arms. That is the last straw, as I immediately start crying as I grip onto him tightly. He holds me, and soothes me as I cry in his arms. Again, he doesn't try to hush me or get me to stop. I don't know how long he holds me. It feels like only a few minutes, but he deserves to know the truth.

I gently push away, wiping my face, but I continue to look down, avoiding eye contact. "I'm scared." I finally look up at him.

"Of what, kitten?" he asks as he runs his hand up and down my arm.

"Of falling asleep."

A look of understanding washes over his face. "Nightmares," he states and not asks.

"Yes." I nod.

He continues to run his hand up and down my arm. "Ya know ya are safe now? No one can hurt ya. Bo and I won't allow it."

"Yes, I know." I give him a small smile as I take a deep breath. "In my nightmares, I see him and he is hurting me. It's just over and over." I exhale and take another breath. I am so frustrated with this asshole taking up inventory in my head. I am angry as I clench my fist and teeth.

"I know he is in jail, and I know he can't get to me again, but I just can't get him out of my head. Why can't I get him OUT OF MY HEAD BEN?" I hide my face in my hands again as Ben takes me in a loving and caring embrace. He holds me again as I cry, his arms soothing as his hands caress my back.

"Is this why ya have been fightin' sleep?" he whispers softly in my ear.

"Yes," I speak into his chest, inhaling his scent on his T-shirt. The calming mix of lavender fabric softener and Ben works its magic and calms me.

"What can I do to assure ya that you are safe and no one will hurt ya again?"

"I don't know. I wish I did." I hug him tighter. Once again, I am feeling hopeless and embarrassed.

When I finally slow down and pull away, Ben gets up, getting me some tissues to blow my nose. My eyes are heavy from my sleepiness as well as the crying. When I am done with the tissues he takes them.

"I will be right back," he says as he touches my cheek. He leaves the light on as he leaves the room and Bo follows him. I can't say I blame Bo, he is probably sick of my crying spells too.

A few minutes later, he returns dressed in a dry T-shirt and lounge pants, with Bo walking right beside him. I sit quietly and watch as he makes Bo lie down on his bed on the floor and turns off my bedroom light. He closes the bathroom door, but leaves it cracked open with a light on before walking over to the other side of the bed. The shirt is sleeveless and I see a band of tattoos on his upper arm and shoulder. It must be some tribal pattern because I don't recognize it. But before I can ask, he surprises me by climbing into my bed. I sit there not knowing what to do.

He props himself up on pillows before looking over at me. "Lie down and go to sleep, I will stay here until ya do."

An awkward feeling comes over me. I am not sure if I am ready for Ben to share my bed. But my body does as he asks as I relax, lie down, and turn on my side to face him. "But ... but you're tired too," I whisper.

"I'll be fine." He smiles. "Now, close your eyes."

I close them but quickly open them again. It is hard because my eyelids feel like they weigh a ton. "Ben, I am being silly, you can go to bed. I will be okay." At this point, I am exhausted, I have to give in to sleep, nightmares or not.

He sinks down on the mattress and faces me, propping his head up with his hand. "You're not bein' silly. Ya have been through a trauma, it's gonna take time to deal with that. Besides, I promised to take care of ya, so this is me, takin' care of ya." He reaches out and brushes a strand of hair that has fallen, out of my face.

His touch is so comforting to me. I really don't want him to leave. Do I dare ask him to stay in here with me all night? Maybe I should be brave and for once in my life say what I want.

"Talk to me. kitten, what's on ya mind?" he asks, making me wonder if he is, in fact, a mind reader.

"You don't have to leave, unless you want to," I whisper, too late to take back the words.

He smiles and touches my cheek as he sinks further

down on the bed. He opens his arms out to me—an invitation that I don't hesitate to accept. I scoot into his arms as he pulls me close, my head on his chest, and I snuggle into him.

"This okay?" he whispers in my ear.

"Yes." I smile into his chest. This is better than okay. This is awesome.

"Ya feel my arms around ya?" He squeezes me. "These arms will not allow for anyone to ever hurt you again. Do ya understand?"

"Yes."

He kisses my head. "Bo and I are both here. You are safe, so no nightmares. Ya will only have sweet dreams tonight. Understand?"

"Yes. Good night, Ben." I smile and finally close my eyes.

"Good night, kitten."

# CHAPTER
## *eighteen*

SLEEPING IN BEN'S ARMS LAST night did the trick, and I must have slept like the dead because when I wake I realize I slept all night with not one nightmare. His arm is around my middle now, just below my breast, as natural as if we have spooned for a lifetime, my back right up against the front of him. I wiggle around to see if I can get up without waking him. Then I am suddenly embarrassed as I realize that my wiggling has caused a certain reaction from Ben.

"Please, don't wiggle like that, kitten, a man can only take so much," he whispers in my ear.

My face instantly becomes hot with embarrassment, making the desire to get out of bed more urgent. "I'm sorry, I just need to get up," I whisper back.

He releases his hold on me and I quickly move away and sit up in the bed, relieved but disappointed at the same time.

"Where ya goin'?" he mumbles in his pillow, barely awake. The sight of him lying in my bed makes me happy. I haven't been this happy in a long time. It feels good, it feels right.

"I'm ... I was ... I am going to go fix breakfast." I struggle with the words as I gaze at the sight of this gorgeous man—in my bed. Smooth, Julie, real smooth.

He opens his eyes and looks over at the time on the clock that sits on my nightstand. It is six o'clock, time for him to get up, anyway. He sits up and stretches his arms over his head, letting out a loud yawn as he looks over at me. He rubs his eyes and chin, trying to wake up.

"No, ya need to stay off that ankle. I will make it. Just give me a few minutes, okay?"

"Sure, I will meet you in the kitchen." I get up and hobble over to the bathroom. This is all new for me and my mind is running around in circles. I am not sure what to say or do. I really need to talk to Holly. When I return to the room, Ben is still sitting in bed, but now he is petting Bo. I grab my crutches and head out of the room. "I will start the coffee."

Ben makes breakfast as I get dressed. Not many options of wardrobe when you have a neon pink bulky cast on your leg. Luckily, the legs in my pajama pants are big enough to accommodate my temporary nuisance. I frown at my reflection in the mirror. The T-shirt and pajama pant ensemble, not to mention a bad case of bedhead, have me questioning myself. How could Ben be attracted to this? The bruises are fading and are now just a yucky shade of yellow. Makeup could fix it, but why bother?

I grab a hair scrunchie from the drawer and tie my hair up in a ponytail. Why fight it? It's frumpy girl again today. I ease into the kitchen minus the crutches. There is Mr. Wonderful at the stove, looking sexy as hell. He gives me a smile, until he sees my lack of crutches for support. That earns me a disappointing frown. Well, what the hell, we both can be miserable.

"I wish ya would use your crutches, ya are gonna to fall, if ya are not careful," he says as I give him a shrug and sit down.

I carefully lift my leg and place it in the other chair. I give him a condescending look. "There, happy?" Geez, will you listen to me? Why am I being so pissy?

"Okay, I guess someone is a little grumpy this mornin'." He pours a cup of coffee and sets it in front of me with my favorite creamer and spoon. "Here, this should cheer ya up." He smiles before returning to the stove.

The smell of bacon fills the kitchen. I love that smell. I sniff my coffee as I take the first sip. I smile as the hot brew touches my lips and taste buds. Ahh, pure heaven.

We quietly eat breakfast together. I called Holly earlier, telling her to come over today instead of Carl. I need more girl time with my bestie. I have so many questions since I am treading new waters here. I have finally found my spark, but I have no clue what to do about it.

Ben finishes cleaning up before coming over to me. "There is a sandwich in the fridge for later. Is there anythin' else ya need? Carl didn't say what time he would be here today."

"He's not coming." I look up to see Ben frowning. "No, it's okay, Holly is on her way. She is going to hang out with me again today."

"Okay, that's good. I will fix supper tonight so promise me you'll stay off the ankle."

"Yes, sir." I mock salute.

He smirks as he slides on his coat. "Since I am gonna be outside, I am takin' Bo with me. He needs the exercise;

he's getting' fat."

"That's not very nice, but yeah you are probably right." I frown knowing until Holly shows up I will be lonely and bored.

He looks around the house before coming over to kneel in front of me. His closeness puts me on guard and I lean back for a second before I force myself to relax. Just great, he was probably going to kiss me but my reaction probably stopped that. I need to get a handle on that or this gorgeous man will never kiss me. He must misunderstand when I frown again.

"Hey, cheer up," he says and carefully touches my knee. "Ya will be up runnin' around like crazy in no time. Ya know, I was thinkin'. The other night I saw the Christmas decorations in the garage. Do ya wanna decorate a tree tonight? I can pick one up on my way home." He smiles.

My face lights up with excitement. I'm not sure whether it is because his hand is touching my knee, the thought of decorating a tree, or the fact he just called my place his home. "Really? Yes, I would love to." I smile at him.

"Okay, it's a date." He cautiously leans in and gives me a kiss on the cheek before standing up. "Come on, let me help ya get to the couch. I wanna make sure ya don't fall." He pulls me up and supports me as I hobble over to the couch. He places my ankle gently up on the couch again. "You ladies be good today and stay off that ankle. Ya promise?"

"I promise." I give him a smile, even though I am disappointed that we didn't really kiss.

"Come on, Bo, time to go." Bo wags his tail and I pet him as he heads for the door. He seems excited to leave with Ben. It is amazing how close they seem. A part of me is a little jealous because it took Bo a little longer to get that close to me. It reminds me of how Jason and Bo were together. "I will see ya tonight." He winks and heads out, with Bo right behind him.

A few hours and too many talk shows later, Holly shows up. I set aside my crocheting as she makes her way inside. She doesn't show up empty handed, as she has several grocery bags dangling from her arms. "What's all that?"

"I am cooking your supper tonight and we are making cookies today." She sets the bags down on the floor. "We are also decorating up this mortuary you call home for the holidays. I want my Julie who loves Christmas back. No more bah humbugs from you."

We spend the day cooking and baking. I explain to her about what happened between me and Ben last night. She listens to me and offers some advice. She knows I lack experience in dating and men, and I am thankful she doesn't tease me about it. Later that afternoon, we settle down to watch a few Christmas movies as I watch her decorate the fireplace. Earlier, I gently placed Jason's flag and my pictures in the hope chest in my bedroom. I felt funny about it at first, but it is only temporary during the holidays.

"Hey, didn't you say something yesterday about Ben being a police officer in the marines?" Holly asks as she places the floral garland on the fireplace.

"Yeah, why?" I carefully finish up the Ben's stocking, putting his name on the red felt stocking with the gold glitter glue pen. Holly already hung mine and Bo's. When she brought me three blank stockings, I just smiled. Even though she didn't come out and say it, I think she is okay with the idea of Ben and me.

"Mike wants to join." She turns, looking at me.

I stop what I am doing and look over at her. "The Marines?" I ask.

"No, but just as bad—he wants to be a cop."

"What?" She nods, confirming what she said. "But Mike never mentioned wanting to be a cop before," I add in confusion.

"I know, right? He changed his major to criminal law and has been taking courses. He is almost ready to go to the academy." She sighs.

"Wow, and you didn't know?" I ask, still in shock by her revelation.

"I had my suspicions but I figured he wanted to do some kind of CSI stuff, but no, he wants to hit the streets."

"So what does this have to do with Ben?"

Holly sits down a moment in the recliner. "Well, when I mentioned Ben's former job to Mike, he got all excited and wants to meet him to ask him questions. And I am hoping Ben can scare him out of wanting to be a cop."

Holly finishes up the supper and the decorating and I beg her to help make me pretty again. Deciding to take things up a notch and let Ben see that I can be something besides frumpy, she helps me find a nice dress to wear and does my hair and makeup. Before she takes off she gives me a thumbs-up. Ben has only seen me at my worse or wearing my waitress garb, and just dressed up nicely that one time he thought I was going out to meet my friends.

I want to look nice for him. I am hoping tonight he will finally kiss me. I mean last night he cuddled me and slept beside me, which I hope will be the arrangement from now on. I am falling in love with him and I don't even want to think of him leaving. It's so funny to me, the moment I stopped looking for love, he found me. Life is strange.

# CHAPTER
## *nineteen*

I HEAR MY CAR PULL up and Bo start barking. I straighten my hair and dress as I relax on the couch, my foot elevated as promised. Holly was nice enough to start the fireplace and light candles to give the room a romantic glow.

The door opens and Bo walks in, coming straight to me, giving me licks and wanting attention as I watch Ben walk in holding some bags, surprised by the scenery.

He looks at the fire, the candles, and then at me. His eyes look me over as a slow smile comes to his face. "Wow!" That is the only word he says. I hope it means he likes it.

"Dinner is ready when you are."

He looks over at the decorated table, but then looks at me again as if he can't get enough. He has a funny look on his face that I have never seen before.

"Umm, let me go clean up, I will be quick, I swear."

"Okay, I will wait."

He turns but looks at me again and glances at me a few times as he smiles and heads down the hallway. I think the man is speechless. Holly was right, this dress is a winner.

As promised, Ben hurries and when he comes back out, it is now me that is in awe. He is wearing some new clothes—a white buttoned-down shirt and black slacks and black boots. He walks in like a runway model and spins around, giving me a show from all angles.

"Looks like someone went shopping." I smile, as I notice he also shaved for the occasion.

"Yep, Carl is payin' me daily for now." He stops at the couch, his hands in his pockets. "I thought my wardrobe could use an upgrade. What do ya think?"

I sit on the couch, wishing I could jump in his arms and dance with this gorgeous man. "I think you look very handsome." I smile.

"And ya look breathtakin'," he says, offering his hand to me. "Shall we go to dinner?" He smiles down at me as I put my hand in his. He gently helps me up and then surprises me by bending down and then lifting me in his arms.

Placing my arms around his neck, I realize our faces are so close. This would be the perfect moment I have been waiting for—the kiss. For some reason the way he is holding me feels different, especially the way he is looking at me. It's not like he is helping me, more like he is wanting me. Is this real or is this just my over romantic mind? My shyness tries to make light of it. "Ben, the table is just right there." I look toward the decorated table, with the candles burning bright, very romantic. I look back at him.

"I know, but I like holdin' ya." Gone is his smile, his expression more serious. Nervous energy is running through my body as I expect him to lean in and kiss me any second now. He starts walking to the table and before I know it, he is setting me down at the table. He gives me a wink and takes a seat across from me. The connection is lost for now, and I could kick myself for opening my mouth and spoiling what could have been our very first kiss.

"So, what are we havin'?" Ben asks, looking at the table.

"Holly made it—baked ham, sweet potato casserole, and green beans. I made a cranberry spinach salad to go with it."

"Sounds delicious. Ya sit tight, I will get it." He gets up, leaving me for a moment as he goes into the kitchen. I take a sip of iced water, trying to cool my overheated body. I can still smell his cologne and feel his body holding mine. Forget the spark, we are in flame mode now. Holly told me earlier to just relax and let things just happen.

He comes out, setting a plate in front of me, before sitting down across from me again. He gives me a smile as he looks over the table again. "Ya and Holly did a nice job. The table is so pretty, I am afraid of messin' it up. What do we have here?" He looks at the wine chilling in the ice bucket.

"Holly thought it would go good with dinner." I smile shyly at him.

"Well, let's find out." He opens the white wine like a pro and then pours me a glass before pouring one for himself. "This looks delicious and smells great. So, Holly did this? Is it safe to say she no longer hates me or should I be careful of the food?" He teases.

"She never hated you, she is just overprotective of me." I shake my head as I unfold my napkin.

"Well, then we have somethin' in common." He

smiles as he takes a sip of the wine.

We start eating, enjoying the dinner and wine. The food is great, but our conversation is on hold as we enjoy our feast. When we finish, I feel like my dress is about to pop. I am so full.

Ben sits back, obviously acting as stuffed as I am. "I am not even gonna ask about dessert. I don't think I could find room." He pats his stomach.

"Did you get a tree?"

"Yes, it's still outside. In a few minutes, I will go get it and bring in the decorations. I see ya started a little already." He gives me a firm look. "I hope ya didn't overdo it, ya were supposed to rest," he scolds.

"No worries, Holly did it all. I supervised from the couch, foot up. I swear."

"Good girl." He winks. He stands up and blows out the candles, before taking our plates back in the kitchen. I sit here feeling hopeless and useless. Stupid ankle. I pour myself another glass of wine. Yep, that's me the good girl, who has a sexy man staying with her and no clue on how to seduce him. He has to be so frustrated with me.

I wallow in my self-pity as I sip my wine. Another glass down and I am starting to feel the effects. I am not much of a drinker. Holly kids me and calls me a cheap date. Ben finally returns to the room and helps me to the couch, only this time, he hands me the crutches and escorts me to make sure I get there with no issues. I regret that he doesn't carry me this time. I need to learn to keep my big mouth shut. He does take my legs and places them on the cushions. He slides off my one shoe and smiles at the color of my toenails. They are painted red and white to look like candy canes. She even painted the ones sticking out of my cast.

"Cute toes. Holly?" He smiles as he rubs my foot.

I relax back. I think I have died and gone to heaven. My foot is so sore, since it has to support all my weight, and Ben's foot massage feels so good. "Uh, huh." I sigh and nod, urging him to continue the foot rub.

He smiles at me, getting my cue as he continues massaging the soreness out. "Feels good, huh?" He chuckles.

"Oh, yeah." I sigh again as I relax and close my eyes. My anxiety is at bay for now. Whether it is because of the wine or Ben's awesome foot massage, I don't care. It feels good to relax. He continues for a few more minutes, before gently placing my foot back on the cushions. I open my eyes and smile at him. "Thank you."

"You're very welcome." He winks as he stands back up and walks to the fireplace.

I watch him as he places another log in the fireplace. I could so get used to this. I look at him and I envision wedding gowns, china patterns, tasting wedding cake samples, and honeymoon destinations. Of course, the fact I started a secret Pinterest board while I was waiting for him to come home, probably helps with the visions.

"Do ya know where ya want the tree?" He interrupts my daydream as he turns and talks to me.

I smile, remembering that, of course, he wouldn't know we always put it near the window. I point to the area Holly cleared out by the front window. "Right by the window."

He turns his gaze to where I am pointing. "Oh, good, that will be easy. Stay right there, I will be right back." He heads to the door and grabs his coat from the hook. Bo gets up and follows him out. It doesn't take him long to return, Bo running ahead of him, as he places the tree by the window and hurries to shut the door. I can smell the wonderful fragrance of the tree. He picked a beauty, at least seven feet tall, and so full and green. Holly hates real trees, she says they are too messy, but I don't care. I will gladly clean up the mess to be able to smell the fresh scent of a real tree.

Ben removes his jacket and heads back to the fireplace. He places his hands out to warm them before turning to face me. He is blowing on his hands now to warm them. "It's gettin' really cold out there." He smiles. How funny to see him now, complaining about the cold, when he was living on the streets just days ago. I don't dare say it out loud to him, though, those days are embarrassing to him, and they are over with now.

"I hope it will snow for Christmas." I comment instead.

"Well, I don't think ya get much snow here, but ya never know." He turns back to the fire, rubbing his hands in front of it.

Ben sets up the tree in the stand and adds water before going out and getting the lights and decorations. He checks the lights first then strings them up, lighting up the tree. He finds the star and places it on top for me, before helping me up on the crutches to help decorate. We play Christmas music on the TV while singing along and decorating the tree. He starts singing along to "Silent Night" and I stop just to hear him.

When he finishes, I once again compliment him. "You have a beautiful voice."

He smiles at my compliment. "Thanks. It's my favorite Christmas song. I learned to play it on my guitar, when I was a kid."

"So what happened to your guitar?"

His smile fades. "Like everythin' else I owned, Renee hawked it," he says as he starts putting away the boxes.

"Did you try looking for it in the pawn shops in your area?" I ask as I continue decorating the tree.

"Yeah, it was sold. It really sucks as my mom got me

that guitar for Christmas when I was twelve. She didn't have a lot of money, but she knew how much I wanted to learn how to play. It was a beautiful black Gibson acoustical. Oh, well." He smiles a sad smile at me before he takes the boxes back to the garage.

I remain quiet, not knowing what to say to make him feel better. Stupid ex-wife. And me, my big mouth strikes again. We were having a good time, and I had to ask him things that bring back bad memories for him. When he gets back, I am going to put him back in a good mood somehow.

I am worried about Ben's bad mood, but then he returns from the garage wearing a Santa hat and smiling. I am relieved. He is so adorable. He refills our glasses with wine and puts up some other decorations, allowing me to finish the tree. It is nice to have someone to share the holidays with again. And I am having the best time I have had in a long time.

"Okay, time to get back off your feet." Ben comes around, taking my crutches and setting them up against the wall. He is cheerful and almost dancing in the way he is moving around. When I think he is just going to help me get to the couch and put my foot up, he surprises me by lifting me in his arms again. I don't know if it is the wine that has him in a good mood, but I don't care. I am in his arms again and that is all that matters. He walks past the couch and heads to the kitchen, humming along with "We Wish you a Merry Christmas" playing in the background.

"What are you doing?" I laugh. He is being so playful; I am loving this side of him.

"I need you to hang something for me." He smiles.

What could he possibly want to hang in the kitchen? "What? Where?" I ask, looking around.

"Right there, on the counter."

I look down to see a spring of mistletoe with a red ribbon. I reach down and grab it, finding the loop of fabric to hang it. "Where did this come from?"

"The guy at the tree lot gave it to me. Hang it up there."

We are standing in the entryway of the kitchen and living room. The nail is still there from past Christmases when my dad would hang mistletoe there, years ago. He joked it was the only way he could get Mom to stop and kiss him during the holidays. Did Ben know about this? Who cares, I am not spoiling this with silly questions.

Ben lifts me a little higher as I reach up and hang the mistletoe on the nail. When I am done, I wrap my arms around his neck. Ben stares up at the mistletoe and then looks at me, his hazel eyes burning into mine. There it is—there's the spark. Something great is about to happen, I can feel it.

"Ya know, the man at the tree lot said it is tradition to kiss your girl under the mistletoe," he whispers, his eyes never leaving mine. His warm breath hits me with the subtle smell of the candy cane he was eating earlier.

My heart is beating fast. I don't know which has me more excited, the fact he is calling me his girl or the fact he is about to kiss me. I know I am blushing and I am sure it's not just the wine. "Did he now?" I whisper back.

He smiles again but one of those dangerous smiles that lets me know really quick that he is serious and means business. This is it, this is finally it. He is going to kiss me. Stay calm, Julie. Whatever you do, don't blow this.

"So, I have a question for ya, Julie," he says as he licks his lips ever so slightly before giving me a mischievous grin. "Are ya ... my girl?"

With that simple question I know my life is about to change. I can tell he is serious, no more joking around, no more tiptoeing around what we are to each other. This is the spark I have been waiting for all my life. There is no way I am screwing up this time.

"Yes." I barely get the word out before my lips are covered with his. He takes three quick pecks before coming in and taking over my mouth. He stands there in the doorway holding me under the mistletoe, kissing me, his arms full with holding me. I am free to touch and hold his face and control how long we kiss. His face is so smooth and soft; I am so glad to touch it now without that beard in the way. His tongue presses on my lips, wanting to enter so I open my mouth, allowing his tongue to dance with mine. It is the sweetest, sexiest, most romantic kiss I have ever had.

I don't see sparks. I see fireworks that would put the annual Clover Fourth of July display to shame. I am so lost in our kiss that I don't even realize when we start heading to the couch. He stops long enough to sit down and make sure not to hit my foot before we start again. This time his hands are free to touch me and he runs his hands through my hair. I open my mouth again, inviting his tongue back in. Now I can taste the sweet peppermint from earlier.

We stop for a minute to catch our breath, our foreheads touching, as we gaze into each other's eyes.

"That's some mistletoe." He smiles. His hands are around my waist, holding me in his lap.

"Uh huh," is the only response I can manage. My fingers are running through his soft hair.

"I have wanted to do that for a while now," he confesses, as he tries to catch his breath.

"Me too." I pull his head toward me to bring his lips to mine, diving right back in to the kissing. Shy Julie is history.

We continue sitting on the couch, making out. Kisses

are now traveling to necks and there is the desire for some heavy petting going on for both of us. My body is aching for his touch as he scoots down and lays us both down on the couch. He is partially on top of me as his hands begin to explore and find my breasts. As much as I am lost in the desire of Ben and his loving kisses, a cloud of darkness starts taking over me.

I start having trouble breathing and a feeling of needing air comes over me as my memories start to interfere with my pleasure. I am seeing flashes of what that man did to me the other night. He was on top of me. He was ripping at my shirt. He was choking me. I am suffocating and can't breathe as I try to push him off me. I stop kissing and turn my head away as I find Ben's hand and try to remove it.

"No, no stop, Ben, please stop," I say, struggling to push his hand away.

Ben immediately stops and sits up as I squirm and get out of his embrace, scooting to the corner of the couch and curling up inside myself. The darkness has found me again. I am in panic mode and can't breathe. I hug my knees and cry, rocking back and forth. I feel him scoot over next to me, his hands touching mine. I look up at him, his concerned look is breaking my heart again.

"Ben, I can't breathe. What's wrong with me?" I hold my chest, expecting to faint any moment.

"Julie, it's okay, just take deep breaths. Breathe, baby, just breathe and relax. You are okay, it's the panic. You're not dyin'. Just breathe through it, like I showed ya before." He rubs my hands.

I am doing the breathing exercise like he taught me, and I start to calm down. It helps that he is no longer on top of me.

"Julie, I am so sorry, baby, I wasn't thinkin'."

I hide my face, ashamed of my reaction. I wanted this

so badly and now it is ruined. I just shake my head, refusing to look at him as I sob. I can only hear myself and the whines from Bo who has come over to comfort me.

He plays with my fingers, until soon, we are holding hands. I look up long enough to see the pain and desperation in his eyes. I reach out hugging him as I fall into his arms, sobbing again against his neck. "Ben, he ruined me. I can't forget what he did. I can't let you touch me." I cry.

"Shhh, it's okay, baby, it's okay. We can take it slow. I am so sorry, I wasn't thinkin'." He holds me tight in his arms, in the safety net that drives my demons away.

"I am sorry he ruined me."

Ben releases me and gently pushes me away so I am looking at him. "Hey, listen to me, now." He takes my chin as I try looking down and forces me to look him in the eyes. "Let's get one thin' straight. He didn't ruin ya, he hurt ya. There's a difference. We will get past this, it just takes time. Ya just need time, baby."

I nod in agreement as he pulls me to him once more. He sits there rocking me like a child once again, allowing me to cry in his arms. He finally whispers in my ear. "I think we have both had enough holiday cheer tonight. Let's go get ready for bed, huh?"

My face is against his chest, his shirt soaked with my tears once again. "Okay, will you sleep next to me again? Like you did last night?" I shyly ask.

"Do ya want me to, kitten?"

I look up at him. "Yes, very much. I feel safe when you lie next to me." I lean up and kiss him quickly on the lips. I hope my issues are not driving a wedge between us.

He smiles, giving me another quick kiss. "Then, of course, I will. I want ya in my arms always." He smiles at me again.

We get ready for bed and this time when he pulls me

into his arms, he kisses me, careful not to be on top of me and send me back into my panic. When he stops, I look at him expectantly. As much as part of me wants to continue the other part is relieved.

It's as if he knows exactly what I am thinking. "We will get there, Julie. I have waited a lifetime for someone like ya. I am not givin' you up without a fight." He pulls me into his arms and cuddles me close to him.

I smile, loving the fact that he understands.

# CHAPTER
## twenty

I AM RUNNING DOWN DARK alleyways. The man is behind me with the knife and suddenly I run right into him as he rips my dress, exposing me. He laughs, forcing me down to the ground. I am screaming for Ben but he is not answering. Why doesn't he hear me? He said I would be safe, that he wouldn't leave me …

"Julie, Julie baby, wake up."

I jerk awake and find myself in the arms of my hero, he is here. He didn't leave me.

"I got ya. I got ya, baby."

I let go of him and see that he is dressed. "Where did you go? What time is it?" I am confused, it seems we only went to bed minutes ago.

"It's okay, it's still early, I just couldn't sleep. I am so sorry, you were sound asleep, I was sure ya wouldn't have a nightmare, but then I heard ya screamin' my name."

My throat is sore; I must have been screaming for a while. I feel something wet on my hand and I see Bo lying on the bed, licking my hand. I reach over and pet him.

"He heard ya first. I was in the garage cleanin' up in there."

"I'm sorry. I didn't mean to scare you."

"Nonsense, if anyone should apologize, it is me. I was sure ya would be okay. You were sound asleep when I got up. I just wanted to work on clearin' out the garage. I want to be able to park the car in there tonight so I can check it. It is getting' so cold out."

"I am sorry, Ben. I know you didn't sign up to babysit such a basket case like me." I try to joke but he is not amused.

"Hey, don't talk down on yourself like that, you're not crazy. Promise me ya won't do it anymore. I don't like it."

I nod and shyly look down. No matter what I do, I say the wrong thing.

"Julie, look at me."

I look up at him, his concerned eyes searching mine.

"I think ya should do as the doc said and go talk with someone. It will help."

"I don't need to. I have Carl and Holly and now I have you."

"Ya do, baby, but sometimes it helps talkin' to someone professional who has dealt with situations like what happened to ya."

"Are you saying you think I need a shrink?" I shyly look down again. He does think I am crazy.

"Hey, it's not a bad thin'," he says. "In fact, if it makes you feel any better, I have been seein' one myself."

"You have?" I look up to see him smiling.

"Yeah. Carl helped me get in contact with groups that help veterans like me. Remember the Marine I was tellin' ya about, how we were helpin' fix his house?"

"Yes."

"Well, he and I got to talkin'. He recommended someone that has helped him with his PTSD issues. So I went and seen the guy. I have only been once, but it's helpin'. I went to ones in the past when I was overseas too, but I was made to go to those by the Corps."

"Why?" I reach for his hand and he takes it, our fingers intertwining.

"I sometimes have PTSD issues, just like you are havin'. Only mine are because of the things I saw and dealt with in Afghanistan. Example, the other day, when I was angry when ya woke me. I wasn't mad at ya, it was just a flashback." He pauses a moment to look at our hands.

I watch him swallowing quietly. He is upset. I reach over and caress his cheek. He touches my hand, kissing it, and placing it beside our other intertwined hands.

He looks up at me, his eyes glistening. "But when I hurt ya ..." He takes a deep breath. He is struggling with this. I just stay quiet and let him finish. "When I hurt ya, I realized I needed to get help. I would rather die than hurt ya, kitten."

"You didn't hurt me, Ben." I lean over and kiss his cheek.

He gets up and peels his T-shirt off. I can see the tattoos, on his shoulder, back, and upper arm. I will ask their meaning one day, but not now. They obviously have a story, and I bet it is something to do with the pain he has felt. We have talked enough about our hurt for one day. He slips off his jeans to his boxer briefs, and I am enjoying the view of his gorgeous body. He is so sculpted, so perfect. My body desires him, wants him, needs him. If only I could get my brain to follow along. He turns off the light and climbs back in bed with me. I ease back down as he pulls me next to him to spoon. He kisses my neck before turning me to face him.

"I just found ya and I don't want to do anythin' to make ya leave me. For a while now I didn't care, after Renee did what she did. I didn't give a damn about myself or anyone else. That's changed now because of ya. I want to be better for ya, and maybe if you see someone …"

"Then I could get better for you." I finish for him, running my hand against his cheek. He leans down and kisses me, nothing hot and heavy, just a sweet kiss between friends that are falling in love.

When his lips leave mine, he smiles at me. "That would be the best Christmas present ever."

# CHAPTER twenty-one

AFTER OUR TALK LAST NIGHT, I finally fall into a peaceful sleep. I am actually up before Ben this time and I cook his favorite breakfast of biscuits and gravy. He isn't happy that I am going to be home alone today, but I insist he leaves. I am getting around much better now, since the pain is almost gone. Later that morning, after Ben reluctantly leaves, I make an appointment with one of the counselors the doctor recommended. She is a woman and that makes me feel better. Holly volunteers to take me in a few days because Ben has some things to do. Checking my calendar, I realize the Legion Hall Christmas party is tomorrow; time has slipped away from me. Carl didn't call me to remind me. Why? I grab my cell and dial him up.

"Hello, this is Carl."

I realize I haven't seen him in days. I miss his cheerful voice, but right now, I am mad at him. "Carl, how come you didn't remind me about the party? You know I help out every year."

"I didn't want to bother you, darling. You have a lot going on right now."

Definitely the wrong answer. I am getting so sick and tired of people deciding what is good for me right now. I am not a child. It is pissing me off. "Nonsense, I help you every year, and this year is no exception. I will be right over." I hang up, not giving him a chance to argue with me. I quickly dial Ben. It is the first time I have called him on the new cell phone he bought the night he brought home the tree. I even took a picture of him in the Santa hat to post on his contact.

"Hey, baby, what's up? You all right?" Damn, even his phone voice is sexy.

"Yes, but I need to get over to the diner right now. Holly is out of town with Mike, otherwise I would ask her. Can you please come get me?"

"Yes, of course, but what's goin' on? Ya sound upset."

"I am fine. Carl is trying to push me out of helping with the Legion Hall party, and he is not going to get away with it. I help out every year. All of you need to stop treating me like a baby." I am in full rant mode right now, and I have no clue why.

"All right, calm down. I will be there in a few minutes." He hangs up on me.

I want to call him back to apologize. I am not mad at him. I am just irritated by this whole ankle mess.

Ben comes in as I am finishing getting dressed. Holly brought over some long denim skirts so I would have something to wear, besides nightgowns and pajama pants. I slide on my left boot, as Ben helps me stand up.

"Thank you, I'm ready, let's go." I smile as I attempt to walk past him.

He stops me short, his hands on my arms. "Not so

fast, I don't think so," Ben says, eyeing me.

"What? Why?" My patience is at the end of its rope.

"Ya forgot somethin'," he says, with the most serious of faces.

"Forgot what? I'm dressed, my crutches are right there, and my purse is by the door."

"Ya forgot to kiss me." He smiles.

I now feel like a first-class jerk. I give him a smile, and mouth the words, "I'm sorry," as I reach up and put my arms around his neck to give him a quick kiss. But a quick kiss is not what he is looking for. He pulls me closer to him, one hand on the back of my head, the other just above my butt, and kisses me deeper and hotter, than ever before. Our tongues dance together again, and I am lost in the passionate embrace. I don't know what has gotten into him, but I am not complaining. When he finally lets my lips go, I am in a daze and forgot what the hell I was in a hurry for.

"Much better, now we can go." He smiles and slaps my behind as he walks out of the room.

"Owe, what was that for?" I call out, as I rub my butt. It surprised me more than hurt.

"That is for forgettin' to kiss me," he says as he pokes his head back in the doorway. "Oh, and for practically bitin' my head off on the phone a little while ago." He grins, heading back out.

I limp out to follow him. "I said I was sorry," I shout out.

"Don't forget your crutches," he yells out from the other room.

"I don't need them." I limp into the living room, holding on to the walls for support.

"Yeah, if ya keep that up, ya will. Remember what the doc said," he says as he comes over to help me.

"Ben, I feel fine, my ankle is fine, can we just go,

please? Stop fussing over me."

He reaches down and picks me up, carrying me to the garage. "Sorry, sweetness, but you're my girl now and that entitles me to fussin' over ya as much as I like."

We arrive at the diner and I sit in the car, staring at the building. I haven't been back since the attack and I feel nervous. I know he is not there and can't hurt me, but I am nervous anyway. I can feel the panic start to build.

"Are ya all right?" Ben takes my hand, bringing it to his lips and kissing it.

I am instantly calmer and feel safe. I look over at him and smile, taking a deep breath. I win this battle with anxiety for now. "Yes, I am now." I reach over and kiss him.

"Let's do this, shall we?" He smiles.

Before we left the house, Ben went back to grab my crutches. He said tomorrow, when I go to my doctor's appointment, maybe I can talk them into a boot cast. For now, he doesn't want me falling and breaking my neck.

I walk in and Carl is surprised, but seems happy to see me. "I am sorry, darling, I didn't mean to leave you out. I just didn't want you pushing yourself." He holds me in his fatherly bear hug.

We sit down in a vacant booth. Ben helps me slide in and grabs my hand, holding it when we sit down. I watch as Carl eyes our joined hands.

"Apology accepted, but I want to help. Keeping busy helps."

"Okay, then you asked for it. Here is a list of everything that needs to be done." He slides the notebook over to me. Ben leans over and looks at it with me.

"Wow, you aren't kidding. Hey, wait, it says here you need a Santa." I look up at Carl sitting across from me. "I thought you were doing Santa. You always do Santa."

"I did too, until I went to rent the costume. Hang on, I will be right back."

I look around and feel strange. I am usually serving food to customers, and now I am sitting here, one of them.

"Ya doin' okay, kitten?" Ben asks.

"Yeah, I just feel funny not working. I will be so glad when this cast is gone."

Ben begins to say something but Carl is back with the suit. I can tell immediately it is too tall and big for Carl.

"Oh, no, that is definitely not going to work for you, but we need a Santa, the kids will be expecting it."

"Well, it will have to be a taller guy to fit in that," Carl chimes in.

Immediately, Carl and I both look at Ben. Ben looks at me and then at Carl and then back at me. "Oh, no. No way! Uh uh." He shakes his head.

I smile. "You would be perfect." I hug his arm and bat my eyes at him. He looks at me strangely before looking at Carl.

"Umm, Carl, don't ya need me to do somethin' tomorrow?" Ben is trying to get himself out of this, but Carl doesn't help. He just smiles and shrugs.

"I am sorry, Benjamin Parker, but you are it. We don't want to upset the kids, now do we?" I say, giving him a kiss on the cheek.

# CHAPTER
## twenty-two

THE NEXT DAY WE ARE at the Legion Hall, getting things ready for the party. I am in the back with Ben, helping him with the Santa suit. To make him feel better, I found my old elf suit and put it on. It took a little sweet talk and a lot of kissing last night to get him to agree to do this. I have a feeling he would have anyway.

"So how ridiculous do I look?" he asks as he adjusts the hat.

"You look perfect—one fine looking Santa." I reach up, wrapping my arms around his neck.

"Yeah, right," he says, looking down at me and smiling.

"No, seriously, in fact, I am finding Santa Claus pretty sexy right now."

This puts a twinkle in Ben's eyes. "Oh, really, is it the red suit or the boots? No, wait, let me guess, it's the beard. Chicks dig the beard." Ben sits down in a chair, and pulls me down on his lap. "So, tell me, little elf, have ya been naughty or nice?" The white fake eyebrows wiggle up and down.

"Well, Santa, I am usually a good elf," I whisper as I run my finger up and down the white fur trim of his suit. I am becoming bolder now and am enjoying the playfulness of having a boyfriend.

"Oh, yeah?" His voice gets lower and deeper.

"But lately I have been thinking very naughty things." I blush because it is true.

"Really? Do ya wanna whisper in Santa's ear what those naughty things are?" His face comes closer to mine.

"Well, Santa, maybe I will tell you later," I whisper.

"Fine, but can Santa have a little kiss before he is surrounded by the brat brigade?"

I smile and lean down to kiss his lips. It is hard finding them with the fake beard, but I manage. The beard tickles so I kiss him quickly before slapping his chest. "Stop being a grump. Santa is supposed to be a jolly fellow."

"Well, then give me a better kiss and I promise to be the jolliest of fellows." He smiles.

I kiss him again, but I pull down the beard, and our kiss goes deeper and longer. I am taking advantage of the fact that for now, the demons are gone and I can enjoy Ben. My lips are saying everything my heart is wanting to.

"Ahem." We both stop and look up to see Holly and Mike staring at us. "If the kids catch you, you will have to explain why Santa is making out with the cute elf instead of Mrs. Claus," Mike says.

"Not to mention this is a G-rated party and you guys were getting way past PG-13," Holly chimes in.

I go ahead and hop off of Ben's lap. "Let's go, Santa,

the kids are waiting."

I walk out to the dining hall and we have a huge turnout. So many people in need of a little Christmas cheer. The children are so excited as they know what is coming next. After passing out some candy bags, I make my way to the corner to watch his entrance.

Ben was grumpy earlier, but just as I suspected, he falls into his role as St. Nick just fine and the kids adore him. Watching him with them makes me think of what kind of father he would be and I fantasize about our own children, sitting on his lap as he tells them a story.

"What, or should I say whom, are you daydreaming about?" Holly says as she comes up to me. We haven't spoken much in the last few days, so she is fishing for info on how things are going with Ben.

"I will give you one guess." I smile over at her.

"Yeah, I thought so. He is really a great guy. I am sorry I was so hard on him in the beginning." She stares over at him. Mike has joined him, helping him pass out presents to the kids.

"Shouldn't you be telling him that and not me?" I laugh. I knew she would eventually warm up to him.

"Oh, I did the other day. We are the best of buds now." She looks over at me and smiles.

"Yeah, right. So what changed your mind about him?" I ask.

"He is good to you and he makes you happy. That's all I need."

I lean over to hug her. That is the best answer she could possibly give me. Having her blessing means a lot. "Thank you, Holly."

"I am just happy to see you join the ranks of the living again."

The event goes off without a hitch and many families and children go home with items to make their holiday a little brighter.

"Here ya go." Ben hands me the suit. We have both changed back into our regular clothes, but it took a while to get the adhesive off of his face.

"Next year make sure ya find one that fits Carl." He rubs his face again, checking to make sure all of the glue is gone.

"Oh, come on, it wasn't so bad, was it?" I hang the suit up on a hanger, leaving it for Carl to return.

"No, I guess not." He turns and looks at me. "It's still early, how about we go on a date?"

"A date?" My eyes widen with surprise. "When?"

"Right now. I wanna take my girl out on our first date."

I love when he calls me his girl. "All right. Where will we go?"

"It's a surprise. Come on and grab your purse. Let's get out of here."

# CHAPTER twenty-three

"**B**EN WHERE ARE YOU TAKING me?" We borrowed Carl's truck instead of taking my car, which has me wondering where we are going.

"If I told ya, it wouldn't be a surprise." He winks, grabbing my hand and holding it. I chose to sit in the middle so I could be close to him.

We drive in the darkness. It's early but the sun is already gone and it is chilly out. It is a dark country road, in an area I am not familiar with, even though I have lived here all my life.

"Ya aren't nervous, are ya?" He gives my hand a little squeeze.

"Should I be?" I look over at him. My worry is written all over my face, I am sure.

"Not at all, you are with me." He brings my hand up to his mouth for a kiss, before releasing it, and placing both hands back on the wheel.

When we reach the corner, I see the glow of car taillights going into the area and when I look over, I see the glow of Christmas lights in the trees. I finally recognize where we are. "Oh, Ben, it's Christmas Park. I have been wanting to come back here for a long time." I am so excited, just like I was when I was a kid. Jason and I loved coming here.

"How long has it been?" he asks as he stops, waiting on the traffic to move forward.

"Oh, wow, thirteen years now. I haven't been back since my parents died." I stare out the window.

"Well, I think it is time ya see it again, don't ya? What do ya say?" He looks over at me, grinning from ear to ear.

I answer him by hugging him and almost jumping into his lap, squealing with delight. I finally top it off with a hot wet kiss.

When I finally calm down, Ben looks shocked but delighted. "I'll take that as a yes?"

I nod in agreement.

Christmas Park is only open on the weekend of Thanksgiving and through Christmas. It is designed especially for Christmas with Christmas lights everywhere. It was a family tradition to come here every year as a family. Sadly, we didn't keep it up after my parents died. It just wasn't the same. Why it is different to me now, I have no clue. I am not going to spend my time rationalizing it. I just want to enjoy it.

Ben pays for our tickets. A gesture I find a little strange because a few weeks ago, he couldn't even buy himself a cup of coffee. Now he is treating me to a date. I don't say a word, because I would die if I embarrassed him. He has come a long way since those few weeks ago. When we get out of the truck in the parking lot, the crisp winter breeze hits us. I pull my coat tightly around me as Ben does the same. Luckily we were both prepared with our scarves, but as I feel around in my coat pockets, I realize I forgot my gloves.

"Oh, shoot," I say, looking up at Ben.

"What's wrong?" Ben asks as he locks the truck.

"I forgot my gloves." I shrug. "I must have left them at the diner."

"No worries." He walks over to face me as he takes my hands in his. "I will keep your hands warm," he says as he takes my hands in his large ones and blows his hot breath across them, rubbing them before taking one and tucking it in his pocket with his. "Keep your hand in your other pocket and we will switch periodically."

"Did you learn that in the Marines?" I jest, rubbing our noses together before giving him a quick peck on the lips.

"Kissin' pretty girls? That would be a negative." He raises his eyebrows as I roll my eyes.

"I meant the hand warming, silly."

"Nope, I am learnin' that as we go." He winks.

We start walking down the path leading to the hayride that will take us into the park. I was able to get the walking cast, making getting around much easier than the crutches. I still hold onto Ben for support so I don't trip. When we get to the wagon, Ben lifts me up, still being careful with my ankle as he places me in the back before hopping up himself.

"Remember, little lady, no jumpin' around, your ankle still needs to heal."

We sit on the hay bales and he is still holding my hand. He wraps his arm around me, pulling me close. This is such a new experience for me. I didn't date in high school and I even went with a group of friends to the senior prom instead of having a date. My brother, on the other hand, always had a girl on his arm. No way was he being forced to take his sister to the prom.

To have a man now calling me his girl, holding me close, and kissing me is such a beautiful and new experience. A part of me that I thought was cold and dead is now warming up with the promise of love. For once in a very long time, I am thinking about the future and not dwelling on the past.

"Are ya warm enough?" he whispers in my ear, his warm breath driving me crazy.

"Yes. How about you?"

"Definitely toasty." He smiles, pulling me closer to his side and giving me another kiss.

The ride stops at the park entrance and again Ben helps me down. He takes my hand and keeps it warm with his in his jacket pocket as we walk together, looking at all the beautiful Christmas lights. There are lights everywhere you look, in the trees, on the pathway, and on the gazebos. It is so magical. There are different Christmas scenes staged throughout, everything thing from famous cartoon characters, to a living room set up with Santa greeting the kids, and a beautiful manger scene.

Ben and I spend a few moments admiring the gazebo decorated patriotically, with red, white, and blue lights. A tree just like the one in the diner is in the center. It is so beautiful. I can tell Ben likes it as he liked the one in the diner as well. I squeeze his arm, so proud that I am standing with a soldier who took the oath to protect this wonderful country we live in.

Occasionally we switch sides so he can warm my other hand. We make our way around enjoying the sights, when we spy the food booths and the fire pits close by. Ben directs me to a bench near one of the fire pits.

"Ya stay here. I'm gonna get us some hot chocolates. That should get ya warmed up."

Someone pinch me, I have to be dreaming. This is such a perfect date. Please, oh please, let there be more days like this in my life.

Very quickly he returns with our hot chocolates and a funnel cake to share.

"Wow, are you trying to put us in a sugar coma?" I laugh.

"Oh man, when I saw these I couldn't resist. I can't tell ya the last time I had a funnel cake." He sits down, handing me my drink.

"Allow me then." I take and pull a chunk off, shaking the extra powdered sugar off before holding it in front of Ben's mouth. Smiling, Ben opens his mouth wide to accept the sticky cake. Before I can pull my hand away, he takes it and puts my fingers in his mouth, licking off the extra sugar. He gives me a wink before releasing my hand. The very sexy act has me blushing, and reminding me that we are out in public. I quickly change the subject before I continue this PDA.

"So, how did you know about this place?" I ask, curious about how he knew.

"Carl mentioned ya used to love goin' here as a kid. I took a chance that maybe ya would like to come here again," he says before taking another bite of the cake.

"Thank you."

"You're welcome. Ya know, this town is pretty cool." He stares at the fire in front of us and is silent for a moment. I can tell something is on his mind, but I am too chicken to ask him to tell me. I don't want to spoil the fun we are having. "I feel like for the first time in a very long time, I have a home." He finally looks my way again. "Thank ya, Julie."

I smile, not knowing really what to say.

We continue walking the park and wearing off our sugar high of funnel cake and hot chocolate before heading back for the hayride to get to the parking lot. Ben is still quiet, only making casual comments. He is still showing affection to me, but not in his normal playful way. Did something tonight trigger some bad memories for him?

# CHAPTER
## twenty-four

WHEN WE ARRIVE HOME, Bo greets us eagerly, still not liking when we are not there at night. But instead of greeting me first as usual, he is more eager to see Ben. Ben is also happy to see Bo, and his smile returns as he kneels down to pet him. I stand there in the foyer watching them. Bo finally comes over to me for some attention.

"I can't get over how quickly Bo has taken to you. It's as if he has known you for his whole life," I joke as I pet Bo. When I look up at Ben, he is no longer smiling. "What's wrong?" I stand back up. I don't like the expression on his face. Something is troubling him.

"I need to talk to you about somethin', but first let me build a fire so we can sit and talk." He walks away, heading to the fireplace.

My heart sinks. I am unsure what this could be about. Stunned, I sit on the couch, not knowing what to do with myself. Ben seemed happy earlier, he couldn't want to break up with me already; we have barely started dating.

Maybe it's something else, maybe he has decided to leave again, or maybe he wants to find his ex. A million different scenarios are running through my head as I watch the man I have fallen in love with as he stands with his back to me, building a fire. When he is done, he comes over to sit beside me on the couch. My stomach is churning. I was right, he is going to leave. I can't look at him. I know I will start crying. What happened tonight? What changed?

"I have been tryin' to think of an easy way to say this, but I realized tonight, there is no easy way. So I am gonna just say it, before I chicken out again."

I finally look over at him, tears welling up in my eyes. "What's wrong?" is all I can manage to say.

He looks so sad. He finally takes a deep breath. "I have been lying to ya, Julie."

I sit there, pulling my legs up on the couch, sinking into the corner. I stare at the fire, avoiding looking at him as I remain silent. Ben hasn't made any attempt to touch me, but just looks at me. I swallow as I feel like at any moment I am going to throw up. The words still playing in my head, "I have been lying to ya, Julie." I finally find the courage to speak, but I refuse to look at him. "I'm listening," is the only response I give.

"Remember when ya told me the story of Bo and how he was your brother's dog?"

The question takes a moment to sink in. This is about Bo? Curiosity has me finally looking at him. "Yes." I am trembling now, not sure where this could be going.

"And ya remember how ya said that when your brother was shot, Bo wouldn't leave his side and they had to get another handler to get Bo away from your brother?"

"Yes." I am confused as Ben takes my trembling hands and holds them securely in his.

"That was me, Julie, I was the handler. That is why Bo knows me. He was with me until I got out." Ben tightens his hold on my hands as I sit there in disbelief. This is not the conversation I was expecting. It takes a moment for his words to sink in.

"You ... were you with him when he died?" I stumble with my words as my mind tries to process what he just told me.

"No, darlin'. He had already died by the time I got there."

I look over at Bo and then to Ben. The odds of meeting the man who was there to help Bo and take care of my brother's body, has me feeling overwhelmed. I look down at our joined hands as Ben takes a deep breath and continues.

"There's more. The day at the diner was not the first time I saw ya."

I quickly look up at him. "What?"

"I attended your brother's funeral. I was the Marine that brought Bo."

Like finding the last piece to a puzzle, everything clicks into place. He was the Marine that offered me his hand when I was sitting on the ground with Bo. I was grieving so much that the memory of his face had faded.

"I didn't know what to say or do when ya sat down with Bo at the funeral. It went against the protocol, but it was obvious ya needed that moment as did Bo. You were right, he wasn't the same after your brother died."

As if Bo knows he is the subject of our conversation, he comes over to us and sits by Ben. Ben reaches down and pets him.

"Bo was assigned to me, and even though we got along, he was havin' difficulty followin' my commands.

He would do the basics, but when it came time to work, he would freeze up. It's not uncommon for them to have PTSD issues after somethin' like that. I worked with him for several weeks, hopin' he would snap of it, but he never did. We had no choice but to send him back to Lackland. I guess they must have decided to just retire him."

"Why didn't you want to adopt him?" I ask.

"I would have loved to, but I was goin' through so much with gettin' out of active duty and Renee filin' for divorce." He continues petting Bo as he looks down at him. "It is a good thing now. He would have been homeless just like me, and besides." He stops and looks at me again. "He belongs with ya."

"I'm sorry I didn't recognize you that first day at the diner."

He smiles, releasing my hands as he puts his arm around me. We ease back into the couch, finally letting some of the earlier tension go.

"It's okay, I mean I looked very different than from the first time ya saw me."

"Did you know it was me that day?"

"Honestly, I am not sure. I mean, when I approached ya, no, I didn't know. But when ya looked up at me, somethin' felt familiar. I couldn't put my finger on it at first. Later I just assumed it was because I was attracted to ya, and didn't think about it much more. Then there was the night ya came to find me." He looks over at me.

"What happened then?"

"Ya brought Bo. When I saw him, that's when I remembered." Bo laid his head in my lap as Ben reached over and petted him again. I stare at the interaction between the two of them. This whole thing is just incredible. Ben sits back again and leans over, kissing my temple and squeezing me closer.

I snuggle into him, in relief that what he just told me wasn't as horrible as what I was thinking it was going to be.

"Tell me what you're thinking? I am sorry I didn't tell ya sooner, but ya had so much already upsettin' ya, I didn't want to add to it."

"I am just thinking how lucky I am for meeting someone as incredible as you. You are a kind and loving man, Ben Parker. You will always be my hero. I am so thankful you were there that night to save me."

"Some hero, if I hadn't been a complete jackass and left ya, ya would never have been there in the first place."

"You don't know that."

"Yeah, I do. If I would have been here, I would have talked ya out of workin' that night or at least went with ya."

"Well, I am just glad you were there that night." I hug him tighter, but he tenses and sits up, looking at me.

"But that's the thin'. I almost wasn't. I only went back there because I had accidently left the scarf ya gave me on the milk crates when I was there earlier in the day. At night I had been stayin' at the shelter, but when I realized I didn't have the scarf, I went back."

"You were at the diner during the day?"

"Yeah, I guess I was hopin' you would come out for your break like ya normally did, but soon I realized ya weren't workin' that mornin' so I left. Ya always work mornings so I never dreamed ya would be there that night."

I get up and crawl onto his lap as he welcomes me in his arms. We sit there holding each other close. At that moment, I can tell he needs my comfort as much as I need his. I kiss his neck and hug him close.

"You were gone for a few days. I thought you left for good."

"I was close by. I was just too embarrassed to show my face to ya after the shit I said."

"We both said some mean things that day." I sit up and look at him. "So what changed your mind to come find me that day?"

"I just realized ya were right and that I was bein' a coward. I realized walkin' away from ya was gonna be the biggest mistake of my life. I was ready to beg and grovel for ya to give me another chance," he says as he lifts my hand to his lips and kisses it tenderly.

"I would have and you wouldn't have had to beg." I smile at him. I am so glad we are okay again.

"Grovel?" he asks as he looks at me questionably.

I shrug as I pull my hand away and pinch my thumb and finger together. "Maybe a little," I tease.

"Oh, yeah?" He starts tickling me and soon we are wrestling around on the couch. Bo decides we are both nuts and returns to the quiet and safety of his dog pillow. When we are both out of breath from laughing and playing, we begin to kiss. Once again, Ben is careful to not be on top of me even in play.

He stops kissing me, looking into my eyes. "I love ya, Julie."

"I love you too, Ben."

# CHAPTER
## twenty-five

"WANT ME TO GO IN there with you?" Holly asks as we pull up in front of the social services center. I am nervous. I have never talked to anyone about personal stuff, only my closest family and friends, and you can count them on one hand. Now, I was about to talk about something so vile and scary, to a complete stranger. I need to do this though. I want to get better so Ben and I can move past this and start a life together. I want him to see that he doesn't always have to come to my rescue, and that I can be strong and face my demons. I look over at Holly who is waiting for my answer.

"No thanks, but can you pick me back up in an hour? We can go have lunch and maybe do a little more last-minute Christmas shopping."

"It's a date. Good luck. You will do fine." She smiles as I take a deep breath and get out of the car.

I close the door and wave her off as I walk through the doors. After I sign in, I go to sit down in the waiting room. My eyes are drawn to the pamphlet holder across the room so I walk over to it. Pamphlets on domestic abuse, drug abuse, alcoholism, and rape, fill the slots. Rape, could you really classify what that creep did to me as rape? I grab the pamphlet and start looking at it. The police called it assault with attempted rape, so they don't believe I was raped. As I start to read, I hear my name being called.

"Julie Walsh?"

I turn, quickly stuffing the pamphlet back in the pocket. I walk over to the woman standing in the doorway who called my name. She is casually dressed with a friendly welcoming smile. Not at all what I was expecting.

"Hello, Julie, my name is Sharon Day, but please call me Sharon."

"Hello, Sharon, nice to meet you." I shake her hand and I follow her to the back. We walk into a small, but comfortable office. Just like Sharon, it is welcoming and casual. She must love horses because they are everywhere you look, pictures, figurines, on the sofa cushions, and blanket. It looks more like someone's living room than an office. There is a desk with a chair in front, but she moves toward the sofa.

"Go ahead and have a seat. Make yourself at home. Can I get you anything? I have water, soda, iced tea, and coffee."

"Coffee would be great."

"Hazelnut okay? I haven't been to the store yet to stock up with more flavors. I just love my new Keurig machine, so much easier than making a pot of coffee."

I am sitting on the sofa and we are discussing coffee? Okay, I will roll with it. She makes me a cup and brings it over in a mug with, you guessed it, horses on it.

"I take it you like horses." I say nervously as she hands me the mug.

"Kind of hard to tell, huh?" She jokes as she walks back to the coffee machine. "Yes, I love horses. How about you?" It is like you are visiting a friend, not a professional shrink. She makes herself a cup and brings over a liquid creamer and spoon.

"They're all right, I guess. I have never been around them."

She sits down on the couch with me. "If you want sugar, I left it over there, make yourself at home."

"No, creamer is fine, thanks."

"I grew up on a ranch and now I have one of my own. I own four horses. They are my babies. So tell me about yourself, Julie."

I feel at ease with Sharon and I tell her about myself. She sits and listens as she sips her coffee. She doesn't butt in or try to take over the conversation, she just lets me speak. For some reason, I do and I start telling her everything about my past, my losses, my attack, and even my new relationship with Ben. The hour appointment is over with before I know it. I feel like we just started. She takes my mug and walks over to the sink.

"I think that is enough for today. I would like to see you every day for at least this week, is this time okay?"

"Yeah, sure." I get up, not exactly sure what to do with myself.

"All right, you enjoy the rest of your day and I will see you tomorrow."

"So did she ask you about the attack, or offer any advice?" Holly has been questioning me ever since she picked me up. We are sitting in a local sandwich shop, waiting for our order. I am feeling more relaxed than I was earlier. They say confession is good for the soul.

"No, she just listened. I told her my life story and I told her what happened to me. She just listened. I have never opened up and talked so much in my life." I smile as I remember how I just sat there and told Sharon all about my life. "It felt good."

"Well, that's good. Hey, since you have a boyfriend now, why don't you and Ben come out with us tonight?"

"Sure, let me ask Ben, in case he is too tired."

"You can come over to our place first for dinner and then maybe we can go out for drinks." Holly takes a bite of her sandwich, grinning from ear to ear.

I hesitate eating, as her words finally register in my head. "What do you mean 'our place'?" I eye her suspiciously. "Are you and Mike living together?"

She nods with her normal Holly enthusiasm. She must have been waiting for a while to throw this bombshell at me.

"Since when?"

"Since a few days ago. We are trying it on for size before heading toward the alter."

I realize that I am a little hurt that she has waited this long to tell me. Since I have been with Ben, Holly and I don't talk as we used to.

"Besides, you're living with your guy and it seems to be working for you."

"Wow, Holly, I don't know what to say. I guess things are changing for both of us very quickly, huh?"

"Yes they are. Speaking of that, have you guys ...? You know?"

I know right away what she is hinting at. Sex is one

of her favorite subjects. "No, not yet, I am still not ready." I stare down at my plate, avoiding eye contact with her, like I am ashamed to admit it. Hopefully she will drop the subject. I decide to give her a little push and quickly change the subject.

"What time should Ben and I be at your house?"

She smiles and doesn't try to bring the subject back up. I am thankful she can take a hint. "Six o'clock." She winks at me.

"Okay, sounds good."

# CHAPTER
## twenty-six

LATER THAT EVENING, THE FOUR of us have a wonderful spaghetti dinner at Mike's and now Holly's place. Holly has come in and added her special touches. It reminds me that maybe I should let Ben add a few things of his own at our place. I smile thinking of my home as his now. I then remember he doesn't really have anything. I wonder if I can change that. After quickly cleaning up, we head out to the local sports bar.

Mike asks Ben many questions about the military police and some of Ben's stories made make me so thankful that he is no longer a Marine. I know he left many things out when he was talking with us there, but it was still enough to make me so glad he is no longer doing it. I am thankful when the guys go to play pool, so we don't have to listen to any more of Ben's war stories.

"What if Mike doesn't change his mind, Holly? He doesn't seem to be turned off by Ben's stories."

I stare across at her as we sit in the booth. She has been very quiet tonight as she tears at the label of her beer. "I know."

She sighs. "Oh, well, I guess I will have no choice but to support him. I love him." She shrugs as she takes a swig of her beer.

We look over, watching our guys. Our guys. I have been waiting for this day to happen. I am in love and enjoying all the aspects of that. Ben is laughing and having a great time. I just watch in awe at the change in him from the days he was homeless. To look at him now, no one would ever know. As if he senses my staring, he turns, looking at me with a smile on his face. He is chalking his pool cue and getting ready to break.

As Holly and I sit there chatting, a song starts playing. It is one we loved dancing to as teens. Holly must be filling nostalgic when she grabs my hand. "Come on, Julie, it's our song. Let's go." She stands and pulls me up with her.

"I don't know, Holly. My ankle is still not healed. Maybe I should sit this one out." I actually just don't like making a spectacle out of myself, and the ankle is a convenient excuse.

"Just stand and shake your money maker, it will be okay." She starts pulling me along, and before I know it, we are on the dance floor. Being very careful with my ankle, we dance to groove. I decide what the hell, the old Julie hated doing stuff like this, but this is the new Julie. Holly is her normal self as she gets into the song and I can tell she is surprised but happy that I am keeping up with her. A couple of guys dance next to us, joining in our fun. It feels good to have fun again, to feel alive again.

Suddenly, the guy dancing next to me, starts getting closer. I back up trying to keep him out of my personal space. I am hoping he will get the hint to stay back, but no such luck, he just comes closer again. I try pushing him away from my personal space, but he must think it is part of my dancing, because he comes around me, pulling me to him. I start grabbing and scratching at his arms, screaming to let me go.

He does instantly but looks at me as if I am a crazy person. Holly starts to come to me, but I am suddenly pulled into a strong set of protective arms. My defenses are up as I push them away. "DON'T TOUCH ME." I shout.

Ben grabs my upper arms, gently this time. "Julie, it's me." As I look up into his caring eyes, I quickly recover and fall into the safety of his arms. Thankfully, he understands my behavior as he hugs me to him.

"Dude, I am sorry, we were dancing, and she just freaked. Is she crazy or something?"

I immediately feel Ben tense. He eases me out of his arms and into Holly's. This wasn't going to be good.

"No, ya fuckin' asshole, just because she doesn't want ya pawin' her, doesn't make her crazy." Ben is in the guy's face, and he looks like he is going to challenge back, but Ben continues his verbal assault. "What makes ya think that's okay, huh?" He pushes the guy back. "Ya wanna see crazy? Ya son of a bitch."

The guy holds his hands up. He seems to have wised up and decided it was best to let this one go. "It's cool, dude, sorry. I ain't looking for trouble." He walks away with his friend in tow.

Ben is tensed, ready to fight; I can tell he is trying to hold in his anger. I pull away from Holly to go to him, touching his arm, and bringing him back, just like he did with me minutes ago. He looks down at me, still angry, but takes my hand, pulling me to him. The song is over and a slow one starts. Instead of going back to our table, Ben takes me in his arms and we start to dance. Mike and Holly join in beside us.

"I am sorry," I mumble into his chest, my tears beginning to wet his shirt.

"Don't," he says. I can hear the anger still in his voice. He is still tense as he holds me. I feel bad, that once again, he has to come to my rescue.

"It seems like all I do is cry. I am so sorry I made you mad."

He gently pushes me out of his arms, just so he can look at my face. I shyly look down, not wanting him to see me cry. "Look at me, Julie." I slowly gaze up at his command. His expression is stern, but not scary. "You are not a crybaby and I am not mad at ya. So stop it, okay?"

I nod as he once again pulls me into his arms and holds me tight.

"I was comin' to stop him even before ya got upset. I didn't like the way he was touchin' ya."

I think about that for a moment. He was jealous? That thought never occurred to me. Like a knight coming to the rescue of his lady in the books I love to read. He was coming to defend my honor and claim me as his. My sadness is quickly washed away and now I can't stop smiling. Then smiles turn to laughing.

"Are ya laughin' at me?" He leans down, whispering in my ear. His normal Ben voice has pleasantly returned.

"No, not at all," I mumble, still giggling. Laughter after tears— what an awesome feeling.

"Yes, ya are." He kisses my ear before taking a playful bite at my earlobe.

I hug him tighter to me. We continue to dance and enjoy each other.

We drop Mike and Holly off and head back home. Ben had stopped drinking after one beer very early so he was able to drive home. I guess he was still in protective mode after the dance floor incident. As we get ready for bed, as I hoped, he no longer sleeps in Jason's room but instead sleeps beside me. I don't even have to ask. I cuddle up next him, my new favorite way to sleep. I still feel bad that he almost fought because of me.

"I am sorry about freaking out tonight. I am glad you didn't fight that guy."

"It wasn't your fault and stop callin' yourself crazy. Ya have been through a trauma, that doesn't make you crazy."

As I listen to his words, I hope that he too takes them to heart. I look up at him. "Neither are you, you know?" I smile, kissing him quickly.

"Sure I am," he says with the most serious of faces. I frown, not knowing how to respond. "I am crazy about ya." He smiles and returns my kiss.

I ease back down in the bed. Except for the fight incident, the night was fun. "You and Mike seem to have bonded."

"Yeah, he is a good guy."

"So, do you think he will make a good cop?"

"Oh, yeah. He'll do great."

"Holly isn't thrilled about it."

"Yeah, he told me that."

"But she said she would support him if he still decides to do it."

"That's good, that is the way it should be."

"I am just glad that you are out of that dangerous stuff now. You are here where you are safe. I don't think I am strong enough to go through what Holly is about to with Mike."

"I don't think ya give yourself enough credit." He scolds.

"Well, I have seen my entire family die. I don't want to have to worry about you being killed in the line of duty."

I hear Ben sigh, as he eases more into the bed. "I'm

tired, kitten. Good night. I love ya." He quickly kisses my lips. Usually we make out a little, but I don't press. It has been a long and crazy night. I can't help but be a little concerned about his quick dismissal. My mind starts going through so many different scenarios that I have to stop doing this to myself. Things are good, Julie, don't overanalyze things.

"Good night, love you too."

# CHAPTER
## twenty-seven

I TELL SHARON ABOUT THE incident at the bar in my next session. She doesn't think my reaction is abnormal considering the circumstances and the fact I am questioning it proves even more that I am on the road to recovery. We talk some more about my parents and Aunt Gina, but then the focus turns to my relationship with Jason.

"So Jason was not only your brother, but your twin brother, correct?" She sits down on the couch next to me. Yesterday she just listened, but today she is asking more questions.

"Yes."

"Tell me about your last conversation with him," she asks and I am caught off guard by her request.

"What?"

"Do you remember the last time you spoke with him?" she asks casually as my mind digs back into my memories.

"Well, yes, of course I do."

"Tell me about it." She smiles and relaxes back, sipping her coffee.

"It wasn't on the phone this time; it was a video feed chat. Those were rare for us." I let my guard down a little and relax too.

"It was November of last year, on a Saturday. I made sure I was off work, so I wouldn't miss it. He wasn't going to be able to come home for the holidays so he had arranged the video chat. He knew I was going to be upset that he wasn't coming home for Christmas, since he had missed Christmas the year before. I got to see him and it was special. We talked about the past holidays, our parents, his old buddies, what foods he missed, and then he brought up school again."

"School?"

"Yes, he was getting on to me again for not enrolling at the JC." I roll my eyes, and then look at her. "Every time we talked, he would bring it up. I swear sometimes he acted more like my parent than my brother."

"Did that bother you?"

"Yes, it bugged me. Like I said we really didn't get much opportunity to talk and he wanted to waste the little time we had trying to convince me to go back to school." I can feel the anger building the more I try to explain. I pause for a moment to calm my emotions, but Sharon is not letting me off that easy.

"Why does the subject of school upset you?"

So much for calming down. I stand up and start pacing the office floor. I can no longer sit still if we are going to talk about this. "It was all he would talk about during our last conversation. I didn't want to talk about that, I wanted to know how he was and about all the places he had been to. He kept pressing on about how I should enroll and how Mom and Dad wanted us to have an education."

I stop and turn to look at her. She is still relaxing on the couch, watching me rant on. "It pissed me off. We only had a few moments to speak and he was wasting it on college talk, and then of course we got cut off."

"Cut off?"

"Yeah, the feed died and I ..." I pause, taking a deep breath as the thoughts of that last time we spoke weigh on my mind. "I didn't get to say goodbye." I start choking up now as my vision blurs. I go ahead and sit back down as a few tears start to fall.

"I didn't get to tell him I loved him and missed him. We just argued about stupid school. He died before we could speak again." I start wiping away the tears that are falling as she hands me a box of tissues. I am glad she doesn't press me to go on this time, as she gives me a few moments to pull myself together.

"I am sure it was only because he wanted the best for you." She finally chimes in.

"You're right. It seems silly now, why we argued about it. I guess that's just what siblings do, right?" And here I go, rationalizing everything again.

"Yes, but you both had special circumstances, being without parents. Of course I didn't know your brother, but maybe in his way he felt he needed to play a more parental role in your life."

I think about that a moment. I think she is right about that. Jason didn't start playing the whole big brother act until my parents died. After that I was no longer his twin, but his baby sis. He would always call me that.

We spend a few more minutes discussing my final conversation with Jason. I realize now why I get so angry when someone brings up the subject of me going back to college. She makes me realize that even though we didn't get the chance to say the words, Jason knew I loved him and he loved me. The fact that he was still worried about my well-being and wanted me to succeed only proves that more.

After my session with Sharon, I drive around town. It feels good to have a little sense of freedom again and being able to drive again. Carl let Ben borrow his truck to go to work, so I could have the car. I made the excuse I needed it to shop, which Ben quickly chimed in and offered to do for me. I love that he wants to help, but after being alone for so long, I just desire a little me time.

Everything seems to be happening so fast in my life while others so slow. I pull up in the parking lot of Clover Junior College. It is almost deserted right now because of the holiday break. I remember touring it when I was a senior in high school but it seemed so scary to me at the time. I feel funny coming here now. Am I too old to do this? I get out and walk to the admissions office.

It is dark when I pull up in the drive. I hit the button on the garage opener remote that Ben placed in the car for me. The door opens and lights up the garage as I pull in. I feel so spoiled, being able to pull into the garage now. It is all thanks to Ben, who has been working in here every night to make it nice for me. It was nice to be alone today, but now I miss him.

I grab the bags of groceries and go inside as Bo greets me. I want to cook a nice dinner for Ben tonight. Hopefully he won't be home late. I give Bo the chew bone I bought and he disappears. I am in a great mood as I put away things. I could definitely get used to this. I grab the package of toilet paper and head to bathroom and without thinking, I walk right in. I am hit with the steam of the hot shower almost immediately as I realize that someone is home already.

I stare at the beautiful naked man in the shower

rinsing his hair under the water. He must have not heard me walk in as he continues on, oblivious to my presence. The man is just gorgeous and while I should be looking away, or better yet, stepping out of there, I can't move. Why did I decide on clear shower glass doors? I can see everything, and I definitely like what I see as I watch the water roll off his body.

I feel like a Peeping Tom, but I can't look away. He is so handsome and sexy that it takes my breath away and it also makes me realize what I want but am too afraid to act upon. My nervousness shows its ugly head as I drop the package of toilet paper on the floor.

This time he hears me as he turns and looks my way. I am horrified he just caught me staring at him, but I remain frozen in my embarrassment. He smiles as he continues as if everything is normal. He is not embarrassed in the slightest. His smile is mischievous and for a minute, it makes me think he is almost daring me to join him.

He opens the shower door and holds his hand out to me. The gesture is so simple but yet so sexy. My body is on fire, and begging me to strip right there and join him. I want to, oh God how I want to. I take a small step and stop, before turning around and leaving the room.

My face is hot not to mention my body as I try desperately to control my racing heart and concentrate on putting away groceries. I say many silent prayers that he doesn't say anything about it and tease me. Why did I run away from him? What the hell is wrong with me? I look around the kitchen. My home is where I run to when things get overwhelming but where do I go now? I walk out to the backyard and sit on the swing. I stare up at the stars, trying to relax, but the chill in the air is making that almost impossible.

"Nice night, isn't it, kitten?"

I look over at Ben who is smiling as he stares down at me. He is dressed now, complete with a jacket and holding one out for me. I smile and take it, slipping it on as he sits beside me. We sit there and swing in a silence so deafening that it makes me feel even more awkward. There is no way I am going to bring up what happened a few minutes ago first. I wouldn't know what to say even if I did. I am still looking up at the stars for answers, when Ben speaks again.

"My mom and I loved to sit and look at the stars. One year for Christmas she got me a telescope and a book with all the constellations."

I look over and smile as he looks up at the stars. He doesn't share much about himself, so when he finally does, I try not to interrupt.

"She worked a lot, supportin' my sis and me, so we didn't have much mom and son time, but I remember that, like it was yesterday." His eyes finally meet mine as I slide over next to him. His arm wraps around me as he pulls me closer to lean me back in his arms. The movement is so quick that it shocks and thrills me. Before I can comment, his warm lips cover mine. I am his willing prisoner as I relax and enjoy his seduction.

His kisses only last for a few seconds so I don't have a chance to panic over his forwardness. He sits back up to give me my breathing room, all the while grinning down at me. In the quiet of the evening, we sit there swinging and enjoying each other. Our hands seek each other out and when they connect, our fingers intertwine together.

"I am sorry if I embarrassed ya earlier."

I touch his lips with my fingertips to silence his apology. I was hoping he had forgotten, so I didn't have to relive the embarrassment of running away like a child. I am tired of running though, and it is time to face my fears head-on. Ben would never hurt me or embarrass me on purpose, and I know that. It is way past time that I opened up and was honest with him.

"You didn't embarrass me; not like you think, anyway." He continues swinging us, and the desire to close my eyes is overwhelming.

"What do ya mean?" he asks quietly, a puzzled look in his eyes.

"I left because I wasn't sure what to do. I wanted to join you but you see I'm not ..." I hesitate as if my virginity is something to be ashamed of. I know the notion of a twenty-three-year-old virgin is not the norm.

"Ready?" A logical assumption as I pause in explaining my position. I should just stop right now and leave it right here. I really consider it, until he continues. "I knew that I shouldn't have put ya in that position, it was wrong. I am so sorry."

I feel the lump building in my throat as I can read the apology in his eyes. No, I can't stand to see him take this on himself. "Ben, it's not that, I am ready. Well, I mean I am pretty sure I am ready, but it's just ..." I pause again. As much as I want to tell him, I can't think of the right words.

"It's just what, kitten?" He bends down and rubs his nose against mine playfully before placing another soft kiss on my lips. He grips my hand tighter, more secure as if he is lending me his strength to continue explaining what's on my mind.

"I'm a virgin, Ben. I have never been with a guy. I have barely kissed a guy, before you," I whisper. "I'm sorry I didn't tell you sooner. I should have told you from the very beginning."

He smiles at me again. "It's okay, I understand." He continues smiling and I am confused.

I am not sure if he is amused by my admission or is

once again treating me like a child. Either way, I am not having it. "No, I don't think you do." I sit up quickly and pull out of his arms to face him. His eyebrows rise up as if he is surprised by my abruptness. "This isn't just about the attack, Ben. I admit at first it was, but I know you would never hurt me like that." I stop the swinging motion with my feet. He remains quiet so I can finish.

"I want you, Ben. I want you so bad, I really do. It's just that I'm not sure if I know how to show you how much I love you and want you. I have been hiding for so long, away from people, afraid to make connections with anyone." While it feels good to finally gets this off my chest, I am embarrassed by my rant.

"This is all so new to me, I just don't want to mess things up."

Ben doesn't say a word as he leans over and kisses me again. It is a gentle and quick kiss, almost dismissive. He stands and faces me. I can't read his expression, so I am not sure what he is going to say. My heart sinks thinking that he is leaving after my confession. He smiles as he holds his hand out to me again, just like earlier, before I ran off.

"I'll teach ya," he whispers as I stare at his hand. I look into his loving eyes as I gently place my hand in his.

# CHAPTER
## twenty-eight

WE SILENTLY WALK BACK INTO the house. We don't stop in the kitchen or even the living room. We walk right past Bo, who is too busy with his rawhide bone to care what we are doing. Ben continues to guide me down the hallway. At first I think that maybe we are going to finish what began in the bathroom, but he walks right past and steps into our bedroom. He leaves me for a moment in the center of the room as he steps away to close the door. I am so nervous when I feel him step behind me.

"Are ya still cold?" he asks as he starts guiding my jacket off my shoulders and down my arms.

"A little," I whisper as I feel him move my hair to the side, exposing my neck. His hand rests gently on my stomach, pulling me to him. I can feel his hot breath near my ear.

"I'll warm ya up." His hands go to the hem of my shirt,

and he slowly guides it up over my head and off. I now feel his warm hands touch my bare stomach. He kisses my shoulder and neck and I close my eyes as I am lost in this passionate moment. I put my hand over his, caressing it as he continues. He stops and turns me to face him. It is as if I can read his mind; I copy what he did as I grab the hem of his shirt, and he raises his arms and allows me to remove it.

When I have it off, I drop it to the floor. I start kissing his chest as I rub my hands through his patch of chest hair. My kisses make it up to his neck and shoulders. He holds me gently to him, allowing me to continue as I feel his fingers on my back, unhooking my bra. I stop long enough for him to remove my bra before I try to continue.

He allows me a few more kisses before he takes over, kissing my neck and working his way to my breasts. No guy has ever made it this far with me. I run my fingers through Ben's hair. His head is at my chest as he continues kissing and sucking and licking my breasts. The sensation is felt over my entire body as my need for him grows stronger. These feelings are not new, but they've been unsated, but I have a feeling that is about to change very quickly.

He rises to kiss my mouth, and our kisses are more urgent and more demanding now. But fear starts building along with the lust. As much as I tried to ward it off, Ben must sense it as he stops. I can't stop the shiver of nervousness that flows through me.

"Lesson one, kitten, is ya have to relax. There's no rush." He smiles, taking my face and kissing me again, and then slowly walks me backwards to my bed. "Sit down and don't move. I'll be right back." He goes into the bathroom and I hear the water running in the tub.

I sit frozen on the bed, not moving one muscle at his command. My breasts are exposed while the rest of me is dressed; I still even have on my shoes. I'm not sure what I should be doing now. Instinctively my arms come up, hugging myself to cover my naked chest. Self-doubt resurfaces. Did he change his mind? Does he want me clean first? What is he doing?

After a few moments, I hear the water turn off. It is dark now except for the light peeking out from the bathroom when he steps back into the bedroom.

"That won't do at all." He walks over to me, taking my hands and pulling away my cover. He pulls me to him and begins to kiss me again and laying me back onto the bed. He kneels before me, sliding off my shoes and socks, and before I can protest, he grabs the waistband of my sweats and pulls them down, my panties in tow as he carefully pulls them off and away from my still sore ankle. I stare up at the ceiling as I am now completely naked for his viewing, and am nervous as hell to look him in the eyes. His hands massage my upper legs and he kisses and works his way up my body. He spends a few moments at my breasts again, before his lips find mine.

"I think a warm bath will knock the chill out of ya and relax ya a little. Come on." He stands and pulls me up. Before I know it, we are back in the bathroom, where this seduction first began a little while ago. The only difference is I am the one naked now. He helps me into the bubble bath he has prepared for me, complete with candles lit around the garden tub.

As he holds my hands, I carefully sit and lean back into the warm sudsy bath. Bending down he gives me one more kiss and steps away. For a split second, I think he is leaving me to soak. I realize that is not the case when he starts unfastening his jeans. He strips for me with such a cool and sexy flare, I feel like I am watching my own version of Chippendales. He is teasing me with his wicked smile, but it is his playfulness that I love and need.

I laugh a little and then I actually do start to relax. The nervousness is slowly slipping away as I watch Ben, my Ben, shed the rest of his clothes and step into the bath behind me. He once again wraps his arms around me and pulls me to him. We sleep like this, but now it's different. Our naked bodies are touching, and it's wickedly sexy.

He starts kissing at my neck again, before turning me to lie across his body. He is at my mouth again, our tongues dancing with one another. Our bodies are slick and sudsy as we touch and caress each other. His hands are exploring me, with no part off the table now as I begin my own expedition.

Instinctually, I touch his manhood and feel it getting harder. I have never touched a man until now and the excitement of that event has me on edge. I slowly begin to stroke him, but then his hand gently removes mine, holding it and squeezing it lovingly. I stop kissing him to look at him, wondering if I hurt him or did something he didn't like. "Did I hurt you?"

"No, darlin', but it has been awhile, and I have many plans for ya tonight, so I don't want to end it too quickly, if ya know what I mean." He smiles and winks.

He kisses me again before I can respond, laying me back and caressing my breasts before his hands slide down my stomach and then my groin and finally to my sex that is aching with need. He massages and rubs and I am enjoying every delightful second. His fingers part my folds as he finds my clit and begins rubbing it.

I am helpless now in his arms, my hands gripping his legs as he continues playing with me. Something is building inside me, and the struggle of wanting it to stop and wanting it to continue, fight each other. His one hand is gripping my breast, while his other hand is rubbing my mound where his fingers strum at my clit, all while he is kissing my neck.

I am on fire. I have neither the desire nor the capability to ask him to stop as I reach the point of no return and fall into the well of orgasmic bliss. The throbbing of my clit and the thumping of my heart are in sync. The release was so incredible that my body lays back on his, unable to move. Thankfully, he is there to keep me from sinking into the water; otherwise, I think I would drown. I stare up at him with disbelief and wonder what just happened.

I receive a knowing smile. "I'll take that ya liked that?"

"Uh huh." I nod.

"We have only just begun, kitten. I have many more moments like that in store for ya."

After lying helpless in his arms for I have no idea how long, the chill of the water turning colder has us seeking fluffy towels and the warmth and comfort of the bed. Ben gets out first, drying off and wrapping a towel around his waist, before helping me out and drying me off. He wraps me in the towel, and we make our way to the bedroom, but he removes it after he turns down the covers on the bed. I slide in as he removes his own towel and joins me. The sheets are cold so my body seeks the warmth of his as we cuddle together.

"Next time, I need to turn up the thermostat," he jokes.

"There are other ways you can turn up the heat," I hint.

"I think I've created a monster." I can't help but notice he is taking great care to not be too overpowering. A few times he wanted to pull me under him, only to end up with us facing side to side. His hands begin exploring again, but this time, he takes my hand and brings it to his penis. He guides me on touching him as I feel his softness begin to harden very quickly. His hand is instructing mine on how to grip him and touch him until he pulls away again.

"I am gettin' ahead of myself. I want to do somethin' first." Before I have time to protest, he is up under the covers, turning me on my back and spreading my legs. He sinks down in front of my opening and begins kissing and touching. I am at his mercy and loving every minute of it. His wicked tongue flicks at the spot where I find my great pleasure and I am finding it very hard to lie still as I grab the edges of my pillow.

Eventually the blankets are removed and I lie there naked as he feasts upon me. Curiosity gets the best of me as I look down at him at the junction of my legs. He has my legs open wide for him as he continues his sensual kisses. A moan escapes my mouth causing him to look up at me, but he doesn't stop and I damn sure don't want him to. In fact, I am lifting up, offering him more, wanting more, needing more, when it happens again—that beautiful release. I feel like I am in this other world, where only pleasure is around me.

Ben starts ascending up toward the top of me, slowly and lovingly. I no longer feel fear as the man I love starts kissing his way up my body. He has chased away the demons that have tried their best to swallow me up. He is now above me, and I feel protected and I feel loved. The look in his eyes tells me all I need to know. He would rather die than hurt me. I caress his face and smile, and he takes my lips again for a kiss.

We are still kissing when I hear the nightstand drawer open and then close. I should be embarrassed that he has obviously found my just in case stash of condoms. Actually, it was Holly that bought them, hoping one day, I might find a guy. He sits up and I watch as he places the condom on himself with no hesitation of how it works.

A second of doubt hits my mind as I have to remind myself, it may be my first time, but not his. He is not only older, but he was married. From what I can put together, he only had sex with his ex, but I haven't come out and asked him. That will be a subject for another time. He is with me now and that's all that matters at this moment.

I remain silent and smile at him once again as he gently lies on top of me. My mind and body are now in sync as we both welcome him inside. I feel the pinch Holly warned me about, but Ben is so gentle and is going so slowly, that the second of pain I feel is no big deal. Twice he has given me pleasure and now it is my turn to give him his. The feeling of having him inside me is the most incredible feeling I have ever experienced.

He is mine, and as I kiss his neck and pull him tighter against me while he makes love to me, I have to hold back the temptation of screaming that fact out to the world. Sensing that I am okay, Ben speeds up his tempo and very quickly, he is moaning and sighing, before kissing my breast as he relaxes. He lies on top of me, not moving, and breathing heavily as I stroke his hair.

As his breathing settles, he looks up at me and smiles. "You okay?" he whispers.

"Yes," I whisper back, unable to control the huge smile on my face. He gently pulls out of me, and once again lies beside me, but only for a quick kiss before he leaves the bed and heads to the bathroom. I remain in the bed, still feeling like I am in some fantasy world. I am officially a woman now—Ben's woman. I am so glad I waited; this is just as I hoped and dreamed it would be. I hear the water running again as Ben comes back into the room. Instead of climbing back in bed, he gathers me up in his arms and heads to the bathroom. The tub is once again filling.

"Another bath so soon?"

"It will help with the soreness." He sets me down and steps into the tub, sitting down as he holds my hand to join him. Once again, I am lying back in his arms, as he gently takes care of me. He doesn't say a word as he washes the evidence of my virginity away from both of us. The way he is being so gentle and caring makes me want to weep. But this is no time for tears. He would misunderstand, I know he would.

After he is done, he gets out. "Soak for a few more minutes. I'm gonna go make the bed," he says as he wraps a towel around him.

I lean back and relax in the warm water and sigh. Damn, how did I get so lucky to find this man?

# CHAPTER
## *twenty-nine*

THE SUNLIGHT PEEKING INTO THE bedroom has me awakening in Ben's arms. After our special night, I fell quickly asleep in these same arms. I don't want to leave them, but it is going to be a busy day, getting ready for Carl's annual Christmas Eve party tonight. I carefully try to get out of his arms, only to be pulled in tighter against him.

"Where ya goin'?" he mumbles in his pillow.

"To cook breakfast."

He releases me, allowing me to leave the warmth of his arms. I quickly slip into my thick robe and slippers, to avoid being chilled. Ben pulls the covers back over his head, not moving. But I could have sworn I heard him moan or was it a growl?

"Any special request?" I laugh as it finally dawns on me that Ben is not a morning person.

All I hear is another response that sounds much like

a caveman.

After the coffee is made, Ben joins me in the kitchen and wraps his arms around me as I am washing a few dishes. Neck kisses and earlobe nibbles are fine, but after last night, I want a little more of a good morning so I turn around and reach up to kiss his lips. I notice our kissing is a little different now. It's more knowing and less innocent. I am no longer shy of expressing my feelings and needs with Ben. He has seen it all, knows it all, and I take great comfort in that. I finally break away from his lips and smile.

"Well good morning to you too."

He smiles, giving me another quick peck before getting a cup of coffee. "What's on the agenda today?" Ben asks, sitting down as Bo comes over to say hello.

"Cooking for me. I have to make some things to take to Carl's party tonight. What about you?"

"Well, I need to finish up that project for Carl today. So I guess I will be hidin' out in the garage."

"When are you going to tell me, or better yet, show me this special project?" I ask as I set a plate down in front of him. He takes the opportunity to guide me onto his lap and I wrap my arms around his neck.

"In due time, my love. All good things come in time. Perfect example was last night. How are ya feelin' by the way?"

"Awesome." I kiss him quickly. "Fabulous." I kiss him quickly again. "In love." I finish with another needy kiss. When I am done, the surprised look on Ben's face is priceless.

"Horny?" he jokes and gets a smack on the arm for that as I try to wiggle out of his arms. I pretend to be offended by the remark, but he holds me tighter and kisses me. His colorful remark, soon forgotten.

After breakfast, Ben goes out to the garage to work

on his special project for Carl. I start getting things ready for Carl's party tonight. I am tempted to call Holly and tell her all about last night, but I will be seeing her later, so I decide to wait. Ben has been out there for hours, and I am beginning to feel lonely for his touch. I almost want to cheer as I hear the garage door open and close.

I hear him walk into the kitchen, but I remain busy at the stove. I don't want him to know that I have been waiting for him to come to me. He comes up behind me again, hugging me to him, and kissing my neck, but then he reaches and sneaks a piece of bacon from the plate beside the stove.

"Hey, that's for the recipe I am making." I chastise him.

"But it's bacon, kitten, and I am crazy about bacon," he says as he takes a bite of the crispy piece.

I shake my head at him, all the while, smiling at his boyish ways.

"Wanna know what else I am crazy about?"

I decide to play coy, to get back at him for the bacon theft. So I shrug. "Nah, not really." I try my hardest not to smile.

"Oh, yeah? Well maybe instead of tellin' ya, I will show ya." He reaches over, shutting off the burner, before picking me up in his arms.

"Ben Parker, put me down! What on earth do you think you are doing?"

"Well, part of me feels like givin' ya a good spankin' for teasin' me." He starts walking toward the bedroom "But I have decided I would rather strip ya naked and show ya what else I am crazy about, since ya don't want me to tell ya."

We spend the rest of the afternoon in bed, as Ben shows me all the things he is crazy about, again and again. When we finally come up for air, we realize it is only an hour until the party and still have to get ready. We scramble around the house, cleaning up, getting dressed, and gathering up the things we are taking to the party. Bo just watches us like we are crazy.

I decide on a festive red sweater and jeans. I would love to wear my boots but it is better to not push it with the ankle. Ben is wearing a cable sweater with jeans and looks so handsome. I make him wear the Santa hat again since he looks so damn cute in it, but he agrees only if I wear the reindeer antlers he bought me. I tie a festive red bow onto Bo's collar. He gives me a look that I know is dog code for, You can't be serious?

We are a little late when we arrive at Carl's house where the festivities have already begun without us. Holly, Mike, Carl, and his new lady friend Evelyn are all drinking, eating, and socializing. I have been to several of these get-togethers in the years past, but tonight is the first time I walk in with someone with me. Everyone welcomes Ben, as he is now part of the family, no one feeling doubtful about him any longer. I know the feeling of joy is written all over my face. Holly immediately grabs my hand, pulling me into the kitchen for girl chat.

"Okay, spill. You're acting funny. Something has happened, hasn't it?"

"I don't know what you are talking about." I decide to make her work for it just a little bit longer.

"Bullshit!" She pours a glass of wine and hands it to me as she pours herself a glass. "You did it, didn't you?"

"Yes." I smile, sipping my wine.

"Well, there is no need to ask you if you are happy. It is written all over your face." She takes a sip of wine. "And his."

"Very."

"So this is it, huh? He's the one?" She walks over and gives me a sisterly side hug.

"Most definitely."

We eat and socialize. I keep my drinking to one small glass of wine, in case Ben wants to have a few beers with Mike and Carl. He is over in the corner of the room talking guy stuff with them. As I talk with Holly and Evelyn, I can't help but look over at him and wait for him to catch my eye. When he does, it is so sexy as he gives me a wink. He is right, he has created a monster. I crave his touch so much; I can't stand it.

Everyone finally gathers in the living room to exchange gifts. Carl has limited seating in his small house, but Ben resolves that by pulling me onto his lap. That is just fine with me.

The room is bustling with activity as everyone just starts opening their gifts. I hear a few oohs and ahhhs about the homemade scarves I made and the picture frames Ben made. I admire his talent with woodworking, and maybe after Christmas I can convince him to look into doing it as a career. I also want to tell him about my decision to go back to school, but I would rather wait until we are alone.

Everyone is happy and smiling as we open presents. Bo is enjoying his large rawhide bone courtesy of Carl. I get my favorite gift of some warm socks, some perfume, and gift cards. Ben gets some Blu-ray movies he has been wanting to see and has missed over the years. Holly gets up and hands us each a gift. It is her special tradition, as she loves to give novelty type gifts to embarrass us. She can't do it at home with so many people, so we let her get away with it here.

When I open mine, I get a shirt that has "I will hook for yarn" written on it. This is typical Holly and everyone gets a good laugh at my expense.

"You love me, you know it." she says as she steps out of the room to refill her wine glass.

Ben starts to open his but then closes it and tries to hide it but not before I witness it.

"What did you get?"

"It's nothin'. I will show it to ya later." He smiles, looking somewhat embarrassed. It must be something very naughty. That thought has me squirming a little on his lap.

Mike opens his and it is a toy cop set that he is laughing about, but I feel Ben tense.

I start laughing until Holly walks into the room and chimes in, "I just thought since our guys want to play cops they should have some practice equipment."

It takes a second for the words to register in my head. I stop laughing and I am confused about what I think she said. "What are you talking about?" I think for a split second as I reach over and look at the present Ben is hiding. I am in shock to see it is identical to Mike's. "I don't understand the joke. Only Mike is going into the academy." I laugh, but no one is laughing with me.

Immediately Holly frowns and pales as Mike looks guiltily at Ben. The whole room is quiet.

I look at Ben, waiting for someone to say, "Just joking," but no one is. My stomach starts to churn as I realize this is no joke. "Ben?"

"I wanted to talk to ya later about it," he whispers.

A wave of despair washes over me, taking away all the fun I was having earlier. In its place, I feel the ugliness of betrayal. "Later? I don't believe this," I say angrily as I get up off his lap before he can stop me.

"Julie, wait."

I hear him but continue walking to the kitchen, unable to look at anyone, especially him right now. He calmly walks into the room and toward me, but I back away from him. I am angry and the last thing I want at this moment is his touch. I can tell by the look of surprise and disappointment on his face that this doesn't sit too well with him.

"Julie, look it will be okay. I was a good cop in the military and I can be one again. It is a good job and I will be able to support us better." He stands on one side of the kitchen island as I face him on the other, separated already, before we've barely begun. I shake my head as his explanation doesn't do anything to make it better for me.

"I told you, I don't need you to support me; that we were okay financially. I have money—"

He cuts me off before I can finish. "That's not the point, Julie."

I realize that maybe I haven't been clear about my finances. Maybe that is why he has this crazy notion. "Ben, I am financially set. Don't you get it? You don't need to work, and you certainly don't need to risk your life. I can support us. Neither one of us has to work." I plead with him, hoping he finally understands. From the look on his face, I doubt it. My confession seems to have angered him.

"No! Ya don't get it. I don't want ya to support me. It's my job to take care of ya now." He points at his chest as his words grow louder. "I want to take care of ya. It's important to me to feel I can provide and protect ya and put assholes like Jackson behind bars so they don't hurt other people."

I stand silent as he continues.

"But it's more than just that," he says more quietly as he comes around the island to stand face to face with me.

I don't back away this time and allow him to hold my hands in his.

"Julie, I can be a good cop. I enjoyed it in the military and I know I would enjoy doin' it again." He squeezes my hands as I look down at the floor. "Don't ya see, Julie, ya helped me see that. Ya gave me the courage and confidence to be me again."

I look up at him. "So this is my fault?" I pull my hands away and walk around the island, separating us again.

"Dammit, NO! Of course not." His voice rises again, so he lowers it as he continues. "Look, I don't want to do this here. We will talk about this when we get home, after we've both calmed down."

My emotions are all over the board, and there is no way I can walk back into the living room and be calm after this revelation. "Don't you mean my home?" I cross my arms in front of me. "I mean it seems it isn't good enough for you now, and maybe it never was." I hear my words and know they are wrong, but I am angry and hurt. My defense is to hurt back, especially now.

Looking over at Ben, I can see that my assault has hit its target by the hurtful look on his face. He stands there gripping the counter, before looking down. He is trying really hard not to yell at me, I can sense it. I feel badly for making him feel this way and I am almost at the point of taking back my hurtful words.

"I am not gonna talk to ya when ya are actin' like this." He finally looks up and scolds me like a child.

That has me over the top, my anger boiling once again. "Fine by me," I huff. "But if you think I am going to sit by and watch another person I love die, you are wrong."

We stare at each other in silence. I finally admitted the one thing, I have feared since the moment I realized I was in love with him, the fear of losing him. But I would rather lose him to a breakup, than lose him to death. Anything but that. I couldn't live through it, not again.

Obviously I have left Ben speechless, not knowing what to say in response. He knows he can't promise me he won't get hurt and he won't die. Who really can?

Realizing that I need to be alone, to work through this, I head to the kitchen door, walking past him. "I am going outside. I need air." I can't look at him right now. I need time.

"Julie, wait, please, we aren't done talkin' about this." He starts to follow me, but I turn to stop him, putting my hands up to guard me from him touching me. If he touches me, I will give in and I can't do that right now, no matter how much my distance hurts him, and me as well.

"Don't follow me, Ben." I look up at him, tears in my eyes. "I need a moment alone, please."

He lets me go and doesn't try to stop me this time. I head outside, my tears falling as I realize what this means. He is going through with it and becoming a police officer, and once again I will be faced with the possibility of losing someone I love. I am not sure if it is the chill in the air, or the chill running through my body that has me shaking. I wrap my arms around myself as I stare out at the houses down the street. Cheerful displays of Christmas lights are everywhere you look.

I feel a jacket touch my shoulders as I slip my arms in the sleeves. For a split second, I think it is Ben, whose concern for my well-being would outweigh my request that he leave me alone. Looking over my shoulder, I see it is Holly. I am disappointed that it isn't Ben, but after the hurtful things I said, could I really blame him for not coming out here?

"Ben sent reinforcements?" I button up my coat as she stands next to me.

"Julie, I am so sorry. I thought you knew. He was going to tell you, but maybe he wanted to wait until after Christmas."

"Ya think?" I wipe my tears as they keep falling down my cheeks.

She grabs my arm, hugging it next to her. "Hey, it will

be okay. He is a good cop, he will be okay."

"You don't know that, Holly. Don't you see the news and hear the reports? Cops are hated worse than soldiers. Once again he will be putting himself in harm's way." I pull away from her and turn to face her. "I can't do it again, Holly. I can't stand by and see someone I love die."

"You don't have the power to stop it. If it happens, it is going to happen. It can happen to any of us. What are you going to do? Lock us all up so you don't have to worry about us?"

"He has done his duty, dammit! Why can't he just be happy with the way things are now?"

"What do you want him to do, Julie, stay home to be your poor little homeless guy that you can take care of?"

For once, Holly is not on my side. I can't help but feel a little betrayed. Her words are also ridiculous, as well as untrue. "That's not fair." Now I am wanting her to leave me alone as well.

"Look, he was honest with you. He enjoys being a cop. Hell, I don't like the fact that Mike is going to be out there either. But if it is what they dream of doing, who are we to stop them?"

I am out of answers; I can't get them to see things my way. I need to be alone. "I need to go. I need time to think. Can I borrow your car?" I hold my hand out, hoping she will give me her keys.

"You're upset. Just stay here, okay? I will go back inside and leave you be."

"I can't. Please, Holly, I will be careful. I just want to go home. I need time alone to think."

She hesitates for a moment, but finally reaches her hand inside her pocket. "Fine, here." She hands me her keys "What do I tell Ben?"

"Tell him I just need time, okay?"

She nods in agreement.

I get in her car and as I am pulling out into the street, I hear Ben yell out to me. I see him in the rearview mirror, starting to chase me but stopping when he realizes I am too far gone. Part of me wants to stop the car and turn around and run to him. However, the part of me that is afraid and fearful for him keeps me driving.

# CHAPTER thirty

I DRIVE AROUND FOR A little while, after deciding I don't want to go home either. Funny, it has always been the place where I feel the safest. Something has changed now. I finally stop when I realize I am at the cemetery. I drove here purely by instinct. I go ahead and get out of the car. Luckily, the street lights give me enough light to find my way through the cemetery, since I don't have a flashlight or phone to help. I finally reach the graves of the ones I have loved and lost, falling to my knees and sobbing harder than I have in quite some time.

"I love all of you and you are gone. Now the man I love ..." I start straightening the flowers by their headstones. "The man that I want to spend the rest of my life with wants to do something dangerous." I take a breath. "Mommy, Daddy, Aunt Gee Gee, Jason." I say each of their names as I look at each cold stone. "What do I do?" I bow my head, sobbing.

My heart is breaking at the thought of one day burying another loved one, especially Ben, who is half my heart and soul. How would I survive it? I have seen too much death in my life. How do these women do it? How do they sit and wait for their husbands, knowing any day they could die? I am not strong enough. How could I possibly be strong enough to do this?

Then I think of Ben's ex-wife. She never supported him. In fact, she cheated, lied, and destroyed him, and all the while he was fighting for our country. While I lay in Ben's arms last night he told me how caring I am and how he wished he would have met me first. He knows that I would have loved and supported him. Boy, did I prove him wrong.

It is no wonder he wanted to wait to tell me. I remember our conversations now, where he tried to tell me before. It was my comments that stopped him. He opens up the door and learns to trust me and I turn around and slam it in his face. As my tears fall, I look up to the night sky. It is full of stars. Aunt Gina loved star gazing. That swing in the backyard was her favorite spot. Shortly before Carl and I had to call Hospice to care for her, she sat out there with me as we talked.

"Julie, I know you have not had it easy and you may think that life has been unfair to you, but you got to remember this, sweetheart. Life is a wonderful and crazy ride, full of ups and downs. Some people get off the ride, sooner than others, but keep riding, baby girl. Enjoy the thrills and survive the falls. Life is full of risks, but it's the risks in life that make it worth living."

I realize she was right. I can shut myself up in my house and avoid everyone. While I may not have to deal with death, would I really be living? In a few short weeks, I have had trauma, but I also have had great joy. My time with Ben has been so wonderful, especially the last few days. Do I really want to throw it all away?

I wanted him to come back to being the man he was and he did that, only to have me be angry with him about it. I am being so unfair. I look at all the tombstones of my loved ones. They were my life and my past, but Ben is my future. I have to love him and support him, as he has supported me these last few weeks. I owe him that.

"I love him, guys, and I know that all of you would be telling me right now to go to him and let go of this. I love and miss you all, and I hope I make you proud." I place a kiss on each stone, saying my goodbyes. I will be back to visit but it is time to get back on the ride.

It is getting late and now I regret leaving Ben the way I did. I know he will be worried and it was wrong of me to run away from him like that. I start driving, but instead of going back to Carl's I decide to go home first. Knowing Ben, he would look for me there.

I arrive at home and the house is dark and quiet, and I notice Bo is not even there to greet me.

"Ben?" I call out. "Bo?" I get scared walking into the house alone. I realize now how protected I felt with Bo and Ben around. Self-doubt resurfaces again as I race into the bedroom. I am relieved to find his things still here. Good. He didn't leave me, although I wouldn't blame him.

I guess he stayed at Carl's or he is out looking for me. I am so stupid worrying him like this. I can't even call him to tell him I am safe, because I left my phone at Carl's. Great going, Julie, you worried your friends now too.

I grab the keys getting ready to head back to Carl's when the door flies open and Bo runs in barking and greeting me. I kneel, hugging him, glad to see my friend. I look up in time to see my hero, my love, my friend, my Ben walk in. I don't even hesitate as I run into his arms.

"Julie." He sweeps me up in his arms, holding me tight. "God, baby, I was so worried. I looked everywhere for ya. When ya left, I got so scared, I didn't know where ya were. Damn, baby, where did ya go?" He holds me tight, not letting me go.

"Oh, Ben, I am so sorry." I nuzzle my face in his neck, kissing him and am relieved he still wants me after the ugly things I said. He kicks the door closed with his foot and walks us over to the couch. He doesn't let go of me, probably in fear I will run again, and sits down with me in his arms. Knowing I scared him and realizing I was being selfish in making him worry, I start tearing up.

"Please don't cry. I changed my mind, baby. I won't do it, Julie." He holds me, rubbing my back.

"What?" I pull away, looking at him.

He wipes the tears from my face. "Baby, I won't do it, okay? I will call them right after Christmas and tell them no. It is not worth losin' ya. I am sure I can find somethin' to do, handy work, construction, anythin'. I just can't lose ya."

"You would really do that for me?" A part of me wants to hold him to it. It would guarantee his safety.

"Angel, you are my life, of course I would. I can find work anywhere." The look in his eyes, I know he means it. I must have really scared him when I left. It wasn't my plan; I just had to think. As much as I love hearing this, I can't do this to him. For as much as I may want him not to do it, I love him too much to not let him follow his dreams.

"I want you to do it," I say quietly

"What?" He is confused and I can't blame him.

"It was selfish of me to act that way, and you knew I would take it bad. You couldn't even come to me and tell me, because you knew I would be upset. I want you to do it, Ben. I won't stand in your way."

"No, baby, ya don't have to say this," he says, shaking his head.

I take my hand, stopping his chin and looking at him. "I won't stand in your way, but I will stand beside you, supporting you, loving you, and cheering you on." I smile and kiss his cheek and then his lips. I have left him speechless.

"Ya mean it, kitten? Are ya absolutely sure?"

"Yes." Before I can say more, his lips are on mine. We recline back on the couch, kissing away all the hurt from hours ago.

He stops us for a moment. I can see the questions in his eyes. "What changed your mind?"

I want to tell him, but it will wait. "Doesn't matter. I love you." I kiss him again.

"I love ya too, so much." He lifts me up in his arms and starts heading for the bedroom. He stops when he hears the clock on the mantel chiming twelve times. It is midnight and officially Christmas morning.

"Merry Christmas! I love ya, Julie."

"Merry Christmas! I love you too, Ben."

★

WE MAKE LOVE AND FALL asleep, only to wake up and make love again. Since the moment he walked in the door, we haven't left each other's side.

All the love making must have exhausted me because it is late morning before I am awakened by kissing and dog licks on my hand.

"Wake up, kitten, it's Christmas. Don't ya want to see what Santa got ya?" He sounds too cheerful to be my Ben. My Ben is not a morning person, but seems to be one today. He sits on the bed, shaking me to get up.

"What are you up to?"

"Me? Nothin', it was Santa."

I pull the pillow over my head. "There is no such thing as Santa."

He pulls the pillow away. "Come on ya Grinch. Get up."

It takes me a few minutes to get up and get my robe and tie my messy hair up. He is not leaving my side and acting strange. Is he still afraid I will leave again?

I walk out to the living room with him behind me. I look to see the same presents under the tree. "What surprise are you talking about Ben?" I yawn.

I hear him whistle behind me. He is still standing in the hallway. "Not under the tree, over here." He disappears down the hall, so I follow. He stands by my craft room door, with a shit-eating grin on his face.

I eye him suspiciously as he opens the door to my craft room and I tuck under his arm to look inside. My jaw drops as I see the room. Gone are the piles of clutter, with items strewed everywhere. Beautiful wooden shelves now hold my crafting items, neatly organized and labeled. An even more beautiful wooden table sits near the wall. I walk inside, amazed by his fine woodworking. I run my hand over the table, I am at a loss for words. "Oh, Ben," I whisper.

"Ya like it?" he asks as he steps inside the room.

I turn to look at him "Like it? Are you kidding? I love it! It is so beautiful." He smiles in relief, as I finally comment on the room. He must have been up for hours to do this. I walk into his arms, hugging him tight. "This is the special project you were working on all the time?" I look up and give him a kiss.

"Yep."

I give him another kiss. "Thank you, thank you so much. I love it."

"You're welcome."

"Now it's your turn, come with me." I take his hand and head to the living room. I drag him to the couch and make him sit.

I go to leave but he pulls me back. "Wait, first I have one more. Sit down."

I sit beside him but then he gets up and heads to the tree. He brings over a medium-size box and lays it on the floor between us.

"Ben, but the room is so nice, you shouldn't have gotten me anything else."

"Just open it," he says. I carefully unwrap the present and Ben helps me cut the taped up box. I reach inside and pull out the wooden case. Jason's flag is displayed inside along with his medals and a gold plate with his name engraved on it.

"Oh, Ben, it is so beautiful." In my life, I never expected something like this. I start tearing up.

"I knew ya were waitin' to find a special case for it. Is it okay?"

"Yes." I am too touched for many words. I set it down and hug him close. "Thank you, it's lovely."

"You're welcome. I am glad ya like it."

Before I start another crying jag, I get up, remembering I have a few surprises for him. "Now, it's my turn."

He sits back as I go to the closet and remove the guitar case, bringing it to him with a red bow. His smile fades as a look of shock comes over him.

"Merry Christmas."

Ben's face is priceless. I know he can't believe what he is seeing. "Julie, ... no way, it can't be." He takes the guitar case, laying it on his lap and stares at it as he runs his hand over it.

"It is. It took me a while to find it, but it is yours." I sit down beside him.

He opens the case and touches his guitar, tears in his eyes. I have made him as speechless as he made me earlier. He carefully closes the case and sets the guitar down beside him, before pulling me into his embrace. "Thank ya, baby, ya have no idea what this means to me."

I feel the wetness of a few stray tears at my neck. "You're welcome." I hug him tighter.

"How did ya find it?"

"I called up the pawn shops in the town you lived in. I was running into all dead ends until the very last one. He remembered the guitar I was looking for, in fact, he kept it for himself after it defaulted. I offered to buy it back from him, but as we talked and I told him your story, well, he just said he was going to ship it to me, free of charge. He wanted me to tell you thank you for your sacrifices. I gave him Holly's address to ship it to and that's that."

"You're amazing, ya know that?" He takes my face in his hands and kisses me.

"I love you, so much. Thank you for finding me and loving me and giving me my life back." We kiss again, but Bo is hungry and nudges his way between us.

"All right, ya win. I will get up and feed ya," Ben says and he starts to get up.

"No, wait. I'll do it. I have one more thing for you." Before he can protest, I get up and Bo follows me to the kitchen. I quickly give him some food, before taking my cell off the charger. Thankfully, Ben remembered to bring me back my purse when he left Carl's house last night in his frantic search for me.

I walk back out to the living room as Ben watches me. I hit the dial button on the number I have preset in my phone. He doesn't say a word, but I can tell he is curious about what I am up to.

"Hello. Yeah, it's me. Merry Christmas to you too." I smile as Ben continues to look at me strangely. "I have someone here who wants to say hello, hold on just a sec." I hand the phone to a puzzled Ben. "It's your sister. Merry Christmas." I smile.

He takes the phone, starting back at me and then at the phone. "Hello, Mary." He smiles. "Merry Christmas to ya too. Yeah, it's good to hear your voice too." He holds his hand out to me and I offer it up as he pulls me to sit beside him. He doesn't let go of my hand the whole time he is speaking.

"Really? Another niece." He squeezes my hand, as I wipe the stray tear falling down his cheek. "Yes, we will have to make time to come see ya and the kids, real soon. Yeah, she is pretty awesome. Yes, more each day." He brings my hand to his lips and kisses it. "Ya have a Merry Christmas too and we will see ya soon, I promise. Love ya too, Sis, bye now."

He sets the phone down and the moment is too much for him as he sinks down into my arms and weeps as I hold him close and cry with him.

*Thank you for reading my first book in the Holiday Love Series. Look for more of Julie and Ben's story in Another Auld Lang Syne coming October 2017.*

## MARIE SAVAGE

# ABOUT THE *author*

MARIE SAVAGE IS A NEW author who is finally fulfilling her dream of publishing her stories. Her first self published book, Tidings of Comfort and Joy, was her NaNoWriMo Winning work from 2015. It is the first book in her Holiday Love Series.

Born and raised in the Florida Panhandle, she has always had a love for reading and writing, with the romance genre being her obvious favorite. Her desire to expand her horizons, led her to join the United States Air Force and proudly serve her country for six years.

While stationed in Atwater California, she met her true love and together they have shared life's beautiful joys and tragic losses. After spending over half her life in the Central Valley of California, she has moved back to her southern roots, where her desire to write first began.

Made in the USA
Middletown, DE
13 March 2018